Suzanne Ruta is a native New Yorker who has lived for long periods in France, Switzerland, Chiapas, and northern New Mexico, where in the mid nineties she co-founded a thriving immigrants' rights group. Her short story collection *Stalin in the Bronx* (Grove Press) was a *New York Times* notable book of the year. Her stories, essays, and reviews have appeared in the *New York Times*, *Grand Street*, *Bookforum*, and many other publications. She lives in New York City with her husband, painter Peter Ruta.

To Algeria, with Love

SUZANNE RUTA

virago

VIRAGO

First published as a paperback original in Great Britain
in 2011 by Virago Press

A CIP catalogue record for this book
is available from the British Library.

ISBN 978-1-84408-642-9

Typeset in Bembo by M Rules
Printed and bound in Great Britain by
Clays Ltd, St Ives plc

Papers used by Virago are natural, renewable and
recyclable products sourced from well-managed forests and certified
in accordance with the rules of the Forest Stewardship Council.

Mixed Sources
Product group from well-managed
forests and other controlled sources
www.fsc.org   Cert no. SGS-COC-004081
© 1996 Forest Stewardship Council
FSC

Virago Press
An imprint of
Little, Brown Book Group
100 Victoria Embankment
London EC4Y 0DY

An Hachette UK Company
www.hachette.co.uk

www.virago.co.uk

To Peter

Part One

Part One

1

Louise

Half an hour early and forty years too late, the story of my life. Three-thirty by the clock in that midtown luncheonette. We were not due to meet till four. How would I recognize him? They didn't put his picture on his book jacket. Tariq said he was tall and scrawny and ascetic looking, with round wire-rimmed glasses, like Gandhi or John Lennon. Either one would do.

Tariq set the time and place for this encounter. My sidewalk savior used to drive an ambulance in Paris. Now he drives a limo in New York but he hasn't lost the instincts of a rescuer.

'I'm accident prone,' he said the day we met in the Bellevue emergency room, 'prone to other people's accidents.' He just happened to be driving by, that afternoon, when poor old Friedrich keeled over on the sidewalk. His forehead struck the pavement, drawing blood. Tariq spotted him, leapt from his car, raised the wounded gently from the gutter and bore him to the hospital where he found my name and number in Friedrich's wallet.

Half an hour later I walked in and saw Friedrich looking

like the SS finally caught up with him. Was he still in his right mind? Blinking back my tears, I tested him.

'Did you hear that, Friedrich? This kind gentleman once lived in Paris, just like you.' Friedrich's mind was unimpaired. When he heard me say Paris, he staggered to his feet and sang the 'Marseillaise.' He remembered all the words.

'A rare display of chauvinism,' Tariq commented, as a nurse came running to shush Friedrich and lead him away behind the swinging doors.

'Oh Friedrich isn't French, he's a Francophile refugee from Nazi Germany. One of many. Look, this was very kind of you, I don't know how to thank you, but don't you have to get back to work about now?'

Tariq told me not to worry, his hours were flexible. He was employed by the French consulate as chauffeur and guide for visiting celebrities from over there.

'Celebrities?' I asked. Jean Gabin? Catherine Deneuve? Bernard-Henri Lévy?

Tariq said it was mostly celebrities no one in New York had ever heard of, which made his work much easier. Right now, for example, he was in charge of an exiled Algerian who'd written a bestseller. He shrugged, 'The kind of thing the French go crazy over for a season anyway, you know how it is with them, it's cyclical and short lived, like May flies. I doubt three people in New York have read this Algerian's book.'

And then he named the man, and I said, 'Really? You're talking to one of the three. I would love to meet Aissa Abderrahmane. Do you think you could wangle me an interview?'

Tariq said that would be easy. 'What paper are you with?'

I lied and said, 'Oh, several.'

'I'm sure he'll be delighted. Just leave everything to me.'

I once knew Algeria by heart. I had it from a direct source, temporarily relocated to France but honest, voluble, and passionate.

'I swear to you, Louise,' my source would say.

'Don't swear,' I'd say to Wally, that was his name, the name we gave him. 'I believe you without that.' But it was a verbal tic he couldn't lose. A rhythmic pacing, spacing of everything he had to say.

Then I lost him, we lost each other. His fault, my fault, nobody's fault? I got tired of trying to assign blame. I tried to put him out of mind, with all his kin. I lived my life without them and forced myself into a willful ignorance about Algeria. I left France, returned home to New York, and married a kindly European émigré, fluent in five languages. I loved my husband, raised my children, and taught Spanish in the city high schools. But my mind was never clear of old distractions, buzz saws, and barking dogs that made it hard to think about the here and now.

'Un jour tu verras, on se recontrera' (*One day you'll see, we'll meet again*), Wally and I used to listen to that song. I don't think we owned the record. But when they played it on the radio, we stopped whatever we were doing and paid attention. It was not our song, we had a whole list of those besides, but its modest optimism flattered our circumstances.

The promise was betrayed, and badly. I wanted to tell this wandering polysyllabic Algerian, Aissa Abderrahmane, what had happened. Reading him had been almost like listening to Wally. Except that Wally when I knew him had a whole world to look forward to, while Aissa's world – a generation later – turned against him, threw him out, and left him stranded on a foreign shore

Wally talked so much I called him my pet parrot. A parrot does the talking in Aissa's book. When the old bird goes missing from a shabby beach hotel east of Algiers, the owner accuses his young male employees of theft and has them arrested and tortured. The parrot meanwhile flies away to France and finds a comfy niche in a public garden but when he learns about the mess he's left behind, he almost dies of grief.

'Don't dwell on your losses,' I would tell Aissa. 'Listen to me instead. Wally and I have a lot to tell you.'

Aissa

I never expected that silly book to become a bestseller. A week after the accident I sat down to write a suicide note. I must have had a lot of scores to settle. Sixty pages later, I knew I would live to complete the screed. The French love pseudo-memoirs. They compared me to Aesop and La Fontaine (talking animals!), they put me on TV, they stopped me in the street to thank me.

Thank me for what? A thousand times better if my wife were still alive and I had died in the collision. She would be a widow, bereft but young and vital, likely to remarry someday and bear children, not my children, but what did that matter? The important thing is that the generations should succeed each other come what may. In the hope that someone someday may get it right.

★

'*Vous n'avez pas la priorité*' (You do not have the right of way).

Why not? What's wrong with me? Why don't I rate? I fought those warning signs at every traffic circle in the heart of France, where they are legion.

'Don't take it personally, darling,' my wife pleaded between naps. She slept to escape her anxieties and mine. Refugees from civil war, our luck seemed to hold at first. We fled with a suitcase of books, and the name of a protector on the other side. A real Frenchman root and branch, son and grandson of peasants in the Berry, the landlocked heart of France, Jean G. taught grade school in Algeria when the country was brand new and desperately poor and dislocated. Fifty kids to a classroom, eager, docile pupils, discipline never a problem, only hunger, lice, TB, and permanently missing parents. A nation of orphans. He fed us stories from those legendary times, he cooked for us, lent us his car when ours broke down, and when I asked about the rent he said, no hurry.

But all his kindness couldn't save us from our fate. One morning that first winter in France a squat butcher truck came barreling out of the fog and rammed our car, passenger side. Horror upon horror, at the inquest I learned who had the right of way. Not me: I should have yielded to the truck driver, who emerged unscathed. My wife died at the county hospital within hours of the crash. I was implicated in her death. They could have tried me for negligent homicide. They confiscated my license and sent me away. And I began to write my book.

The Minister of Culture sent for me and asked with exquisite courtesy if I would consider a trip to the United States as an ambassador of *la Francophonie*, French spoken outside the national boundaries. It would have been cowardly to

7

refuse, with Arabs getting so much bad press in New York. I accepted without conviction.

In the first year of the war on terror, I expected and was given a hard time at passport check. They pulled me out of the line, fingerprinted me, questioned me about my background, left me waiting for an hour and finally released me with a standard greeting, 'Welcome to the US. Enjoy your stay.' Tariq, my minder, apologized for the dubious reception. His 'powers,' as he mysteriously called them, did not extend into the domain of Homeland Security. He was a Turkish Kurd, an emigrant like me. I liked him immensely, but the idea of cruising the city in a limo with tinted windows was repugnant. I gave him the week off and set out to explore the town on foot.

New York was deep in mourning. Monuments of bronze and cardboard, mounds of flowers, and swarms of candles. Teddy bears. I tried to imagine them transposed to Algiers, barely recovering from civil war. It didn't work. Our unshakeable regime demanded we forget the violence they provoked and then prolonged, and as for the Islamists who tried and failed to take them down by force of arms, well, it has all been swept under a rug the size of the Sahara.

There was nothing in Algiers and never would be, to match the memorial wall outside a downtown Manhattan hospital, where a hundred anguished families had posted snapshots of their loved ones. Those hurried pleas had long since served their purpose, but no one had the heart to strip away that random cluster of young men in basketball gear, brides in their finery, college grads with gown and mortarboard.

'The face is the evidence that makes evidence possible,' says Levinas, the French moral philosopher. What about a wall of missing faces?

8

'Yes, what about it?!' one of the portraits mocked me. I took another look. Second row from the top, between a beaming Trinidadian accountant and an Ecuadorian head waiter in starched shirt and black bow tie, my wife stared down at me. The resemblance was too strong to be coincidental, the name change didn't fool me. I knew that photo. I took it myself the day she graduated from university in 1987. She flashed a teasing smile and brandished her rolled-up diploma, warning the world that now she was armed for combat. Had I been given a great gift? Was the universe about to bend its laws for me? Maybe all I had to do was dial the number scrawled beneath the photo, and all would be well.

I dialed the cell phone Tariq had given me. It rang and rang. Then Tariq appeared out of nowhere and took the phone away. Had he been trailing me all week? How could I have missed him?

'This is not what you need,' he said quietly and handed me his handkerchief. He was right, my face was damp. I blotted it and followed him to the waiting car.

From then on I was docile to Tariq's commands. I gave interviews uptown and down. Always the same questions: why is your country so violent? How did 9/11 change the world for you? I was tired of debate. It was a relief to find myself just sitting and listening to Louise. More of Tariq's prescient machinations?

'Why me?' I asked when I discovered she didn't want to ask questions. She wanted to talk. A confession of sorts.

'You'll know when you have heard me out.'

'And why now?'

'I had to be old enough to understand how young I was in 1961.'

1961, possibly the nastiest year of our last long war

against the French colonizers. Nastiest, except for all the others.

'You must have been a child then,' I said. She shook her head.

'Kind of you, I was twenty-one.'

'And you were where? Not in Algeria with the war on? In France perhaps? Where you met one of ours. A combatant?' The dashing rebel army that swept all before it, including the hearts of European women, later disappointed when our liberators morphed into the crabby bureaucrats of a heavy-handed dictatorship. A story one had heard before. Divorce, Algerian style.

'It was in southern France. But Wally was not a combatant. He was just a nice guy trying to survive.' And after a pause, 'We were good friends for a while, but in the end I let him down.'

'YOU let HIM down?' This was a new twist on the old tale.

'But I intend to make amends,' she disregarded my skepticism.

'Amends!' – Surely she knew that where I came from we didn't do amends, apologies, or reconciliations. We did grudges, feuds, vendettas, massive reprisals, rushed burials and enforced silence. Now I was curious, if wary.

'I would like to be brief and to the point. *Veni, vidi, vici*: I can't match that standard of terseness, however. Actually, this may run a while,' she said, and I could see how an odd mix of mischief and melancholy could have led her into trouble at one time.

'What year were you born?' she asked. '*Sans indiscrétion.*'

'1965.'

'Just so,' she said mysteriously.

'Just so,' I agreed and waited to hear more.

10

2

Louise

I always hated injustice. I was my father's daughter, in that way. My father was a radical, a rebel, he never held a gun or dynamited a haystack, but in his youth he roamed the US, east to west, penniless and hungry, in search of heroes, anarchists, socialists, and legendary labor leaders. I knew their names, their songs from early on. But by his forties, with a wife and children to support, he had acquired another set of friends, former Communists maimed for life by a terrifying trip to Moscow in 1929. These bloodless, ingrown men became his mentors, they made his career, fed him tips he turned into front-page stories for the news-paper where he wrote for a few successful years, until the paper folded suddenly, in the mid-fifties, leaving him stranded. My mother went to work while my poor father sat home and reminisced about old times. I was his captive audience. He fed me legends that kindled my imagination and my sense of justice. But when I began to seek for myself – at lectures and ban the bomb marches – the kind of company he kept as a young man, he called it a betrayal.

'It's you who have betrayed the man you used to be,' I told him in the heat of argument, sorry the minute I said it because it's wrong to hit a man when he is down, but I did not apologize and he did not forgive me. From then on and until I left home, we no longer spoke. He would cross the street in order to avoid greeting me. If I saw him first, I ducked into a doorway to spare him the ordeal of a face-to-face encounter.

In those years of domestic cold war, I would have been lost without my uncles. The men my mother's sisters married brought the air of other worlds into the stifling closeness of our de facto matriarchy. My uncles had fought in the war I was born too late to know, except by hearsay and the vaguest memories. I say fought, but I doubt any of them ever fired a gun, except in target practice, or to test their aim against some hapless jungle fowl.

Uncle Sid had been photographed in Europe, in his Eisenhower jacket and overseas cap. He saw tremendous desperation in Brussels, women who would do anything for a pound of coffee. In northern Germany he saw – he didn't like to talk about what he had seen. For example, he had never told his wife, but he would tell me because he knew I was keen to travel and when I got to Europe and saw the museums and cathedrals I would have to find a way to fit it all together – high culture and great buildings and what Uncle Sid heard at Bergen-Belsen in the fall of 1945. By then it was a displaced-persons camp, they had cleaned it up, but he heard stories that could turn your hair white overnight. Not his hair, of course, he joked, he was already bald in 1945, beneath his jaunty soldier's cap.

Uncle Max served in the Pacific, a dashing mustachioed captain in the medical corps, armed with vast quantities of DDT. He fought life and death battles with malaria and yellow fever. Aunt Phyllis knew him all of three weeks when they married, and three weeks after that he shipped out from New Orleans and she didn't see him again for two years. But he sent delightful letters on the thinnest airmail paper, grass skirts, suggestive carvings in exotic lightweight woods inlaid with opalescent shell fragments, and tiny photographs of himself, bare-chested in shorts, in the close company of small dark men who dressed the same way, not by choice but because they didn't own a shirt among them. Uncle Max was a radical, he believed in revolution from below, and might have stayed on as an adviser to the Philippine guerrilla movement post war, if Aunt Phyllis hadn't been waiting for him. And then the children came, my cousins, three of them in just five years.

'A family is easier to start than stop,' Uncle Max joked. 'Remember that in due time, little child.'

He called me 'little child,' a direct translation from the Yiddish. I would have walked through hell for him. He claimed to know me better than I knew myself, warning, 'You have a very soft heart, just like your Aunt Phyll. You want to be careful where you leave it, it will melt like tiger butter.'

In 1954 there was a great family reunion, when Aunt Nora returned from Europe for the first time since the war. Nora had connected with history in the most direct way: she married it. Her husband, tall handsome Uncle James, was British; they met in New York in wartime and left for Europe in a convoy of ships in 1943. The convoy took six weeks to reach Ireland, circling as far south as Brazil to avoid German submarines. Aunt Nora and her husband were real and vivid, they had known danger and food rationing, and had seen the bombed-out streets of London with their own eyes, before flying off to Lisbon, where Uncle James was sent on a secret mission. Back trouble kept him out of the RAF, Aunt Nora hinted to me the after-noon she cornered me in an upstairs bedroom, where I hid to read André Gide's notebooks. I had already figured out that I was meant to live in France, and in order to be ready when the time came, was reading my way through the entire shelf of French literature at our local library.

'A horrid man, that Gide. I'm sure I don't know what he can tell you that you need to know. How to pick up young men in the public baths?'

I was fourteen and hadn't the faintest idea what my beautiful expatriate aunt was talking about.

'Your accent is quite good, James says so and he's the expert. But there's a lot more to it than what they teach in school. You know that, don't you?'

'*Naturellement*,' I said.

'The place to learn a language is in the streets and cafés. I suppose you know Sartre by heart?'

'Not yet.'

'Revolting man, he looks like a blowfish. We used to see him at the Flore in '49. I don't know why you want to learn French anyway. Italian is more beautiful. Don't ask me, ask Stendhal. The Italians are no easier to know, down deep, but at least they like to play at being friendly. Social life is just a game, a *commedia dell'arte*. The French no longer bother with the social graces.'

'They don't teach Italian at my school,' I said, hoping my aunt would take pity on me and whisk me off to Europe, and I would be home free years ahead of schedule. Aunt Nora and Uncle James had no children of their own and disapproved of the way their nieces and nephews were being raised, coddled they said, in the soft bosom of their respective families. Aunt Nora believed in boarding schools, hard beds, cold showers, lumpy porridge: the regimen of the future king of England.

'I could send you to a school where you'd learn Latin and Greek. James says that's the only real foundation. But your father would never let you out of his clutches. You'll have to win some big important scholarship, you'll have to wow them into letting you go off alone. A pity, it will be harder for you later, when you're eighteen or twenty. It may even be too late by then. You'll be an Amurrican, a New York provincial, no worse provincialism than flourishes right here on these sidewalks. Well, I got shut of it, I suppose you can too.'

'Of course she can,' Uncle James swept into the room, clasped his large hands around my waist, and lifted me so my feet dangled in midair, then set me down again, lightly, lightly.

'Practice walking with a book on your head, that's my advice to you. Chin up, shoulders down, bottom tucked under, for that Audrey Hepburn glide . . .'

'She's reading Gide,' Aunt Nora told James, to shock him.

'Well, why not? In the original? Of course. Good way to build vocabulary. Never mind, I'll send you something better.'

He sent me *Poil de Carotte* by Jules Renard. It was his own schoolboy copy, he had learned French from it as a young orphan lad. French lit. was full of orphans. So was British for that matter.

From then on Uncle James and Aunt Nora visited the States every two years, staying long enough to plant new seeds of doubt and discontent in my mind. James was full of scorn for his brothers-in-law, my beloved uncles. Although courteous and deferential in their presence, when alone with me, he would exclaim, 'Ye gods, grown men drinking milk!'

15

He limited himself to specific complaints. It was Nora who condemned wholesale the slack moral fiber of postwar America. She advised me to get myself to Europe at the first opportunity. Uncle James was a graduate of Cambridge University; he had been turned down by the RAF because his back was too long to fold into the cockpit of a fighter plane. But he had been in London in the Blitz and never talked about it, because, as Nora said, burnishing his reputation behind his aching back, he exemplified the qualities – stoicism, service, lack of self-regard – that had sustained the late great British Empire for two hundred years. Aunt Nora mourned its passing.

'There has been no morality in international relations since the passing of the British Empire,' I once heard her say. That statement sounded wrong on the face of it, but I never argued with my aunts and uncles.

But I couldn't stop them from arguing among themselves.

'Europe?' Uncle Sid spat the word out like a bad seed. 'Vastly overrated. Your Aunt Nora has sold you a bill of goods. What do they have we don't have here, except some shameful history? I know, you've read all those moralists, Camus and Sartre and the rest of them, with their manifestos and their Nobel prizes, all that high-toned debate is just double-talk. They're trying to explain away their shabby war record, not theirs personally but, let's face it, France did not distinguish itself and as for Germany, forget it, you're not planning to go to Germany any time soon? I would seriously advise against it.'

I was ready to go anywhere the Fulbright committee in its wisdom chose to send me, but rather than argue with my uncle, I assured him I was asking for a grant to go to France, since I spoke some French.

'Don't stay away too long, you're needed here,' he said

affably. 'If our so-called Uncle Sam hadn't sent me, I would gladly have forgone the pleasure. Try me in a few years, right now Europe is low on my list,' he concluded, sounding old and tired and full of incontrovertible knowledge, his Old Testament voice was how I thought of it. My Uncle Sid seemed to have been born with the dark, deep-set eyes, and well-defined eyebrows of a grieving prophet.

Everyone had advice for the departing child, I was just a spoiled child, although twenty-one that summer, and a college graduate. Or if not spoiled, naive, susceptible, and untested.

'You have something any European man would want,' my Uncle Bud, the lawyer in the family, warned me.

'Really, what's that?' I asked, not fishing for compliments, just feeding him his lines. I did that with all my uncles but especially with Bud, our stand-up comic.

'Your American passport. Of course you're cute and friendly too. Too friendly, if you ask me. "*Una bócca da baci*," you know what that is? That's Italian for "born to be kissed." Your aunt would kill me if she heard this, but someone has to tell you the facts of life. Remember this: you can only put your ass in one place at a time. *Capisci*?' Uncle Bud was not Italian but he claimed to be on close terms with important members of 'the Mob.'

Uncle Sid went to the basement of the new ranch house in a brand new suburb, and came back with his old Eisenhower jacket.

'I wore this when I was mustered out, don't you love the lingo?' I loved his unerring sense of the absurd and his proactive generosity.

'Take it along, you never know. When I was over there, the army-surplus look was all the rage. Granted that was fifteen years ago. If you find something more in line with current fashion, buy it, and I'll pick up the tab. Agreed?'

17

Uncle Max was tender, motherish. 'We want you to go and have a great time, but remember, if something happens and you change your mind, just jump on the nearest conveyance and come straight back to us.' Why so pessimistic? I wondered. Did he have so little faith in me? No, it was the Zeitgeist, the world historical framework he mistrusted.

'France is in a bad way; your aunt and I have the real story from our contacts over there. Not too many people realize that France has been at war uninterruptedly since 1939, without a break. I see it's news to you too. That's all right, you'll find out soon enough. Thousands of young men your age or barely older have been drafted and sent to die in Algeria. The US as usual has played a double game, supporting the Algerians in public speeches while supplying the French with helicopters and trucks at the same time. You'll read about it in the papers over there, it may not affect you, personally of course, but France under de Gaulle is not a progressive place, not the ideal by any means.'

Paris lived up to its postcards – the city was all spectacle, with a glamorous stage-set flatness I knew I'd never pierce. The book stalls along the Seine, the wide vistas up and down the river from the Pont des Arts. Madame Cheval apologized for weeping in front of twenty Fulbright scholars as she recalled waiting at the Gare de l'Est in summer 1945, for the returning deportees from the camps.

'The way they looked, we could not have imagined . . .' She gave up trying to describe what she had seen that day. Earlier she'd made a graceful little joke about her comic name. She wore a beautifully cut gray suit with a nipped waist. Her humor, elegance, and painful memories were all connected somehow, as Aunt Nora had already intimated: the aesthetics of tragedy. Later I wondered why no one in

18

the room offered a steadying hand or a Kleenex to poor Madame Cheval, assailed by unspeakable memories.

And what to make of this? At an outdoor café table on the boulevard Saint Michel not far from the Sorbonne, a group of students razzed a beggar. What had he done to earn their hatred? Weren't they afraid of adding insult to injury? The *clochard* was clearly down on his luck, their mass insouciance, and their crescendoing catcalls shocked me. The cruel self-indulgent Paris I discovered in fall '61 made me want to flee. No matter how correct my grammar or my accent ('*Vous parlez rudement bien le français,*' was the ambiguous compliment), I was a foreigner, an object of indifference if not outright scorn. Even to be addressed as 'Mademoiselle' could make me cringe with something like shame; it sounded more like mockery than welcome.

When Wally called me 'Mademoiselle' something else was going on. Rueful tease, he held me at arm's length until the day I fell into his arms.

3

The scholarship committee allowed us recent college graduates a month in Paris and then shunted us off to the provinces, presumably for our own good. And that is how I wound up in Cularo, in the Alps, alone and far from home for the first time.

My first friend in France wore a long raincoat with a round collar that marked him as an American import. I found him exotic. The US is a big country, and I'd never been to his home region, the state of Arkansas. Rigid Southern Baptist upbringing, two much older brothers, pillars of their local church, staked him to his European fling.

'They want to hear about my wild life in the dens of iniquity. Not too wild or they'll call me home again in a hurry. The Draft Board will do that anyway. I'm here on borrowed time.'

He was a cheerful gossip with a nice dry self-deprecating sense of humor. He called himself 'a bland white-bready kind of guy.' I was intrigued. He used expressions I had only read in Faulkner novels like 'Go suck an egg.' I fascinated him for the wrong reasons: there were no Jews in his hometown.

He had not given his staid brothers their money's worth, he kidded. No wild life, just a slow romance with a French girl he'd met that summer. He'd followed her to Cularo for the fall term. She'd set her cap for him, which he found flattering but troubling too. If only he could be completely sure of her and of himself. He had asked Josette to sleep with him and set his mind at ease, but she was not amenable. He'd managed to kiss her a few times but that was all. Why was it so difficult to overcome her resistance? Did she sense that he was somehow lacking, did she have his number, or was she waiting to be bowled over?

'I'm not a great bowler,' he lamented. 'I'm a sort of a milquetoast, can't you tell?'

'I'll bet that's what she likes about you,' I told poor Charles, who was tall and lanky and looked a bit like Jimmy Stewart in the movie *Harvey*. He bared his soul during long walks along the parapet of the town's famed fortress. Cularo: a mountain at the end of every street, the travel posters boasted, which was true enough, except those chilly iron-gray mountains did not raise your perspective, they walled it in. They trapped the morning fog inside the narrow valley where the streets ran along the banks of a grayish, rushing river. A sad, sullen place, full of bicycle traffic. Central heating was apparently unknown. Students huddled by stinking gas heaters, washed in cold water, and accepted their landlords' ban on visitors of either sex at any hour of the day or night – visitors who ran up the electric bill and shouted in strange languages, disturbing the natives' hard-earned rest.

'The trouble is not within you,' I finally told Charles. 'It's in your surroundings. Let's run away.'

Charles loved the idea. Neither of us had seen the Mediterranean yet. *Thalassa, thalassa*, I inveighed. That was

21

Greek for the sea. My Aunt Nora in London had been warning me in letter after letter, 'DON'T LET YOUR STUDIES INTEFERE WITH YOUR EDUCATION.' But even without her advice, I would have found it easy to abandon the university in midweek: stuffy lecture halls, impossibly haughty professors, juvenile classmates trapped between misplaced awe and unfocused resentment.

We left town together the next morning. I tied a change of clothing into a bundle swinging freely from one end of a long stick. I don't remember where I found the stick but it was just the right length.

'I'm gone with the Jews and Gypsies,' Charles quoted his favorite Karamazov, Dmitri. (Ivan was a cold fish and Alyosha's feminine side scared him.) Love of Dostoevsky spurred Charles to learn Russian in college, but that was only part of it. Studying Russian was a way of needling his rock-bottom conservative parents.

My airborne bundle wasn't practical for hitchhiking. Within half an hour I dismantled it and stuffed the contents into Charles's small valise, along with a stinking alcohol stove that came in handy later for making tea. We left Cularo around ten a.m. in a covered truck bound for Montélimar. The driver and his mate stuck Charles in the back of the truck, under the tarp roof, and told me to climb into the cab between them. I was absurdly trusting in those days, incapable of recognizing or anticipating malice. In twenty years, no one had ever harmed me intentionally. Unintentionally was another matter of course and worse in a way, because you can't defend yourself against the unwitting or the uncontrolled harm done you by your parents, say. You just wound up feeling sorry for them, and forgave them in advance for anything they did, regardless of the pain.

The truckers dropped us, unharmed, outside Montélimar and I made Charles walk into town so we could try some nougat, the local specialty, a honey candy with ground almonds, and then we trekked back out to the highway and waited for an hour and a half in a chill wind till a doctor in a roomy Citroën stopped for us. He warned us amicably that Marseille with the Mistral blowing was unbearable, why didn't we go on to Corsica? It was only a quick hop and there it would be warm, sunny, and French speaking. I was keen and Charles was content to follow my lead.

But first we had other business to attend to in our double bed in the hotel room (one star) near the Vieux Port in Marseille. Our request for chaste twin beds provoked such merry scorn we quickly reneged and asked for *un lit double*. Exhausted from the journey we fell into bed without undressing and slept like babes. Next morning, however, things took another course. Charles made the first move probably, but he knew I wouldn't turn him down. After all the sad confessions, how could I have refused him? He needed proof of his virility and within half an hour of waking, he had it. Outside it was sunny, but the room was still cold when he shouted in climactic gratitude.

'I worship the Jews.' Still in his Dmitri Karamazov mode. I was surprised but not offended. I was not 'the Jews,' I was just myself, a New York girl, with rabbis somewhere in the family tree generations ago in Lithuania, and if Charles couldn't see that, he had been badly educated. Never mind, he was so pleased with himself, and I was pleased with myself, because I liked to give pleasure when it was easy to give, and his warm limbs in the cold bed tangled agreeably with mine. He was so much taller, it was like meeting a giraffe on close terms, more zoological than sexual, but friendly, very friendly, by the nature of the deed.

He was a sweet kid. He just had some growing up to do. That night we shipped out for Corsica. We not only saw the Mediterranean, for the first time, we plowed through it, fourth class in deck chairs and ratty blankets. It was freezing on that open deck, there were no other passengers, Charles was seasick and then fell asleep. I stayed up all night, euphoric, counting stars.

I never meant to steal Charles from Josette. We were following a trail above a steep gorge outside Corte, moving slowly through the tall scrub, listening to the rushing creek far below. To our left, along the mountain track, ran a barbed-wire fence where a small goat had tangled his horns. I held the lines of barbed wire apart while Charles freed the terrified creature. As we watched it bound away into the maquis, Charles leaned over and asked me, half joking, to marry him.

Of course I said no. I was sure he would return to Josette in time, or someone like her, a cautious young woman with straight blond hair, a good skier, a good Catholic or preferably a Protestant his family would welcome.

But it was not to be, at least, not yet. Back in Cularo three days later, he ran to Josette and made a full confession. She broke down and wept, he told me that same night. My landlady was more offhand than some and the bed in my furnished room was in a kind of narrow closet, behind double doors. And there Charles sat, fully clothed and wept and beat his breast (Dmitri K.) and asked what he should do? He'd never meant to make another person as unhappy as he had made poor Josette. He was a monster, he deserved to die.

'Go back to her,' I told him. 'She needs you.' I was not being magnanimous. I loved Charles as long as I was sure that I would lose him to the other woman and be left to suffer my abandonment in peace. Once he came bounding back to me, things looked different. How could he be so indecisive?

'I love her but I want to be with you. May I stay the night?'

In his wretched state, I didn't have the heart to throw him out. Two women's rejection in one night would have flattened him.

4

Charles met Wally at a bus stop at the northern end of town, where the mountain torrents that once turned mill wheels now powered the turbines of a large industrial suburb. Wally with his haversack slung over his shoulder, was returning home from the electronics plant where he worked six days a week. They struck up a conversation about names. Wally teased Charles about his quintessentially French name. Charles de Gaulle, Charles Trenet, Charles Aznavour. Ray Charles was the exception that proved the rule. Charles got even by Americanizing Wally's exotic, doubly exotic, name: Clovis Ahmed Ouali. Charles scrawled 'WALLY' on a scrap of paper from his jacket pocket. Ahmed Ouali, renamed Wally, was delighted. He was always ready to try something new. His real name, the one his father gave him, was problematic for an Algerian, he admitted. Clovis was king of the Franks, baptized a Catholic around AD 500. I forget the exact date. Wally knew it. It was part of the history every schoolboy in France's global empire was expected to regurgitate on demand.

'He's like a Frenchman but much nicer,' Charles told me. 'His father served in the French army for twelve years. He went through all of World War One from start to finish. Clovis was the name of a French officer he respected and who respected him. They were at Verdun together.'

'He told you all that at the bus stop?' I asked Charles. 'The bus must not run very often.'

'Well, he didn't waste much time. He talks a lot and fast with an intensity, almost like you, but different. Every other sentence is, "I swear to you. *Je te le jure.*" I told him he didn't have to put himself on oath, that I believed him without that. He found that very funny. But it also touched him in some way. He shook my hand and thanked me for the kindness. Odd, no?'

'Why odd?' I asked; it simply showed the man was starved for friendship. While they waited for the bus, Charles told Wally about our trip to Corsica and Wally told Charles he had been foolish to hitchhike around France in wartime. He might have been kidnapped, held for ransom, and killed his parents with worry and grief.

'He's a bit of a scold,' Charles said. 'I told him so. He laughed and said that was the way with older brothers in Algeria. They're expected to keep the rest of the herd in line.'

Most of the Algerians who worked in the factories north of town, building the circuit breakers, the high-speed railway cars and ski-lift gondolas of the new consumer society the kids would noisily reject in 1968, lived four to a room in damp medieval streets along the river. Wally had a furnished room all to himself in a drafty old manor house on a side street not far from the main square. The solid bourgeois family that once lived there appeared to have been wiped out in a catastrophe that left no heirs. The derelict four-story building had an elegant mansarded roof and a grand central staircase with a wrought iron banister. The upper floors were boarded up. A distillery occupied the ground floor. Wally lived directly above it, as we saw when he invited us for tea on Sunday afternoon.

He was waiting by the big front door when we arrived and led us up the winding staircase to his room. Narrow and high ceilinged, it appeared to have been split off from a vast reception hall. The furnishings too looked like abandoned relics of mid nineteenth-century high bourgeois lifestyle. A tall brass bedstead, a standing closet of some noble wood, cherry or walnut, and an enormous low desk, piled with books and manuals. In a corner, behind a screen was a sink with one faucet. The lone window was deep set with heavy creaking shutters. We navigated by artificial light.

We had been in town eight weeks by then. No one had invited us home for dinner or even for a cup of coffee in a bar. Wally was hospitable by nature and tradition. He had a reputation to uphold. We felt the strain and then the charm of being wrapped into a rite where every step was anciently prescribed. He boiled water on a hot plate and poured it into a battered yellow tin teapot, with green tea and a bunch of mint (where did he find fresh mint in the Cularo winter?), added mounds of sugar and then, holding the pot aloft, poured the steeped brew into tiny glasses inscribed in gold with Arabic script. He served the tea on a round brass tray set on a shaky tripod. Polished to a mirror shine, it gave us back our faces tinted the same reddish gold as his. It made us instant kinsmen.

He set out a plate of pastries from the bakery two blocks away: cream puffy things that tasted of the badly refined gas called *mazout*.

'Americans like sweets,' he said. How did he know? He didn't say.

28

What did the writing on glasses mean, I asked Wally. He apologized for his ignorance. The public schools of *Algérie Française* taught only French.

'What did you think of him?' Charles asked me later.

'He looks like a cross between Albert Camus and Sammy Davis Junior,' I mocked Wally in self-defense, because I had already noticed his calm vivacity, his hyper-alert eyes. Around his sturdy neck he wore a red bandana, like Russ Tamblyn in *Seven Brides for Seven Brothers*. The bandana was essential equipment, he explained, with a shy grin. He couldn't fall asleep without it draped over his eyes.

'The Alpine sun too strong for you?' Charles asked.

'Or do you travel back to Africa in dreams?' I chimed in.

'Mademoiselle is witty,' Wally said. He meant at his expense, but he didn't mind. *Au contraire*. He addressed me in third person to sidestep the question of *vous* or *tu*, I thought. But even when we got past *vous*, which happened pretty quickly, he continued to address me in third person for a long time.

We were not Wally's first Americans. Those were the Anglo Saxons who made the disastrous landing at Oran in November 1942. Hundreds died on the ships under enemy fire. Many were lost at sea. The survivors took over the town two days later. Wally was twelve that year. We were infants.

He was our first North African but we didn't say so, in case it sounded rude. Anyway we weren't interested in Africa per se. It was Wally who intrigued us. We thought he was unique.

When I sat on the high brass bed, an outsize museum piece, my feet dangled well above the ground.

'That bed becomes you,' Charles teased in his waspish way.

'This must be the bed where Henri Beyle was born.' I

shut him up, by invoking Cularo's illustrious son. Wally asked who Henri Beyle was.

'You mean they didn't teach you that at school? They were wasting your time,' I said. Wally said they probably taught it at the *lycée*, but he never got there, he left school at the age of twelve. He'd been playing catch up ever since, he nodded toward the pile of books on the old desk.

I believe it was that same afternoon, on our first visit, that just for fun, I proclaimed the Republic of Wally. I walked the length of the oddly truncated room, marking off the capital and the hinterland, the mother country and the colonies.

'Tut, tut,' Wally clicked his tongue against his teeth, 'no colonies . . .'

I continued, 'With Wally as president, prime minister, and ambassador plenipotentiary, free to enter into binding negotiations with representatives of foreign powers, including but not limited to the United States of America.'

'Direct negotiations,' Wally added, 'with no French interference or oversight.'

'Of course not,' I agreed.

'But the negotiations are conducted in French,' Charles butted in.

'French is the language of diplomacy,' I pointed out.

'The status of Arabs in French Algeria' Wally said, 'was like the status of women in most places. They were not full citizens . . . unless they converted to Christianity. They were subjects.'

'Women can't convert to masculinity,' I made a quick hash of his analogy.

'That's true,' Wally conceded happily. He liked to argue, he didn't mind being proved wrong. He liked it best, he told me later, when I talked rings around him.

'And in the Republic of Wally men and women enjoy equal rights from birth, is that not so?' I did a little Socratic number.

'Also true,' Wally agreed.

'You mean you never voted in an election?' Charles demanded.

'None of us did, not even my father, who rose to sergeant in the French army. If he hadn't been an Arab they'd have made him a colonel at least. As for elections, the rules were always rigged, and the vote count, *o là là*. Ten kinds of fraud. We stayed away.'

'What about taxes? Did you pay taxes?' Charles continued, very senatorial.

'Of course. Every time you buy a pack of cigarettes in France.'

'No taxation without representation,' Charles and I chanted in unison. We told Wally about the Boston tea party. He wondered what happened to the men who hurled the tea overboard. Were they shipped back to England in chains, to rot in dungeons?

'Of course not,' we said. Dungeons had no place in US history. Unthinkable.

'You know how many Algerians are sitting in French jails right now?' Wally asked. We had no idea. Neither did he, he confessed. But the number was high, well into the thousands. That was a conversation stopper. We observed a moment of embarrassed silence for the uncounted prisoners.

Wally spoke first.

'Our republic, as you are pleased to call it, Mademoiselle, is a very small island.'

'An island or an oasis?' Charles asked.

'You know I never laid eyes on the desert? I hope to see

31

it some day, when all this is over,' he waved his hand like a magician, like Prospero striking the set. By 'all this' he meant the war, prison, exile. What pathos in that gesture, I already regretted my burbling joke about a private republic, a contradiction in terms.

Wally's so-called republic was a small, unheated room in a condemned building in an enemy country. Yet his cheerfulness was authentic. That was when I began to fall for him. What came before was banter and play-acting all around. Something must have showed in my face, some fleeting sadness, because he took quick action to restore the upbeat mood.

'Mademoiselle, will you do me the honor of selecting the first number?' He handed me a stack of 45s, on loan, he said, from a pal at work.

That was the era of the 45, the single, cheap to acquire, cheap to produce, a boon to collectors and musicians both, lightweight and easily traded, like matchbooks or paperbacks. The format didn't leave room for heavy marketing, the kind of long convoluted show-offy essays the French crowded onto record jackets. You got to hear the latest music, fresh grooves, still running with the juices of creation and for an added bonus there was, unlike with CDs, the flip side, not the hit of the week, the top of the charts, but a runner up or afterthought, that sometimes, '*inopinément*' as they say, turned out to be the real thing, baby. That year I developed a whole theory of the flip side, the law of unintended consequences, the literary value of far-fetched analogies, and committed it to paper, French-style box-you-in graph paper, and even showed it to my professor, the sacred beast at the *Fac. des Lettres*, who was not convinced.

Confronted with that tall stack of 45s, we deferred to

Wally's superior knowledge of French pop culture. That afternoon he introduced us to Leo Ferré's sentimental slangy ballads with catchy titles like *Paname*. *Paname*, the gutter name for Paris. A precious first lesson in slang, never forgotten.

'Why aren't we there?' I asked when the record stopped.

'In Paris?' Wally said, on the *qui vive*. 'I tried it, you know. Too many cops hassling us on every corner, asking for our ID, our pay stub. I got sick of it. It's calmer here.' He stood up and changed the subject. 'How about some more tea? I can have it ready in a minute.' He paused and then added, 'I could have stayed in Paris, the Latin Quarter, the Champs Elysées, La Régie Renault. (I could see he got a kick out of naming those places, that had rejected him.) But if I'd stayed in Paris dodging the *flics* we would not have met. That would have been a shame.'

Our Sundays from then on belonged to Wally. Tea ran into dinner. He threw some chicken legs and rice into a pan on the hotplate, with unlikely additions – olives, raisins, almonds, lemon peel. He stored his victuals on the stone ledge between the shutters and the bay window. We ate right from the pan, with our fingers. He showed us how. Not a grain of rice was lost. After we ate, he brought a damp towel to clean our hands. He fussed over us like a father with his children. His own children were far away across the water. He slid open the desk drawer and carefully extracted a miniscule snapshot of three bright-eyed faces. As if to correct for slippage in the last generation, his children bore solidly traditional names: Mohamed, Ali, and Nour. Mohamed was serious and steady, as befits an oldest brother, although only seven years of age. Ahmed was quick witted, the class clown at six. Nour had it all, brains, beauty, and tender mischief; how could he tell all that, I wondered, about a two-year-old he'd never seen? They would stay in school for as many years as they could stand, he swore to us, and then some, he would see to it, and not just ordinary subjects like math and engineering but languages, Chinese if they wanted or calligraphy or Greek philosophy.

'You are the American dream personified,' I exclaimed. 'Determined to see that your children have more than you do.'

'But that's the Algerian dream,' he looked me straight in the eye. 'Do you think you have a monopoly on hope? Excuse me for saying so but the whole world wants what I want.' He meant 'and what you have,' although he was too polite to say it.

We nodded, chastened. We didn't mind the lecture. *Au contraire, ô confrères.* Not so, dear colleagues. Wally was cute when he was kidding, he was even cuter, we agreed, in solemn mode.

Almost from the start, he took it on himself to correct our French. A born teacher, firm but tactful, taking over where the European refugees who taught me French in New York had left off.

'It's not *le règle, la règle*, feminine. You make so few mistakes, I thought you wouldn't mind if I pointed them out to you now and then.'

'Of course not,' we said.

On the other hand, he was sparing with praise because he himself had been on the receiving end of too many stinging compliments. You speak such good French for a foreigner, a North African, an immigrant. Worst of all, he told us, were those, and they were many in France and overseas, who gauged your fluency by the color of your

34

skin and hailed you right off in a form of pidgin French known in the colonies as '*petit Nègre.*'

Learning French, he insisted, was not that big a deal. '*Ce n'est pas la mer à boire.*' It's not like swallowing the sea. He had a great supply of odd phrases they never taught us at school.

'Which sea is that?' I asked.

'The Mediterranean, don't you think?' he replied, without missing a beat. I was his straight man, he was our star performer. Some day we would take our show on the road. Meanwhile we had a lot to learn. Who would have thought the French could be such stinkers? Wally's first day of school, first lesson, he told us later that winter, was on the battle of Poitiers, Charles Martel defeats the Moors, invading from al Andalus, AD 732. The lesson reinforced with a sharp-edged ruler brought down hard on the palm of his hand.

'Your poor hand,' I said, looking discreetly for scars of this brutal treatment. His hands were sturdy, muscled, and calloused, like catchers' mitts. His right hand met his arm at a strange angle, as if he'd been strung up by his wrists. That year there were busy torture cells in central and suburban Paris. We never heard of them. But it was clear to see that someone, somewhere had messed with Wally's arm.

'This?' he laughed. 'It was a soccer accident.'

He was a goalie and played a horizontal game, diving head first into the fray.

'Do you know *le foot*?' he asked.

I said no.

He said, 'The goalie is a team unto himself, he doesn't wear the team colors, he isn't governed by the same rules as the rest; he's allowed to grab the ball with his two hands, that's how I tripped and landed on my wrist, see there. I blocked the goal, but it cost me my career.'

'Why is it crooked?' I asked. It looked as if his right hand had been severed from his arm, given a quick quarter turn, and reattached, catch as catch can. A bad repair job.

'They let the student doctors practice on me, *un melon, c'est normal.*'

'What's that?' I asked.

'That's what they call us, they have all the names for us that you could want: *melons, ratons, bicots, troncs de figuier, chameaux, bou*—' I made him stop, I couldn't stand to hear it, how could people be so cruel? And yet at the same time, it excited me to think that I had crossed the line, without paying attention, and wound up on his side, with the rebels, outcasts, underdogs, the *bougnoules*, and I already knew that I would make it up to him for all the insults and botched surgery, the interrupted schooling, I would fight his fight, and show the French the error of their ways. Take that, Cularo.

I didn't know the French were racist, my teachers didn't teach those words when they were prepping us for tests, *dicté, passé composé, complément d'objet direct.* They could have warned their students. Camus could have said something in *La Peste.* But it was my own fault. No one has a right to be that naive.

And who taught Wally his one complete sentence in English? He carried it around with him for decades, like a coin from a foreign currency, stranded in his pocket, since the days after the landing in Oran. I pictured the scene. A skinny thirteen-year-old Wally helping some GIs change a tire, bringing stones to block the wheels of their jeep parked on a steep incline somewhere above the harbor, or running to retrieve a bolt that rolled away, and later being offered gum and candy and asking brightly for a chance to inspect the motor of their amazing vehicle. The colonel

and the staff sergeant washing their hands in a nearby fountain, including him in their ablutions, then saying, 'Get in,
kid, we'll take you for a ride,' making room between them
for the boy in short pants and tattered sandals, whizzing
along the coast road, while from sheer good will they
taught this promising street Arab one salient fact about
himself, 'I am a colorèd man.'

5

The call from his Draft Board reached Charles in December. He would have to return home at once. He asked me to go with him, but the invitation lacked conviction. He knew I wasn't ready to leave France. I had only just arrived.

'Move to the big city,' I told him. 'New York is full of girls like me.'

He could have said, 'Oh, but you're unique.' He did not protest. A healthy sign, although it rankled.

I saw him off at the train station, heavy hearted after all. Now I was alone in Cularo, walled in by those stone mountains. I could have gone skiing but I was afraid of heights. I went back to my room and tried to read Thucydides. His Athens seemed impossibly remote, a democracy that tyrannized its neighbors and heartlessly destroyed rebels. How did the Athenians eliminate the men of Melos? With swords and spears? The great historian doesn't say. The women and children were sold into slavery. To unlock Thucydides's terse paragraphs was a worthwhile project, but maybe not for me. Someone knocked at the door of my room. I looked up and there was Wally in a gray jacket I'd never seen before, his shoes shined, his moustache freshly trimmed. He had come, he announced, to take me dancing. Between tango and Thucydides, it was no contest. I accepted the invitation at once.

I worked my way through college as a typist. Losing battles with stacks of flying carbon paper and erasers, headaches and eyestrain meant the wherewithal to pay for escalating school fees, carfare, and dentists' bills. Greek was my only luxury.

'What can you do with it later?' my parents asked.

'Crossword puzzles,' I told them. Or, trying to sound practical, 'Impress the Fulbright Committee.'

But really, I loved the language for itself. Homer's sovereign humanity, Sappho's tantalizing fragments. Sophocles's slangy courtroom drama, *Oedipus the Tyrant*, was my favorite. I will go back to it some day. There's something in the story of an infant son 'exposed' at birth that even Freud missed. Wolves roamed ancient Greece. 'Exposure' is a euphemism. King Laius threw his own son to the wolves.

But that night, in all innocence, Wally came to my rescue. When he said, 'Let's go dancing!' I was more than ready.

'Not so fast. Got a scissors?'

I brought them without asking questions.

'Sit down,' he ordered. 'Wait, do you have a towel? You need a good hair cut.'

'Do you know how?' I asked.

'Where I come from everyone's a barber, tailor, or shoemaker as needed.'

It took him a while to comb out the snarls in back. It was the first time he touched me. Neither of us spoke.

'*Petite sauvage*,' he said when he was through. 'Who raised you? I've been wanting to do that for a long time.'

At the *bal musette*, the chilly open-air dance hall, three members of the National Liberation Front stood on the sidelines, looking for trouble and finding it. Killjoys, they surrounded Wally on the dance floor just as he was showing me a nice sinuous turn. You can't dance the tango in a straight line. Cutting me out, these three guys in leather jackets edged him to one side and hectored him in Arabic for having fun while, as he translated for me afterwards, his countrymen were dying. He resisted their bullying at first, in a language I would never understand, then fished in his pocket and handed over the fine they demanded.

'What were they doing at the dance? They came just to police you?' I asked Wally as we walked back to town at a brisk pace.

'They collect fines to pay for their beer,' he said. 'But let's not talk about misfortune. Your landlady let me in earlier tonight. Think we'll have the same luck again?'

Unlike the rest of her breed, my landlady, Madame Genoud, was not a snoop. Kindly and distracted, she came into my room at six each morning with a small bucket of coal to feed the stove that heated the entire apartment. As if to make up for that unavoidable indiscretion, the rest of the time she remained invisible, behind closed doors, communicating with her tenants by a series of notes in bureaucratic French.

'Please be so kind as to pull the chain briskly,' affixed to the wall of the water closet.

'*La pomme de terre en robe des champs*' (the potato in field jacket) was what Charles called her in her long brown wool skirt and mysterious underpinnings. To me she seemed as remote as a peasant in a painting by Millais. I was startled to find her in my room that night, when we returned from the forbidden dance. The door of the infamous coal stove was flung open. Smoke poured into the room. Wally didn't wait for introductions; he stepped right past Madame, filled

40

a basin with water from the corner sink and tossed it into the furnace.

'The line is plugged somewhere. How do we get to the roof? No, wait, let's try from here.' Suddenly he was a volunteer fireman, rapping out orders.

'Get me a wire hanger, quick.' As I struggled to uncoil it, he snatched it from me.

'Let me do that, it will go faster,' and thrusting his arm into the stove, he prodded with the wire till a tangle of branches and soot fell out onto the floor.

'This is part of a stork nest. I've never seen one up north before. They always came to us in the spring.' Wally scooped up the mass of straw and twigs and set it in the sink.

'Do storks nest in Cularo?' he asked Madame Genoud, who recalled that in the last spring of the war, an unusual number of storks had been sighted around town, probably because their accustomed habitat was a battlefield.

'Even the birds were refugees that year,' Wally said. 'And lately?'

'We haven't seen them,' Madame said. 'But then, I'm not in the habit of walking on the roof.'

'Of course you're not, Madame,' Wally agreed. 'That would be highly inappropriate. Why don't I go take a look around and see what else is waiting since the great war for a high wind to tear loose and drop down your chimney.'

'Not the great war, the last war,' Madame corrected him. 'But look at your jacket, it's all full of soot. Give it to me, I'll take a brush to it.'

'And meanwhile I'll inspect the roof.' Wally removed his thin jacket and handed it to Madame Genoud, who blushed with pleasure at the sudden turn of events that put a young man's garment into her hands.

41

'It's very kind of you, Madame,' Wally said ceremoniously.

'It's very kind of you. Later maybe you would be so kind as to help me rekindle the fire in the stove.'

'By all means, Madame. Don't stay here, the air is bad, go with Madame into some other room. I'll meet you there,' Wally ordered me. In a few minutes he was back again, to report that the roof was clear, although he might want to inspect again in daylight.

'But where do you come from?' Madame Genoud asked Wally, in amazement, as if he had dropped in from another planet, with impeccable timing.

'Rue du Dragon, do you know it?' he replied, deadpan.

'If I know it? My father was born there. My daughter is right there. You may have seen her.'

'Alas, Madame, I don't believe I've had the honor.'

'Oh yes, you have, the fountain, at the corner of rue Fourier, the small bronze statue in the wall niche, an allegory of Virtue. My daughter was the model for that work. The sculptor was a family friend.'

'And were you pleased with the result?'

'As a likeness, it's quite good, but I don't walk that way often. I have to prepare myself, I choose the moment, you understand.'

Wally nodded gravely and threw me a quick sidelong glance, a warning to keep still.

'She was twenty-four in '44. She joined the movement. They used her as a courier, I worried about her going back and forth into the hills. "Don't come see me," I told her, "it's not worth the risk. You're safer up there with your friends until it's over." But that summer there were terrible battles, the Germans had our kids surrounded; they burned whole villages. Some people said they saw the fires from

42

here, but that could not have been. Have you been in our *Vercors*? Famed for its beauty. We used to go for long treks in the summer.'

She collapsed into the nearest chair, with Wally's jacket spread across her lap. She smoothed the folds with her right hand, distractedly, raising little gusts of ash.

'Would Madame drink something about now?' Wally proposed, as if he were her host and not the other way around.

'Good idea,' she agreed loudly and stood right up again. We followed dutifully into her parlor. I hadn't seen it since the day I moved in. With its dark heavy furniture, its general absence of images, icons, and family photographs, it recalled an austere French Protestant church. She opened a tall standing closet and half disappeared inside it, reemerging with a small bundle wrapped in dark blue velvet. She peeled back the wrap to reveal a plaster cast of a woman's face, with a high forehead and marked widow's peak.

Wally studied it intently. 'There's a strong resemblance to her mother. But you're sick of hearing that. Life is unjust,' he added, redundantly, I thought, but Madame Genoud seemed to take comfort from his restatement of the obvious.

'You don't get used to it,' she agreed. 'My husband died of grief, essentially. *Enfin*, that's how it was back then.'

Wally had finally run out of words. And I was at a loss too, although I felt that after three months under her roof, during which I had completely failed to guess at the tragic contents of my landlady's closets, I ought to be able to find something to say. All my life I'd heard from father, mother and a dozen aunts and uncles about the great historic cataclysms, revolutions, wars, depressions, the unimaginable horrors I escaped by being born too late, although in some places 1940 was not exactly a safe year. But I was not born in those places. An American, a New York Jew, a lucky little girl, like the fairy-tale character who has to travel far from home in order to learn how to shudder.

'Is it a death mask then?' I blurted out.

Madame Genoud looked at me, uncomprehending. It was a while before she spoke.

'Well no, it couldn't be you see. There was so much destruction, so many fires. The sculptor did this years earlier, as a study for the bronze on the street corner. A life mask, you could say,' and she disappeared into her cabinet of marvels and produced a bottle of chartreuse, the local brew of an intense chlorophyllic green, an entire Alpine meadow distilled, by clever monks, into a pint of 100 proof liquor. From a glass-fronted cabinet she took a tray and three small glasses, which she filled and passed around.

'*A votre santé*, Madame,' Wally said before he drank.

'Oh, my health is a matter of complete indifference to me,' Madame said. 'To yours,' she emptied her glass in one go.

'Such indifference is in itself a sign of good health,' Wally replied, doing his best to leaven the gloom.

'So much the worse for me,' Madame Genoud said. 'But you are right. I'm as strong as a horse.'

Then, since the air in my room would be unbreathable for some time yet, my chivalrous companion invited me to spend the night at his place.

It was not a long courtship. I shocked Wally with my prompt acquiescence. All he had to do was lay a hand on me – on the nape of my neck, to be precise – and I was his.

44

'I didn't think we'd wind up here tonight,' he told me after the first onslaught. 'You could have kept me waiting a good long time.'

There it was from the start, that strange disconnect between his two roles: seducer and genial adviser. He was grooming me for life, from the wings, as it were. Some day he'd shove me on to the stage to face the audience, and then he'd vanish. All that was foretold in his remark. But he was right. It was too much, too soon. I was not at ease with him that night.

The fault was partly his. Whatever he said about his willingness to wait (perhaps all he meant was that I deprived him of the pleasure of anticipation), he threw himself into the breach with brisk alacrity, stunned and scraped me with his quick hard kisses. He was a man crying fire in a tiny theatre with no audience but me.

And then he fell into a sudden deep sleep. It was almost comic. He worked fifty hours a week at that mysterious factory, on his feet among the heat, screech and metal dust, although you'd never know it to see him outside working hours, scrubbed clean and smooth as a peeled peach. While he slept beneath his red bandana, like a condemned man blindfolded before a firing squad, I kissed his scars, his mangled wrist, the streaks of motor grease tattooed beneath the smooth skin of his capable right forearm, and finally the all but invisible small tear, dating from his seventh year, when he was circumcised.

'What are you doing?' he woke with a start, and gently pushed my hand away from the evidence of carnage wreaked against his tender flesh.

'I never liked to be touched there,' he said, guarding his manhood. Then he relented, 'But go ahead, if it pleases you.'

'Some other time,' I said. 'You need your sleep.'

'*Ma pauvre Louise*,' he said, the first time he'd attached that epithet to my name, clearly a term of endearment, but all the same.

'Why "*pauvre*"?' I asked. But he was already asleep again, behind his red bandana.

6

Wally was an eager, impatient lover, but so tired after his long work day that he fell asleep immediately after the act, although if I woke him with a gentle shake, he apologized affectionately, but then fell asleep again, mid sentence. I accepted the fact that in the unjust world that bound him, he was his own man on Sundays only.

One Sunday when we had spent the whole day in bed, I found a way to tell him what was on my mind.

'You know, when we make love, I feel left out. You're like a diver, you make your little dive and then you vanish.'

I had hesitated to speak, for fear of offending him, but he seemed, on the contrary, delighted to be made the butt of my sharp wit.

'*Tu as de ces expressions à l'emporte-pièce,*' he exclaimed and described, from first hand experience, how an *emporte-pièce* – a kind of die-stamping machinery – could cut through steel like butter. He repeated my cutting remark all week, a propos of nothing, and each time it made him laugh all over again. I relished his unflappable good humor, his cast iron ego, Monsieur Beaufixe, but nothing changed between us, till the next weekend when we were in bed on

Sunday afternoon and he started talking round the subject. I found myself confessing that apart from Charles and the fellow student, best forgotten, who took my virginity on my eighteenth birthday, this lovemaking business was all very new to me.

Then I took a deep breath and confessed that in my dismal college years I used to masturbate while studying. Aristotle's *Metaphysics* in a bad translation drove me to sin many times, I admitted with tears of shame streaming down my face.

Wally waited for my sobs to subside and then said with endearing gravity, '*Tu croyais tomber, tu es tombée dans mes bras.*' An acrobat of unexpected kindness.

He got up and paced the room and then returned with a proposition. At home, the women had a style he thought would suit me, if I was willing to experiment. I said sure, little imagining what was in store, while he went for his razor and a soapy towel. He returned and shaved my pubis, my *mons Veneris* – I taught him the Latin term – he was tenderly absorbed in the delicate task as if I were a piece of intricate machinery entrusted to his care. He didn't rush, and when he had finished he admired the results, as if that's all that had been wanting until now, and when we made love immediately thereafter, the mood established by this Pygmalion-like effort held, and in its expansive heat, my inhibitions melted for the first time. Afterwards, he said sagaciously, 'Now I see what you need. You need a lot of preparation.'

Pleased with his discovery, he lay back and smoked his cigarette, full of thoughts he sometimes shared with me and sometimes, I suspected, did not. And later, as we were dressing to go out for a long walk, he hugged me and said, 'You see, even with *ma légitime*, my lawful wedded wife, her pleasure counts as much as mine. Even more, I swear to you.' The dismissive word dismayed me, poor *légitime*, on her shelf, and all the rest of us in a great endless swirl, anonymous and interchangeable. Was that his view of womankind? Not really, I decided. The crude French lingo of the streets and soccer fields obscured his real nature, his autochthonous tact and sweetness.

I could have run to Paris on weekends like a sensible American co-ed on her first trip abroad. Instead I stuck with Wally. I became his concubine, his version of an odalisque, shaved, scrubbed, pampered, and perfumed. Of all France had to offer, I wanted only him and his embattled country. I sided with Algeria against France, replaced the Louvre and the Sainte Chapelle with a vision of the little bandstand in the main square, ringed with eucalyptus trees, in Wally's torrid African hometown, founded 1872 by colonial fiat after the local tribes were 'pacified' – a bureaucratic euphemism – in a series of horrific campaigns where the French had the advantage in firepower and ruthlessness. I memorized his father's military service record and his mother's proofs of total unconditional love. My own family had imploded, here was a sterling replacement. Wally was my father, mother, brother, sister, lover, in no particular order. He was used to caring for a ragged crowd of women, children, and infants. All the love he couldn't give the home team, he squandered on greedy little me. He resoled my shoes, restitched my hems, cooked me dinner on week nights and weekends, urged me to upgrade my skimpy wardrobe, scrubbed my socks in the sink with his own when I was tired, brought me tea in bed when I had cramps.

I continued to show up for classes at the university, but it seems to me that everything I learned that year I learned from him. He taught me French grammar, syntax, history, and slang. Table manners without a proper table. Cooking, politics, and religion, all in the same pot.

He heaped treasures on me from his great store of essential knowledge.

- For the java – a lumbering waltz that is almost a polka – each partner places his hands at the small of the other partner's back to form a kind of whirling pretzel. The Parisian waltz is lighter, speedier, the placement of hands is in the traditional manner.
- Kremlin Bicêtre is the name of a large prison outside Paris.
- Edith Piaf's grandmother was Algerian, but played no part in the singer's upbringing.
- Henri Martin was a sailor and a pacifist who went to prison rather than fight for the French Empire in Indochina.
- Red wine is best drunk with a meal of bread and Camembert.
- De Gaulle's wife was known as *tante Yvonne*.
- When Piaf, meaning little sparrow, stood in the wings of the Olympia theatre, waiting to go on stage, someone said '*la môme piaffe*,' from the verb *piaffer*, meaning to stamp your feet with impatience, like a horse.
- The two coldest things in nature are the hands of a hairdresser and a woman's backside.
- A Muslim who makes the pilgrimage to Mecca earns the title *hadj*. It stays with him for life.
- Orange-blossom water combined with orange segments and sliced onion makes a delicious salad.
- Messali Hadj founded the Algerian national movement. His rival Ferhat Abbas was a pharmacist and a good man overtaken by events. Both men lived in France for many years and married Frenchwomen.
- Sardines *en escabeche* are a great delight but the tinned variety sold in France is not the real thing.

- Those little lumps in batter when you're making crêpes are called *grumeaux*, they should dissolve but do no harm.
- The bed is a place of repose.
- When you are invited to dinner it is rude to lift the lid and peek into the pot without first asking your host's permission, even if you and your host cohabit.
- The credo of Wally's religion (he always said '*ma religion*,' never 'Islam' which would have sounded pompous) runs: There is no god but God, and Mohamed is his prophet. In euphonious Arabic, *La ilaha illa 'Lah Mohamed rassoul Allah*. This is the absolute least you can get away with knowing and still call yourself a believer. It's called the *Shahada*.
- Some men pray only when strictly necessary. Others take every pretext, before shaving, say, or lighting the day's first cigarette.
- A man's moustache should be kept well trimmed; if clipped too thin, however, it will soon grow back.
- Cleanliness requires the use of a horsehair glove or bone-dry washcloth to scrub away the dead outer layers of skin from the body at least once a week. For places out of reach, the lower back, the shoulder blades, a friend or close relation can be asked to help. Bathing is best done in company.
- Piaf discovered Yves Montand, his real name was Ivo Livi, he grew up in Marseilles, the son of poor Italian refugees.

Wally was cool, if he wasn't cool he would not have survived, but he was probably not hip, we never danced the twist, he didn't own a single Miles Davis record. He loved the tango and the paso doble, dignified, straight up and down, with intricate footwork. I loved them too, under his cheerfully strict tutelage. Later I read, in some snooty American memoir of fifties Paris, that *le jazz hot* was the property of

51

Left Bank intellectuals while the paso doble was for the working class. Wally was definitely working class, but he was also a foreign prince in disguise, and when we danced the samba in the corridors of our crumbling palace, there was no one to stop us.

7

Those National Liberation Front boys who hustled Wally off the dance floor were right of course. 1961 was a cruel year in France and Algeria. The OAS (Organisation Armée Secrète), French army renegades, colonial diehards, Foreign Legion dropouts, and Christian terrorists pursued a bloody strategy of spite. They planted explosives in the Paris Stock Exchange, the Galeries Lafayette, at radio stations, and newspaper offices. They targeted de Gaulle himself, but failed. In Algiers and Oran, meanwhile, their commandos shot into Muslim crowds at bus stops. These daylight massacres were known, unforgivably, as '*ratonnades.*'

We knew all this, we read the papers, but we didn't talk about the news. Cocooned in Wally's room, on New Year's Eve, we simmered snails in garlic sauce on the hot plate – our *souper de réveillons* – and exchanged gifts. He gave me a dictionary of underworld slang compiled by two Paris police inspectors. '*Je pige que dalles*' (it's a mystery to me) and '*tu as les portugaises ensablées*' (you must be deaf) sent us into gales of laughter. So did '*une carte de France*' (a map of France), defined as the traces left in a man's pyjamas by a wet dream.

'What utter chauvinism,' I exclaimed. 'Do you know what we are? We're a pair of Francophonies!'

No matter how passionate or candid our exchanges we held something in reserve – our mother tongues. Wally asked me what phony meant. That was easy, I quoted Sartre, world expert on bad faith and lack of authenticity.

'You really think we're phonies?' Wally sounded hurt, as if I had accused him of outright dishonesty or putting on airs.

Wally never addressed me in Arabic, I pointed out. I never spoke English to him. French was the fragile scaffolding for our staged encounters.

'But besides what we say, there's what we do,' he said with casual aplomb. He did not mean only in bed, he meant all of it, hotplate dinners and long walks around the city after dark. One night outside the Parc Mistral we met a local woman stranded with a flat tire on her old Peugeot. Wally set to work and changed it in a flash and when she tried to pay him for his labor, he refused with such good grace, she flashed me a rare smile of warm, bemused complicity.

My gift to him was a long winter coat, the kind the Algerian delegates to the ceasefire negotiations at Evian wore in news photos. Mid-calf, double-breasted armor for men appointed to make war by other means. I took a bus all the way to Geneva to find that coat. It cost a fortune. In fact, it ate up a whole month's scholarship check, rent, meal tickets at the student cafeteria, and all. That was fine with me. Since the French were said to finance our Fulbright scholarships in repayment of Marshall Plan loans, I reckoned that France in fact bought Wally his first winter coat. Simple justice and long overdue. He tried it on, he checked it in the mirror, pleased with the way it swung around his legs, but then he hung it in the closet and there it stayed, till I moved in with him in mid January. When freezing nights left a thin layer of ice on the floor, the coat of soft navy blue cashmere topped the pile of ragged blankets on our bed.

His first thought when he saw the coat must have been, poor kid, she means well but she doesn't have a clue. It was tacky to bargain, even mentally, over a gift that came from the heart, but I'll bet he thought of what those three hundred new francs would have bought his family, or mine for that matter. For himself he would have been just as happy with a packet of pipe cleaners. The coat was an overlavish gift, I myself was a lavish gift, extravagant, beyond his means. Once I moved in, his room, his republic as I called it the day we met, was an occupied country.

He must have had misgivings all around. He was not a cad. Granted Americans were generally invulnerable, women, all women, ran tremendous risks. But then I turned up every night, dropped my book bag in the doorway, flung my arms around his neck, and the question was moot. '*Force majeure, ce n'est pas la mer à boire.*' It's not like swallowing the sea.

Sometimes we went straight to bed but mostly we ate supper first. Wally liked to cook for me, he said, because I was easy to please, and so grateful for small attentions, it was almost corrupting.

We went to movies that winter, like everyone else, but discovered our tastes clashed. Wally hated Godard's *Breathless*. Any Algerian who killed a cop, even by accident, would have been arrested in five minutes flat, along with twenty of his closest relatives, instead of the weeks it took Jean Seberg to betray her ex-boyfriend to the police. Wally's idea of a good movie was a cloying melodrama about a honey-voiced boy tenor dying of TB. The death of Joselito, sentimental product of Franco Spain, brought tears to his eyes. I teased him, he scolded, miffed. He was a simple man with simple strong feelings, close to the surface. Later it struck me that the horrid little orphan with the golden voice might have reminded him of his own sons, trapped de facto fatherless at home. That was no excuse for bad taste however. One ought to be able to tell the difference between art and reality, even in wartime.

So I put my lover to the test. I bought a copy of *Le Rouge et le Noir* and gave it to him with trepidation. Could I live with a man who didn't love Stendhal? Would I have to move out? Wally read the book on his lunch hour for two weeks and, to my great relief, qualified easily as one of Stendhal's 'happy few.' He identified with Julien Sorel, the novel's hero, a poor peasant from the Jura who nearly marries the daughter of a marquis. In fact there were some uncanny resemblances. Their lives followed the same path, he said.

'But you were not beheaded,' I pointed out. Julien Sorel's life ended at the guillotine.

'No, you see,' Wally turned his head from side to side, the better to display his sturdy, unscarred neck. But the book unleashed a flood of memories in him, as if Stendhal ('the only Frenchman who never patronized me') had handed him his own life on a platter, to be passed along. Sunday afternoons in the brass bed, cigarette in hand, he told me his life story, 'in weekly installments,' I teased him, while tracing the straight line from his navel to his groin, the royal road, with a desultory finger.

Wally was nineteen when he crossed to France for the first time. Right off the ship in Marseille, something caught

56

his eye. A hunk of bread lay in the gutter, a shocking sight. Where he came from, bread was sacred. It was as if he'd landed in a country where ghouls gorged on human flesh, scattering body parts at random. And so they had, not long before. He remembered his father's stories of the European wars, and was ready to turn back. And then, still seasick and anxious, he couldn't help himself, he vomited right there in the street. By that evening, he had rallied. He found work as a dishwasher in a large, noisy restaurant near the Vieux Port. He slept in the storeroom, unpaid guardian of thirty-pound bags of rice, flour, and pasta. He gained twelve pounds in one month, and realized he'd been hungry all his life.

In time he conquered France, not by the sword but with a bunch of white carnations. After a week in hospital with his mangled wrist, he ran to the nearest flower stall and bought a large bunch of white carnations for the head nurse, a Breton nun with rimless glasses and a potato nose. She received his tribute in stunned silence. Finally she spoke, 'We are all God's children.'

'I never doubted it, *Ma Soeur*,' he said. He would have kissed her forehead but wasn't sure it was allowed. Then he went outside to wait for the nurse, an attractive woman in her thirties, who had advised him on the choice of flowers. (He would have gone with roses; too sensual for a bride of Christ, she said.) She took him home with her that night. Her husband was an officer with the French army in Madagascar, she was free to do as she pleased, and it pleased her that year to instruct a young North African fresh off the boat, in the ways of France. Women's ways, all new to him who had no sisters. One day she dressed him in silks and pearls and took his picture, with his pretty face and widow's peak. (This was before he grew his moustache.) But when her husband returned home on leave, she warned Wally to stop coming round and changed the lock on her door. That too was part of the ways of France.

Wally's mother knew everything about him, in advance, by instinct or nervous, affectionate spying. Rising from a midday nap he goes to take a drink of water from the jar in the dark cupboard. His mother hands it to him, smiling, 'My son is a man. You turned over in your sleep, revealing all. Don't worry, I won't blab.' Wedding plans already in her head, her son just turned fourteen.

On his wedding night the women of the family, one family as bride and groom were cousins, waited outside the nuptial chamber to receive the bloodied sheet. Wally's brothers spiked his coffee with pepper as a precaution. His wife's aunt armed her with a long straight pin. When she drew it from beneath her skirts, Wally grabbed it and jabbed himself, hard, in his thigh, right through his baggy pleated trousers and then he told her to give him the sheet, quick, and, as he had already worked as a *métallo* in France by then, he had no trouble gauging exactly where to smear the blood. His wife, as instructed by her aunt, pricked her fingers with the pin and their blood mingled on the sheet. They were like kids, playing tricks on their elders. They were not strangers after all, they grew up on the same street, but people had warned his wife that France had given her husband some crazy notions.

The craziest was his insistence on dragging her along to France in early '55 with their two small sons. In the Charente Maritime he worked in a factory that produced tanks, boilers, and oil drums, the hardware of postwar domestic comfort, central heating, and hot water on demand.

Like Inspector Maigret and J. Robert Oppenheimer and

other deep thinkers of the mid twentieth century, Wally smoked a pipe. His third year at the factory, he discovered a major error in a blueprint and pointed it out to the engineers. If it had been their error, they might have resented an opinion emanating from the factory floor, but since the culprit was the boss's unloved son and heir, they were glad to hear from Wally and recommended him for a bonus, denied of course, and bought him his first pipe, a symbolic promotion to the class of men who, like themselves, had time to fuss with the apparatus of smoking during working hours. Smoking was forbidden on the factory floor where he stood nine hours a day in clouds of spraying motor oil and metal dust. His salary supported his family in France and in Algeria, and the liberation movement, which collected a small monthly cut of every migrant worker's salary to finance the war at home.

He rented a peasant house, two small rooms below an attic storeroom where the owner stored his potato crop. Wally convinced the reluctant landlord that Algerians don't eat potatoes. He whitewashed the walls inside and out, tacked straw mats over tenacious damp rot. They raised laying hens, planted a garden, and the boys started school and learned to read and write good French. They all worked hard, it was the real *douce France* like in the song. Until the day he woke up late for work and slapped his wife's face, because the coffee wasn't hot enough. She forgave him. She blamed France, overwork, and isolation. He blamed the traditions of his country where men had all the power and all the say. He blamed himself, and gave in to her plea that she be sent home, that summer in 1960. The war would soon be over, they thought, then. She was pregnant again (was she pregnant when he slapped her? I did the anxious arithmetic) and wanted to give birth at home.

France had been hard on his sons. Village life was tightly wound with the round of Catholic holidays, not theirs, but all they knew. From time to time, he sat them on his lap and explained as best he could. 'You are not from here. At home we have our own saints, you know, and saints' days, we bathe, we dress in white, we say our prayers, and then we celebrate, food, music, and galloping horses and riders in long capes and rifles going off, the women trill with pleasure. Wait, you'll see. Meanwhile, just remember, *Vous n'êtes pas d'ici*.'

8

I once saw Wally hit a man, or rather, knock the unlit cigarette from between his lips. It was in a café near the university. I had asked Wally to meet me at this student hangout after work, a bad idea, as by the time he arrived, a pale-faced regular named Edouard, with a red moustache – not a student, a hanger on – had invited himself to my table and was holding forth on Wilhelm Reich, reading passages aloud from *The Theory of the Orgasm*, to see if he could make me blush. He could. The blush had faded by the time Wally arrived and tossed a pack of cigarettes on to the table, itself a gesture of contained rage, perhaps, although it didn't strike me at the time.

Edouard was rumored to be absurdly wealthy. His family were said to own shares in South African gold mines. Wally didn't know this. What he objected to was the casual way the young man helped himself to his Disque Bleus. Before the cigarette was lit, Wally knocked it from his face.

'Touchy, aren't we?' Edouard was pleased with this new chance to embarrass me. I was deeply embarrassed.

Wally was not. 'It's polite to ask before you help yourself. Go on, help yourself.'

Edouard smiled and shook his head. 'I wouldn't dare. You might give me a bloody nose. You know, this is exactly how the whole mess began back in 1830, the bey of Algiers struck the French ambassador with a fly swatter, or a fan. Not sure which it was, reports differ, maybe it was both. A fan could be used as a fly swatter and probably vice versa, don't you think? The French demanded satisfaction, with their army and navy as enforcers. Good thing for you I have a phlegmatic nature. I don't take offense. And I have no army or navy at my direct command. OK, see you around,' he left us, patting my head on his way out.

'You overreacted,' I told Wally. 'That guy is on our side. He brings in banned books from Belgium for your book-seller friend.'

'Guys like that have no respect for anyone. You deserve better and you should demand it,' Wally lectured me. '*Bon*, let's forget it. What would you like to drink?'

'A big cognac,' I said. He laughed and ordered me a double cognac. He thought I was a bluestocking, he liked to see me drink now and then. His ordered something called a *bière panachée*. Beer sweetened with grenadine syrup. No accounting for tastes.

The student class and the working class didn't mix in Cularo. The races didn't seem to mix much either. To buy a tin of sardines or a Camembert was an ordeal: the grocer's wife giggled knowingly, as if we were a risqué joke, a walk-ing innuendo. Our only truly liberated zone was Albert's bookstore by the river.

Albert was a French Jewish intellectual who sold books out of a small space on a damp street lined with couscous shops. He chose that location to make a statement and because the rent was cheap.

Albert's father emigrated from Minsk Gubernya to the Jewish section of Paris, around 1924, time enough to learn his way around town, but not to lose his well-founded mistrust of vested authority. When ordered to register his Jewish family with the police in the first days of the Nazi occupation, instead of complying as so many did, he moved his family to the countryside deep in the Savoie. Albert never talked about his years in hiding but he must have lived in intermittent terror, passing as the son of a large peasant family whose authentic offspring resented and threatened the intruder.

After that kind of beginning, his loyalty to a certain idea of France was almost as mysterious as Wally's. But Albert didn't live in France, he lived within a circle of leftist friends and students who came to the bookshop, where French army deserters waiting to slip across the Swiss border knew they would find guidance. The store was barely wide enough for two to stand abreast. Behind the shelves in a makeshift kitchen, Albert and Wally would sometimes play chess on a Saturday night, while I read Fanon in a contraband edition smuggled into the country, as he was banned in France.

Also dead, Albert told me. Fanon had died that winter of leukemia at Walter Reed Hospital in Washington DC. He was not yet forty. I read slowly and reverently. Fanon the psychiatrist, diagnosing the intimate wounds inflicted by racism, made brutal sense. Fanon the theorist of revolutionary violence did not. Albert dismissed that side of him.

'Fanon didn't teach Algerians to fight, we French did that. We drafted them into all our wars. Mexico with Maximilian, Nouvelle-Calédonie, Verdun, the Moroccan Rif, Monte Cassino, Indochina . . . Where did Wally's father learn his French? Not in school, in the trenches.'

'Wally is a pacifist,' I said, making it up as I went along and because I felt it was true, at some level. The Edouard episode was an exception. Albert smiled knowingly. He exuded a good-natured patience, like a monk who knows that God will wait while he clears the path. He even looked like a Franciscan monk, full faced, tonsured by baldness, with his baggy corduroys hanging like a monk's robes.

'Did he tell you that?' he asked.

'Check,' Wally announced his latest move on the chessboard. He did not take part in our political discussions.

'*O là là*, she's deliberately distracting me, it's all a plot,' Albert joked, as if there was any danger of his losing this or any other game. He was a grand master.

So Wally was not an all out pacifist, but neither was he a combatant in the war of liberation. Would Fanon despise him? I once asked Albert in private. He laughed and found a passage in *The Wretched of the Earth* that answered my question.

> In those underdeveloped countries which accede to independence, there almost always exists a small number of honest intellectuals, who have no very precise ideas about politics, but who instinctively distrust the race for positions and pensions which is symptomatic of the early days of independence in colonized countries. The personal situation of these men (breadwinners of large families) or their background (hard struggles and a strictly moral upbringing) explains their manifest contempt for profiteers and schemers . . .

The breadwinner of a large family could only be Wally. I was glad to know he had a place in Fanon's canon, and relieved that Albert knew about the large family and yet approved of our friendship. It was almost as if my Uncle Sid, a baldy like Albert, had given us his blessing.

Then Albert asked with tact, 'Tell me, *pitchounette,* you must have a large family of your own.'

I didn't like where this was headed, but I knew how to cut it short. 'My father is an anti-Stalinist,' I told Albert, the Communist, sure he'd get the point. I was ashamed of betraying my father to his enemies, but it was his own fault for having so many enemies: pinkos, fellow travelers, comsymps, Stalinoids, and useful idiots. Their errors, misjudgments, and outright lies filled him not with sorrow or anger, but with a smug self-righteousness that troubled me from the time I recognized it, in my teens. When he banned me from visiting my subversive aunts and uncles, I saw them on the sly. I felt sorry for my father but I lied to him without regret. His politics repelled me. Ideology was spit, paper, and long hushed phone calls, behind closed doors, with his old Washington cronies.

'But that has nothing to do with it,' I corrected myself to Albert. 'My family don't travel. I send them cheerful post-cards every week. They don't ask questions. They probably imagine I'm up to something, but they'd just as soon not know.'

'*Petite rebelle,*' Albert flattered me. I was not a rebel. I made no claims in that regard. All I wanted was to bask in Wally's careless warmth, without counting the cost.

Albert had me all wrong. Not only was I not a rebel, I was barely a citizen of my own country. In the struggles of my generation – civil rights, ban the bomb, the Vietnam mora-torium – I was a non-participant. The only cause I ever defended with heart and soul, was Wally, in a brazen debate with a professor. My fellow students were appalled.

65

I found them pretty appalling too. In large groups they became a raucous mob. Packed into the student cafeteria they engaged in shoving matches while waiting on line for their ration of herring salad, horsemeat steak, and stewed prunes. Like a bunch of twelve-year-olds alarmed by the first stirrings of desire, they uglified their impulses, belches instead of kisses, elbow digs, and knee thrusts instead of embraces. They hurled hunks of bread across the room and attacked anyone who wandered into the cafeteria in head-scarf or beret with cries of 'Chapeau, chapeau,' upholding what they claimed was an ancient student custom. At evening lectures, they heckled visiting professors cruelly. I saw them reduce one old coot to tears and drive him off the stage. It's true he was a bore, droning on, in a kind of medieval scholasticism about the sources of Rimbaud's best lines in the work of his predecessors, reducing the *poète maudit* to the status of a semi-plagiarist, moved by a dismal – but to the speaker apparently comforting – conviction that there was nothing new under the sun.

Casually cruel in large groups, in small classes the bread-throwing sons of the bourgeoisie turned cowed and respectful. I was made to feel like the class clown for talking back to old Professor Chiunsi. I had sought him out because his name appears in *Guermantes' Way*, as a guest at the Prince de Guermantes' evening parties in about 1905. What secrets must be warehoused in his large domed hairless skull. So what if his voice bleated and his dentures rattled when he spoke. Age and infirmity guaranteed his authenticity and wisdom. Or so I imagined.

Wrong again. His teaching was crabbed and repetitive, the feeble kickings of a man on a life raft. And when I wrote my term paper without his prior approval, he all but accused me of *lèse-majesté*.

'First of all your writing swarms with Anglicisms.' He used the verb *pulluler*, suggesting gnats or midges. I was vermin in his eyes, or my writing was. Wally was outraged when I told him.

'You came all this way to study with the guy, and he goes out of his way to humiliate you. Now you see what we were up against. What else did he say? Did he at least respect your ideas?'

My ideas! Wally had such faith in my ideas and my brains, he thought I'd be a lawyer or a teacher. He oiled my little Olivetti portable, admiring its sleek lines, and cleaned the keys with alcohol. He rigged a lamp so I could work late in a small pool of light, while he slept on the far side of the bed.

From time to time I glanced over at my lover with the bandana draped over his eyes. The firing-squad look: Mathilde de la Mole said it in *Le Rouge et le Noir*. The only men worth knowing in the nineteenth century were those who stood under a death sentence. Everyone else was a petty striver on the make. Writing within arm's length of blindfolded Wally, I reinterpreted Stendhal, taking account of what I saw, felt, and suspected. It was more than clear to me, it fizzed in my blood, like nascent desire.

When Prof Chiunsi dismissed my entire train of thought, I tried to hold my ground, so that when I gave Wally a full report that evening, he would not scold me for collapsing before spurious authority.

'Could you be more specific?' I dared to ask the good professor. I had seen my women classmates shrink against the walls to let him pass, giggling with sheepish pleasure when he nodded or stooped to mutter, 'Good day, ladies,' in their general direction.

He read the line I chose as epigraph for my brief paper: it contained the essence of the great Beyle novel, I thought.

In the ordinary course of events in the XIXth century, when a powerful member of the nobility meets a man of true feeling, he murders him, exiles him, imprisons him or so severely humiliates him that the other is foolish enough to die of grief.

'For the powerful individual you substitute the French army; for the man of true feeling, you substitute one of the Algerian rebels. You think Stendhal condones terrorism, do you?'

'I don't know if he condones it, but he remembered the revolution, he understood the dynamic of class warfare.' I quoted: 'A revolution is bloody in exact proportion to the atrocity of the abuses it is called on to uproot.'

'Hmm. You seem to have committed the entire novel to memory.'

'Not yet,' I answered with crazy daring. 'In the nineteenth century it made sense to see Julien Sorel as a peasant's son from the Jura. Born destitute or as he says, "quite precisely, without a scrap of bread." He could starve to death and no one would care, is what he means.' (Here I was simply quoting Wally.)

'Julien has no status, no claim on anything except the fear and hatred of the upper classes. In the twentieth century – and Stendhal, in 1830, claimed to write for men a hundred years after his time – it makes sense for his hero to set out from farther away. From Algeria, even.'

'Hmm, let's stop right there. I regret to inform you, Mademoiselle, that you are the victim of a basic misconception. You take a few lines out of context and embed them in concrete. But the model for a novel by Stendhal is not a marble monument, or a Chicago skyscraper. It's a conversation in a drawing room, among people who engage in

68

rapid-fire, witty, inspired, debate for its own sake. In the course of one evening, many viewpoints are offered, examined, taken to extremes and then discarded. Nothing is fixed, everything's in flux. Stendhal craved novelty above all. "I require nine cubic meters of novelty a day, the way a steam engine needs coal."

'Now let's see what else you've singled out for over-emphasis.' Prof Chiunsi skimmed the rest of my poor garroted paper. 'Aha, this too!'

'There are no authentic passions in the nineteenth century, that's why the French are so bored. Great acts of cruelty are committed, but without cruelty.'

'You call this a prophetic statement. I call it a reactionary one. Stendhal adored the Italian Renaissance – life as grand opera, passionate loves and hatreds, jealousy, revenge, and outsize ambition. Again the lust for novelty and drama, for enormous egos, heroic individuals, and the fascination with the Corsican gangster who set Europe on its ear. Tell me, what comes to mind when you read that passage, "In nineteenth-century France great acts of cruelty are committed, but without cruelty?" Shall I tell you what I hear? I hear the fatigue of a great nation that has spent itself in the revolution and the Napoleonic wars, and needs to go to ground, to hibernate for several boring decades. *Le Rouge et le Noir* is a novel about a country slowly boring itself to death. And what is the cure for boredom? A war of conquest in Africa! Another *jour de gloire*!'

I knew that wasn't true. I had read enough history to feel certain that Stendhal (unlike Tocqueville, for example) would have denounced the scorched earth campaigns of the 1840s that left western Algerian devastated and decimated for two generations. When Wally's father volunteered for the French army, he went for the enlistment bonus. It went by weight, Wally told me, so much per pound of human flesh. His father was a slight man, the bonus was small, but it fed his family for a while.

Prof Chiunsi was a good man. He knew Algeria. He had gone to teach at the University of Algiers, when de Gaulle came to power, but realizing there was no place left in the city after six years of war, for peacemakers and bridge-builders, Muslim or European, he retreated to Cularo. I learned this later and certainly not from him. In that age of rigid hierarchies, it was unthinkable for a professor of his age and standing to pour out his heart to a brash, unprepared student from across the Atlantic. So from the height of his ancient pedestal, he scored debating points, an easy victory. My wasted year in academia, if not for Wally.

9

Wally and I fought for the first time that winter. In a last ditch attempt to derail the ceasefire in Algeria, the Christian terrorists of the OAS, planted a bomb in the Paris apartment house of de Gaulle's Minister of Culture, André Malraux. He was out that morning, in February 1962, but a four-year-old girl in the same building took a face full of shrapnel and was left blind in one eye. The atrocity hit home. That week there were massive protests in Paris. The Paris police included many returnees from the colonial wars who despised the demonstrators. Eight young people were killed in the crush. The day of their funeral there were demonstrations all over France, even in Cularo.

Wally said that any protest at this point in the war was too little, too late. He had no desire to participate. If he went along, it would only be to keep an eye on me. I told him I was not a child, and could manage without his supervision. And if things got rough, unlikely in Cularo but you never know, he was a more obvious target than I was.

'You mean with my *tête de melon*?' he said. I had impugned his courage, struck a raw nerve. I thought I knew every nerve in his body. Mistake: just because a man is an effusive talker, doesn't mean he's telling you the whole truth all the time. There are reticences and lies of omission. Blank spaces on the map to be filled in. Geography is a slow science, I have not mastered it yet.

When the time came, we marched together in a great peaceful demonstration, after dark, under the usual cold drizzle. My fellow students, the lecture-hall hecklers and the lunch-line shovers, whose brothers had been killed or maimed in the long war, found their voices at last. We took over the city, ten or twelve abreast, holding our banners aloft, like giant tickertapes. Not mob rule, but strength in numbers, solidarity and history. We chanted slogans from the thirties, '*Le fascisme ne passera pas.*' The street had come to life and we were part of it. Wally had a million French allies that night.

That wasn't how he saw it, however. He said it took the shock of Frenchmen killing Frenchmen on French soil to arouse French consciences. Maybe he was right. Someone clearly got the message. Six weeks later, the ceasefire was signed at last. The satirical weekly *Le Canard Enchaîné* was Wally's favorite newspaper. He was teaching me to decode its abstruse puns and arcane allusions. But anyone could get the point of that week's banner headline: '*MERCI DE GAULLE.*' The war was all but over.

Wally spotted Davy in the crowd that night, several rows ahead of us, a big blond guy with a big blond dog in an elaborate harness.

A blind protestor, now that took courage! Wally exclaimed, suddenly his cheerful bossy self again. He had read about the young man in the local paper. A California chess whiz with a golden retriever named Sasha, who answered to forty-three distinct commands. Davy confirmed the press reports.

72

'Sasha does everything but play chess and I may still teach her,' he told us over a quick plate of spaghetti that same night. He returned often for a meal and a chess match with Wally. Davy always won and Wally was always as pleased as if he'd won himself. He adopted Davy like a son or a kid brother. They had so much to tell each other, I sometimes felt left out.

Davy projected confidence, or tried to. On his second visit to the room on rue du Dragon, he demanded a chance to get acquainted in the proper way. We were to hold quite still while he ran his hands over our faces. All his other senses conspired to replace the missing one, he told us, patting us discreetly but avidly. Voices were essential. He never forgot a voice. They had colors. Wally's was warm and sooty, like a well-banked fire. Mine was spiky, like a spill of carpenter's tacks, he said, while kneading my shoulders.

'Blind people give the best massages,' he boasted. I thought he was overdoing it and was about to break loose, when Wally signaled me to be patient with this friend he treated with almost superstitious deference, as if he were a prophet or oracle.

Davy played the role to the hilt. He gave us the once over with his fingertips and then uttered his opinion. Sort of like those birds they keep in cages at the carnival, I told Wally later, letting them out only to peck at cards that tell your fortune. He said I was a pitiless rationalist and should be ashamed.

'Congratulations,' Davy declared the results of his tactile researches. 'You two are a perfect match.'

'How can you tell?' Wally asked, intrigued. There was a lot that Davy didn't know about us yet. So far our conversations had dealt with chess, France, Camembert, and Sasha who had been with Davy by then for eight years, since he

73

was thirteen and lost his sight to meningitis. Sasha was his best friend and alter ego; they had grown up together.

'I know it sounds corny, but I have a sixth sense. I'm sensitive to minute vibrations,' Davy answered Wally. 'Only kidding, that's California talk. But seriously, I can just see the two of you in Palo Alto, you'd fit right in. Wally needs to learn more English first. Why don't we teach him?'

'You go right ahead,' I said. I was beginning to mistrust Davy and his way of taking charge of us, as if we were a figment of his imagination, which to a degree we were. Wally had his native realm, his areas of expertise, his sunny essence, and I would have followed him to the far ends of the Sahara if he had asked me, but I could not imagine him at home in the US. Its sheer immensity would dwarf him, reduce him to the status of a fresh off the boat immigrant non-entity. But I didn't argue with Davy. Sooner or later he would learn the truth about the perfect couple – our days were numbered. We had known that from the start. There was a built-in escape clause to our friendship.

In the end I told Wally we had to set our enthusiastic friend straight. To leave him in the dark so to speak was tantamount to lying. Davy would be hurt when he found out. What could wound him more than to learn we had been tiptoeing around him, exchanging winks and signs under cover of his infirmity? Wally agreed at once and said he'd talk to Davy next chance he got. Two days later Davy came by at four p.m., all alone with Sasha. The dog was the great facilitator in our lives that spring. She set a standard for honesty we couldn't hope to match. Wally said she had more *nif*, meaning nose, meaning self-respect, than most humans he had met.

'So, Wally told me about the two of you,' Davy came right to the point. 'Bummer.'

74

'Yes, he's going to abandon me one of these days,' I said lightly.

'And you'll abandon him,' he had the gall to tell me. 'Or would you follow him to X . . .?' He casually dropped the name of Wally's village as if it were a mere dot on a map and not mysterious forbidden ground, off limits to me.

'I would go there if he asked me,' I said. Now it was my turn to lie. I was furious with this meddling prophet. 'But he won't ask me and now you know why. So let's just drop it, all right?' I begged and turned to Sasha, sitting by patiently and above all silently.

'Good dog,' I said and patted her. Bad man: Davy took the hint.

'I just came to drop off this postcard I received today. It's Santa Cruz. Wally wanted to know what my hometown looked like. I guess I said some foolish things. I feel like I blundered into a French movie starring, I don't know, maybe Simone Signoret? You know what I mean. I'm new in town. I guess it shows.'

'We're all just blundering along until the axe falls,' I said. Davy didn't get it.

'The guillotine, the end of our allotted time,' I played a part too, the brittle sophisticate, relieved when Wally's arrival interrupted the performance. I was awfully glad to see him just then. I loved what I saw. Would I have loved him if I couldn't see him? He wanted me, he confessed when we had been together a few months, from the day my skirt hiked up while I was rolling down a hill in juvenile abandon, and he caught a glimpse of my thighs. Or say he loved the prospect of my thighs. The rest came later. Davy would figure it out for himself in his own sweet time. Meanwhile that spring Wally taught him how to dance the samba, volunteering me as the straw partner, or taking the

75

female role himself, in his eagerness to help Davy learn to lead like a man. I wasn't jealous then, I loved to watch Wally dance. He was a natural. Put him down anywhere in the world and he would catch the beat and run with it.

In April Davy left on a whirlwind tour of Italy. Sasha stayed behind in Wally's care. It meant rushing home from work at lunchtime and back out to the factory again, but he did it happily. Sasha was a phenomenon of nature and culture, an *interlocuteur valable* (bureaucratic wartime French for a trustworthy negotiating partner) with her own brand of intelligence. I would gladly have helped out, to spare Wally the midday rush, but although we spoke the same language, the dog did not trust me. When I called her by her rightful name, she just lay there, deaf, and disconsolate. When Wally broke into comical Americanese, 'Come on, Brownie,' she sprang up, raring to go. She knew with him no harm could come to her. And she had been trained to obey a male voice.

10

'There's a letter for you. One of your froggy friends, the handwriting is unmistakable. C.A.O. – Charles André Ormesson?'

'Not quite,' I restrained myself. I wanted to grab the letter and run away with it before my aunt had a chance to learn of its arrival. Her mind was like the little mill that never stops grinding, in the fairy tale called *Why the Sea is Salt*. Once Nora saw the letter she would insist on knowing who wrote it, who his parents were, if they had money, whether his intentions were honorable, and whether I had slept with him yet (not wise if money was involved, those conservative Catholic families demanded purity in their women). Finally, she would insist on reading the letter and might even dictate an appropriate reply that I would have to scramble to keep her from posting. A contest of wits and wills I was bound to lose in the end, or maybe in the beginning.

Give me the letter, please? I didn't say it, I just smiled, while kind gentlemanly Uncle James repeated, 'froggy penmanship,' without malice of course, all in good fun. He had after all been a French master himself at one time; now he directed the Wimbledon College of English. He was on holiday at a borrowed cottage in Leicestershire, where I had been invited to spend the Easter break, my first visit to England ever. I came over from France on the boat and the night train, made an early connection at St Pancras and hitchhiked with a kindly older couple who went out of their way to drop me on my uncle's doorstep, not liking to see a young thing standing in the road, they said, because there was no telling.

I possessed, according to my aunt, an absurd sense of safety, an innocence dangerous to myself and others. One thing to get yourself in trouble, but what about your mates? It made a good story to tell, although there was no one to tell it to, but the three of us, who already knew it. But Aunt Nora never minded repeating herself.

'César Antoine Olivier, Clovis Arnault Ornière.' My eyes must have given me away, because my uncle pounced at once, 'Ye gods, I guessed it, didn't I? Fancy naming your son Clovis, why not Vercingetorix or Asterix? The family must be a retrograde lot, Pétainistes perhaps? What's he studying, this Clovis? Poor chap, they must rag him mercilessly.'

'He's not a student,' I defended my loyal correspondent.

'What, not a student?' Aunt Nora in her cook's apron, and kerchief knotted at the nape of her neck like a stalwart wartime munitions worker – a style that worked well with her jet black hair and prominent widow's peak, she pointed out – came from the kitchen and promptly commandeered the conversation.

'I hope he's not a shoe salesman, you wrote us about all those shoe shops in Cularo. When peasants come into a little money, that's the first thing they spend it on, after pigs and chickens.'

Then she spotted the letter in her husband's hand. 'The shoe salesman has written you a letter. You gave him our address, did you? I hope he's not planning to turn up here unannounced and throw himself on our hospitality?'

'Oh no, he can't just take off when he likes, he works six days a week. Fifty hours, it's legal in France, imagine.'

I blurted out the truth for once, in my eagerness to keep on my aunt's good side. (But which was her good side? It was always shifting.)

'I see. Of course we know just what you can mean to a man who works fifty hours a week,' my aunt canvassed her husband with flashing eyes. He nodded in sober agreement.

'We're in love, actually,' I defended the truth, now it was out. 'I'd marry him in a minute,' I added. Now that was a lie again, but it felt like truth in the telling.

'I'm sure you would, but he hasn't asked you. Am I right?' my aunt replied at once. And of course she was right, although for the wrong reasons.

'Come to the table, you two, your letter will keep till after.'

Uncle James laid the letter on the mantelpiece in the chilly front room. No fires to be lit till teatime, lest the neighbors, seeing the smoking chimney, accuse the American wife of corrupting her British husband to a shameful softness.

After lunch my aunt and uncle lay down for their siesta, a habit they acquired in Portugal during the war and still clung to in colder climes. Not that I ever questioned their habits. Each morning I took my bath in the tepid water where first uncle, then aunt following, sat for a half hour. Britain had borne the brunt of the war and was still recovering. Rationing was over, but self-imposed rationing of bath water was a patriotic duty, Nora explained; I did not question her. She was the only woman in the family who had seen the war in Europe. My American uncles were in the army, a huge swaddling bureaucratic institution. Nora and James were attached to an institution too, Her Majesty's government. James was something at the British consulate in Oporto, near the Spanish border. Nora hinted at trips to the border to receive groups of Jewish children smuggled out of Spain. Uncle James was secretive and non-committal. Yet I remained in awe of this couple who crossed the Atlantic in a convoy of troop ships in January 1943. Nora's wit and beauty drew her into the thick of things in every epoch; not like me, clinging to the margins, a cold room in Cularo, and a hopeless attachment to a man I had no intention, because no hope, of marrying.

I set out for a walk across the fields. Lambs gambolled, clumped daffodils recited isolated lines from Wordsworth. Poetry in this locale seemed almost a given, a mere reporting of what nature threw at one, with a fine careless rapture. Shelley or Keats? James would know but tall, slender James did not like to take walks. His aching back confined him to a semi-sedentary existence. Of course he never mentioned it, leaving it to Nora.

'James is in pain but you won't hear of it from him,' Nora announced, sometimes to me in private, sometimes in James's presence, prompting a cheery, 'No, indeed' from the silent sufferer.

Exhilarated by the revelation of an English April, blue sky, fluffy scattered clouds, the silly sheep, and the vocal daffodils, I actually forgot about the letter till I reached my favorite yew tree, a mile from the cottage. There I recalled it with an inner yelp of joy.

First I'll read it, then I'll commit it to memory, then I'll tear it to pieces and swallow them, I thought. That was both the safest course and the most satisfying – to ingest something Wally had produced with his own hands, his right hand on the pen, his left on the paper, two whole pages, would strengthen the pact between us. Our *Accords d'Evian*. Wally was my one and only *interlocuteur valable*, my ideal negotiating partner.

Uncle James would have hated Wally, wrong height, wrong color, wrong religion, wrong social class. The rest might be forgiven; class was the killer. That way Wally had of clicking his tongue against his teeth, in disagreement. I had tried it once in Nora's hearing and had been sharply reprimanded, 'Don't do that, it's vulgar.'

As usual, my aunt was at least partly right.

Wally, I hated to admit it, had a surface accretion of vulgarisms; inevitable in a rolling stone with only a grade school education and native wit to guide him. He reveled in silly riddles that circulated at the factory:

> *Quelle est la différence entre un gosse et une femme?*
> *L'enfant aime le chocolat, la femme aime le choc au lit.*

But James cherished his own brand of schoolboy humor:

> 'Tickle your ass with a feather?'
> 'I beg your pardon, what did you say?'
> 'Particularly nasty weather.'

The same silliness, upper-class version.

Wally's letter made me blush. He was dreaming of my lovely white thighs, but also, lest I think him crass, of my sharp mind. Meanwhile he was keeping company with 'our beloved Sasha.'

Along the path, I picked dandelions and made solemn wishes, before scattering the seeds. For my father, peace from his torments, for my mother and my brother, respite from my father's black moods; for all the others, health and wealth and trips to Paris, to see for themselves. It was hard being the only one to travel, a privileged pariah in the family.

The day I turned up on my aunt and uncle's doorstep, Nora was as charming as could be; fed me crustless cucumber sandwiches and treacle tart she'd baked especially, with Lyle's golden syrup and Devonshire clotted cream, and listed all the places we would visit. I sat huddled by the fire in my uncle's woolen bathrobe because my clothes reeked of *Gauloises*; the whole of France reeked, no one noticed till they crossed the border, Nora joked with great good humor and scratched delicately at my skirt and sweater with a little nail brush dipped in soapsuds, a trick she'd learned once from a French landlady who did not believe in washing clothes by immersion, because it wears them out. While my reeking garments aired on the clothesline out back, I was made to try on all my uncle's shirts till we found one that suited Nora's unerring fashion sense, a long dress shirt of creamy challis, minus its detachable stiff collar. It came to just above my knees, a most becoming length, my aunt reminded me years later, during the mini craze. She was always years ahead of the trend.

She waited till next morning to attack my hair, pulling a fine comb through my tangled locks.

'Don't just sit there with your eyes shut; you can't afford to be so passive. Pay attention, learn to make the most of yourself. You're not Princess Anne, you know, if you want to marry a rich man, you'll have to work at it.'

'Who said I want to marry a rich man?' I asked, carelessly, in the languor of the moment. My first mistake. Treacle turned to gall, a long harangue, a pent up flood of grievances. Where had they been the day before? Waiting on tiptoe in the wings? Or not yet hatched? Or cunningly suppressed till the right moment? Whatever the answer, on the morning of my second day under my aunt's roof I learned the painful undeniable lesson, that I was criminally selfish. Instead of studying in France ('What are you studying? Why do you bother? You know you'll never have an original thought!'), I should have left school at sixteen, gone to work to support my family, and groomed myself to marry a rich man, to insure my mother, Nora's long-suffering sister, a comfortable old age.

'Don't you think your mother deserves that much from you?'

But you ran off to England in wartime, I wanted to reply, leaving your widowed mother frantic with worry. I held my tongue, out of respect or to be honest, simple dread of Nora's wrath, the ungainsayable truths she could utter when provoked, while the vein in her left temple throbbed and Uncle James listened from behind the closed door of the study (the tiny cottage had a study!) for a sign the squall had passed, as it always did, quite quickly.

'James, don't cower in your corner, come see what I've done with Louise's hair. You must never travel without a private hairdresser,' she told me. The worm had turned; fatal flaws were only foibles after all, quaint, and quite forgivable.

'Well done, good show,' James boomed. 'Don't hang around in dreary Cularo, you're wasted there, go to Rome, and sit in a café on Via Veneto.'

'Just what I was thinking,' Nora agreed. 'She could be in

83

the movies; Gina Lollobrigida was discovered in a café on the Via Veneto, you know.'

'I can't act,' I objected.

'Neither can she, the directors tell her what to do and she does it.'

'But don't marry an Italian,' James warned.

'Unless he's an Agnelli or an Olivetti,' Nora added.

'Even then,' James objected. 'Italians make jealous husbands.'

'Whom shall I marry?' I asked, feeling reckless with possibilities.

'Marry someone who'll let you alone,' James said, peevishly, as if he wished he'd thought of it in time himself, and retreated to the study, where he was left alone for the rest of the morning, while Nora took me shopping at the Marks and Spencer in Melton Mowbray. She bought me a pair of black pumps, a black corduroy vest to wear over James's long dress shirt *sans* collar, and a funny looking green raffia hat, like an inverted shaggy lampshade. I thought it looked awful but Nora insisted I had a classic face for hats and should never be without one.

By teatime the spell broke again and I learned I was a wretched ingrate, burying my nose in a book, in silent contempt of loving aunts and uncles. Show off, reading Dostoevsky in French, who was I trying to impress? Fake intellectual, like my parents, proud of their poverty, their ignorance, although they were too ignorant to call it that. I sat silently, eyes open but downcast, under the assault. After tea I kissed them both goodnight, went to bed, and cried myself to sleep. And so a pattern was set, as changeable as English weather, sun, then clouds and squalls, then sudden scatterings of sunshine, then another squall or two. Then bed, tears, and fitful sleep.

I did not ingest the letter after all, but stored it in my pocket, a talisman against Nora's attacks. Wally was my *wali*, my protector, in Arabic, a language I endowed with magic properties. Desire that deserted me in bed, blossomed in his absence. Out in the fields, I lost all track of time.

Nora called me to my senses.

'You're late for tea again.' Smoke blew from the chimney, near sundown.

'Drop your shoes here in the doorway, James will clean them for you later. I know, you'd just as soon do it yourself but we can't stop him, I've tried, believe me, and it's hopeless. You know after his mother's death, he tagged after the servants in that gloomy house in Gloucestershire. The old earl, his uncle, couldn't bother with a boy of twelve, no one expected it of him, and a year later they sent James off to a quite decent public school, which is what you call a private school in the US, you know that don't you? And then to Cambridge. James thinks you should see Cambridge while you're here; once you've seen it you won't want to leave but you will need to go back, pack your things, ship them here, and when the term is over, you can follow. That seems the best plan, don't you think? And then we'll see about next year, it may be too late, you'd have to take exams, of course you'd have no trouble passing them, but they're only given at fixed times, the schedule was set three centuries ago, and brooks no exception. Well, James will make it his business to find out, once he's finished rescuing your shoes, that is. Now what?'

'I'll think about it,' I said ungraciously. 'The offer is most generous.'

'I get it,' Nora said. 'You're still mooning over your shoe salesman or whatever he is. French, is he? You never said.'

'Oh, yes,' I did not have to stretch the truth. Wally carried a French ID card, like all Algerians in the last years of the war. His said '*français musulman d'Algérie, FMA*,' to mark the difference with those of European origin.

'Good looking, is he? Married perhaps? I'd much rather he was, you know. Just being practical, since no one else in this family is capable of keeping the realities in mind. Oh, I know they bought you matching suitcases and winter underwear. But did they tell you anything that you might need to know about the facts of life? No, of course they didn't, your mother lives in terror of your brother learning there is such a thing as SEX. For that reason alone, she's glad to have you half a world away. At least here, you're no threat to his innocence. Oh, I'm sorry, I've touched a sore spot, I see. Well, that's the way in families. Here, use this,' Nora handed me a crumpled hanky, stroked my head once, experimentally, and then withdrew her hand.

'I do know how you feel, I have feelings too although I don't indulge them. If I asked James to uproot and find a post at some backwoods college in the US, he'd do it in a minute, for my sake. It's for my sake we hang on here, when he could be a shining light in cow-town academia. Can you imagine, with his looks, his manners, his diction, they'd be wild for him? I'd probably be jealous. That's not why we're here, however; we live in England because my sisters wish to keep me at arm's length and I oblige them. In my generation, I am the pariah, as you are in yours. And you thought no one understood you. Sorry, kiddo, you're transparent.'

'Oh, Nora, do shut up,' James intervened from the doorway and vanished.

'All right, I see your point. Young love will run its course.' Nora relented briefly. 'One last bit of advice, and then I give

86

it up for good. Do NOT talk about your abortions. No one wants to hear that stuff. It's just like going to the toilet.'

She's trying to trick me into a confession, I thought. But there was nothing to confess. The word alone gave me the creeps. Or was this Nora's own confession, typically oblique? Of course she would have wanted children of her own and as for James, the early war orphan, a recalcitrant niece was a poor substitute for the son he never had. Poor man, poor woman. Nora's speechifying came at you so fast and fierce that you were almost bound to panic. But if you kept your cool, behind the blitz and blather there was sorrow at the core. Big-hearted Wally would have pegged Nora at once for an unhappy older woman.

'Be kind to your aunt, she's your mother's sister,' he would have said, tautological and deferential.

Charles called it Wally's Biblical, or better, his Koranic mode. I longed to talk to Wally. But it was just as well I couldn't get him on the phone; Nora would have found a way to listen in.

Uncle James and I set out for Cambridge on our own. Without Nora at his back, he turned quite voluble, found new targets for his ragging, and then gave it up altogether, so that in the end I enjoyed his company, and even managed, over lunch in a dark pub, to draw him out a bit. He and Nora met in spring of 1940 in a Greenwich Village club. The Vanguard, had I never been there? I shook my head.

'Well, next time you're in the States, go see if it's still there and drop me a line, will you?'

'Of course,' I said, eager to serve this intermittently kind, mysteriously reticent and possibly tragic figure.

'We visited the hospital when you were born. Your mother sat in bed with the newspaper on her knees, tears

87

streaming down her face. She had read about the fall of France. So you see, it was pre-destined.'

'What was?' I asked.

'Why, your affinity, or should I say, your tender sympathy, for all things froggy. What does he do in life, this Clovis of yours? We know he's not really a shoe salesman.'

'What difference does it make? I'm not going to marry him,' I said, after some hesitation.

'Bravo, that's the spirit. All right, we'll drop that line of inquiry, shall we? And go look at my old digs in Ewart House.' We walked along the paths under the lovely trees. Only the dons in their long gowns trod the perfect lawns, by ancient right and privilege.

My uncle's old rooms, up a dark staircase, were small, dingy, and low ceilinged, but peopled, in his mind's eye, with a brilliant crowd of linguists, poets, and barristers to be.

'The war was looming but we paid it no mind. Youth is immortal.' In the entryway the names of those who fell in the last war, James's war, were engraved upon a stone tablet, affixed to the wall. Eleven names, I counted quickly.

'Did you know these people?' I asked, ghoulishly, a second-hand shudder at best.

'We're all survivors of something or someone, aren't we?' James said with his usual offhand politeness.

Nora was watching for us on the doorstep, and ran to put the kettle on for tea. When we were seated round the little table, she began again.

'Well, so its decided then, is it? You'll spend the fall term at a crammer's and sit the exams a year from now?'

'What about the Via Veneto?' I asked churlishly.

'That's the fallback plan, if you fail the scholarship exams,' Nora was unflappable. 'But you won't, with your brain. Thank goodness someone in this family knows how to use their noggin. I can't wait to get you out of that provincial hole. Whose idea was it in the first place to bury you alive in the French Alps?'

'The Fulbright people choose our destinations,' I said. 'I wanted to leave home the quickest way.'

'You could have left school at sixteen, worked, saved, and gone to Paris on your own.'

Nora left school at fourteen, the week her father died. Everything she knew she taught herself, she liked to say, or learned from James. James taught her diction, protocol, and Anglo-Irish history, which was the history of his family, who went to Ireland with Cromwell and were rewarded with great estates but later lost them, gambling. James taught Nora how to pitch her voice an octave lower. If she'd had better teeth, she would have been an actress. James would have been her coach and manager. Of course the timing was all wrong, the war, their travels, Italy. No one could be considered educated, who had not lived a year in Italy. I was ready to believe that. I hated to hear Wally say he didn't like Italians, you couldn't trust them, unlike the Spanish. His best friends at home were Spanish, they always kept their word. Such narrow judgments weren't worthy of the man I loved, I felt, although I didn't argue with him, since it was all hypothetical. He could not afford to travel; I couldn't yet, but would someday, without him. Given his prejudices, it was probably just as well.

'So it's all settled then,' Nora repeated. 'You'll go back and pack your trunk, I can't believe you lugged a steamer trunk to France, like some prewar dowager millionairess.'

The old timers' dance, Nora explained en route to the village that night, was not something she herself would take part in, but she liked to watch the locals enjoy themselves. These people, tradesmen, and artisans from hereabouts, who gathered once a month at the social hall, were nothing less than the backbone of a great nation. Their modesty and courage had won the war and saved mankind from German barbarism, French dishonesty, Austrian sloppiness, and all the rest of it.

'So if some sweet old codger asks you to dance, you accept graciously, and give it a whirl. These people are our neighbors, you understand, we don't want them to think we're standoffish.'

'Throw your niece to the wolves, will you?' James's jesting had an edge to it. He was angry with Nora about something. They had had words behind closed doors while I was dressing for this evening out. I hoped it wasn't about me.

The man who tapped me for the tango had a white moustache and a head of stiff white hair; he could have been an older, a much older, Wally. He was taller, thickset, and ruddy faced, but with the same erect bearing, light on his feet, and careful to mark a polite distance between us.

'I'm on me best behavior, your aunt has her eye on me, she's one woman I would not care to cross,' he joked, as I spun away from him and back again, stopping well short of frontal contact.

'Thank you so much for the thought,' I parroted a phrase Nora had taught me. All week there had been lectures on the formulae of English courtesy and diffidence. At the grocer's for example: 'I wonder if I could possibly trouble you to cut me a few slices of that tempting baloney.'

'Thank YOU, young lady,' my partner replied. 'Just visiting these parts, are you?'

'I'm spending a year in France,' I said.

'They're champions at the tango, they nearly invented it, as I recall.'

'So they claim,' I said.

'But you don't believe them?'

'I'd like to,' I said.

'Then do. You're too young to be suspicious, if you follow.'

'My sentiment exactly,' I pronounced the words without thinking, as I often did with Wally, letting the minted phrase speak for itself, taking things farther and faster than I meant them to, trusting him to find a right and decorous retreat.

Nora tapped me on the shoulder.

'Excuse us,' she said to the old gent. 'We're just about to leave.' As we went out the back door she hissed, 'It's very good of you to dance with these old coots, but you don't have to flirt with them. I never saw anything like it. No wonder you're in trouble back in France.'

'No trouble, no trouble at all. I was just making polite conversation. Where's James?'

'In the car, come on, we're going home.' They had been arguing again, behind my back, and kept it up all the way home. I tried not to listen. It was none of my business, I told myself, although I felt at fault for bringing strife into their settled household.

'Who taught you how to dance the tango?' Nora attacked, in the chilly front room. 'I'm going to tell her the truth, James. Don't try to stop me.'

'I wouldn't dream of it; what would be the point? We all know you're unstoppable,' James said and went to put a light under the kettle.

'A good thing too, or I'd be married to some Communist in Brooklyn, dodging those nasty committees. And as for you . . .' but as he was out of earshot, she did not persist. Then she dropped her voice another octave, if that were possible, and a great many decibels, and in a hoarse whisper, as if rehearsing a penance after confession (three Our Fathers, two Hail Marys) said, 'Your mother should have split your father's head open with an axe ten years ago, instead she kowtows to him, and neglects the education of her children. Someone had to take an interest in your well-being, as long as you're in Europe, continental Europe, or the UK, or the colonies. It's all one to me, I'm responsible for your safety, I have the obligation and the worry, do you understand, the worry. How do you think I feel when my young niece receives lascivious propositions from strange men, at my private address?'

'You read my mail. You had no right,' I jumped up. I didn't care about the rest, I wanted Wally's letter, the precious mark of his strong hand.

'Where is my letter?' I demanded.

'That piece of trash, I burned it in the fireplace at four p.m. today.'

I nearly bumped into James returning with the tea tray. He had timed his absence to avoid the squall. Coward!

'No tea for you?' he asked. Was he really so oblivious? I mustered the cruelty to test him.

'Nora burned my mail while we were out.'

'Well, no harm done. You'd read it and committed it to memory,' James said, the giveaway.

'You wrote to him, you wrote to Wally,' I accused my aunt, hoping for a strong rebuttal.

'Just a brief note,' Nora said coolly, 'to tell him you no longer wish to hear from him, as you are preparing to enter Cambridge University next fall. I signed your name, it seemed the quickest way to make the point.'

I bolted from the room.

'Oh Nora, now you've done it, I told you one day you would go too far,' James remonstrated with his wife, in that light arch tone of moral abdication I would never understand. Nora at her most impossibly high-handed acted from conviction. James simply stood aside, laughed, or sneered, or both.

I went to pack my bag. It didn't take me long. What to do with Nora's many gifts? I hadn't wanted them, too many strings attached. I wanted only to spare Wally pain. I wanted to be back with him, in our room, a cave where neither reality nor falsehood could enter. I should have told Nora the truth from the outset. So you see, we never planned to marry, it's out of the question, we're just hanging out together for a while, and if we break each other's hearts, so be it, that's what songs are made of; in France all stories finish as a song:

> les feuilles mortes;
> un jour tu verras;
> mais si je n'ai rien,
> aime-moi quand-même.

Our connection is one big *quand-même*. Nevertheless. Don't begrudge us that. The tears were running down my face by now; so sentimental, just like Wally at his worst. The door opened, Nora slid into the room sideways and sat at the foot of the bed.

'Take it all,' she gestured toward the fiery orange scarf of what she called 'prewar georgette,' the strand of opaque amber beads, a gift from some Italian poet she had known in Venice years ago, the shaggy lampshade hat.

'I know you're upset,' Nora said, a tremendous concession

from this woman of steel. 'But someday you'll see, you will thank me.'

'*Un jour tu verras*,' I recited numbly.

'I heard that song at *Le Boeuf sur le Toit* in 1948; that funny little Algerian with the big nose, a sort of French Jimmy Durante; he was opening that night for Juliette Greco. You could have gone to Paris and had your fling there, with more panache. I hate to think of you with a provincial shoe sales-man,' she added, sounding truly wretched, as if demoted back into her plebian family.

'He's not a shoe salesman. His family owns great estates in North Africa,' I lied extravagantly, vengefully. 'Vineyards as far as the eye can see. He looks like Albert Camus, he comes from the same stock.'

'What do you propose to do now?' Nora asked, intrigued by the mention of great estates.

'I'm going back to Cularo a few days early. I would have had to go no matter what.'

'If his family is rich, why does he work so many hours?' Nora pleaded.

'Algeria is going through a great upheaval, they're going to lose everything they had,' I went on with my fairy tale. 'He has to help out.'

'Well, I hope you know what you're doing. Go to sleep, we'll wake you at six, James will drive you to the station.'

But I didn't trust them, either of them. I sat up all night writing letters to Wally in my head. At daylight I phoned for a taxi from the neighbor town. Nora came out in her bathrobe and commiserated. 'You didn't sleep? Neither did I.'

'I'm sorry to have caused so much commotion,' I said, seeing Nora pale and diminished, a tiny woman really, although she packed a wallop.

'You're not sorry at all, you're stubborn, stubborn and tough, like your mother. How do you suppose she puts up with that petty tyrant? She models herself after him and passes it on down the line. Well, write and tell us your plans. A love affair like yours is not a plan, it's an accident.' But she allowed me to kiss her cheek, and grabbed my hands in hers at the last moment, as if to keep us both from drowning. When I looked back from the departing cab, James stood alongside Nora, waving a jolly lighthearted farewell, goodbye, good riddance, his gesture said. Other people's children were a terrible nuisance.

I phoned Davy from the Gare de Lyon. I tried the number half a dozen times, till I found someone in the dormitory who agreed to go find him.

'I know someone who's going to be very happy,' Davy said when I announced my imminent return.

'I sent him a letter. If it gets there before I do, tell him not to open it.'

'Too late, he got it yesterday, he came to see me early this morning. He was late for work and he was crying.'

'Tell him to disregard it, tell him I changed my mind the minute it was mailed. Crying?'

'I'll try to catch him this evening. What time will you be there?'

'The train leaves at four. I'll be in at midnight.' I wished Davy hadn't told me about Wally crying, it terrified me to think I had the power to make him cry. In every love affair (Stendhal said) there is one who loves more. That was as it should be. Why upset the balance now?

But how could the letter have arrived so quickly, overnight in fact. Unless it was sent by express mail; unless it was mailed days ago, impossible, unless Nora intercepted

Wally's note when it arrived, and turned it over to me only days later, after posting her bogus reply. Derisory and demoniacal, and yet, flesh of my flesh, my mother's older sister, the expatriate, the exile, the righteous, the forlorn. I would tell Wally the whole story, set a test for him. If he forgave Nora's machinations, I would forgive him for shedding tears in front of Davy. Those tears that no one saw (I being absent, Davy being blind) except the one who shed them, irked me mightily. How dare Wally cry for me when we both knew and agreed – it was *prévu dans les accords* – that he would leave me someday, that I would be abandoned and bereft, when he returned home to his family. I fumed until it dawned on me that this was Nora's plan, precisely. She meant to drive my lover crazy, opening a wedge between us. She won't get away with it, I vowed, and checked my watch again, for the third time in ten minutes. Cularo was at the end of the line, the end of the world, behind the jagged mountains.

Wally had a midnight supper waiting on the little table by the window and a sprig of lily of the valley in a glass, since it was 1 May. The French clung to their little rites, like everyone else.

'*O Clovis, tu es mon seul vice,*' I exclaimed, my spirits restored. He expected to find me beaten down, maybe even literally beaten by my family, forced to write that letter that cut him to the quick, although he smelled a rat, suspected treachery, not from me of course but from my blood relations. Families were all alike. They thought they owned you. They did own you. He took the letter seriously for just that reason. He said, 'You call me Clovis so you can play games with my name, go ahead, I don't mind, I know you mean no harm.'

'That's not the reason,' I said. 'I prefer to call you by the name your father gave you, it makes me feel as if I've known you all your life. As if . . .' Words failed me. I went and sat on his lap, and burrowed into his shoulder, the way lovers do on park benches in songs by Georges Brassens.

'*Mon clou de girofle,*' I murmured. *Girofle* in English was clove, short for Clovis.

'Your mind doesn't stop for a minute,' he said. 'First I was a sin, now I'm a spice, and if I was just a man, wouldn't that do?'

'You know what I love best about you?' I ignored his question.' The color of your skin, it's so honest, I can't look at white men any more, they always seem to be hiding something, do you know what I mean, or hiding from something . . .' Even fine-boned Uncle James was a lying cheat.

'Mademoiselle is turning racist,' Wally said patiently. He would let me talk myself out, he understood that after ten days with family I was a nervous wreck, and then . . . from the table to the bed was a short hop.

'No, I swear, it's not that. I can't stand my own color either, I want to be repainted the same color as you, know what I mean?'

'We could give it a try,' Wally said, caressing the nape of my neck. 'Where would you like to begin?'

11

'What will you do today?' Wally asked me every morning, before he left for work, keeping tabs on me. Now classes were over I was a free woman for the first time in my life. I could sleep late or go swimming when the pool opened or stay indoors and look for trouble. Trouble came thick and fast since the March ceasefire. It came in little square envelopes posted in Algeria. They overflowed the drawers and lay scattered on the desk. Their contents were a mystery to me, I studied the stamps, French stamps – Algeria remained part of France until July – and the handwriting, identifying only two correspondents, Wally's half brother Daoud, and Wally's wife, whose name he never mentioned. Instead he said '*Ma femme,*' in the same modest way he always said, '*ma religion.*'

Aunt Nora would have read these letters, as by right. I had my self-respect. These letters were not meant for my eyes, their authors had never heard of me and quite likely never would. Wally and I were thick as thieves, yet there was a part of his world and his life where I did not exist. Knowing this gave me what I called an 'ontological ache.'

One day in late May I retrieved the mail from where it lay, at the foot of the grand stairway, and found a postcard from my father, the first all year, with a scrawled question, 'What are you plans?' And another letter for Wally from the home front. By now I knew the names of Wally's younger brothers; there were three of them, miraculous survivors of the war, living, with wives and children, under their father's roof, although they might well disperse later on. How many children in the household? '*Une vraie ribambelle,*' Wally said and claimed he had lost count.

I held the latest envelope against the little bedside lamp, trying to decipher a line or two. If I asked Wally he would read the letter to me, he had done so in the past. They all ended in the same way: '*Nous vous embrassons cher frère, chacun pour son nom*' (We embrace you dear brother, each according to his name), that touching, Biblical formula, like naming day in Paradise.

The ache set in again. I felt sluggish with the weight of a whole world from which I was excluded, locked out as surely as Wally's wife was locked in. The mirror symmetry of our positions made us sisters, I told myself, waving the envelope over the steam from Wally's little tin teapot where he had brewed tea for me a thousand times – till the seal gave way, as if opened by an unseen hand, a helpful or, more likely, a hurtful djinn.

'*Cher frère,*' why does she call him brother? (It's like cousin, you know we're cousins, I imagined Wally saying.) 'We await your return home. In France we lived like everyone else, every day there were errands to run in the village. The grocer's wife expected me at ten a.m., each day, old Madame Fontaine, an unusually kind woman.

'Now your big brother confines us to the house; so be it, since to protest would cause your mother grief, but if you don't come soon who knows what will be. He talks against you, he calls you the "*roumi*," the European, even to your children, they're terrified of him, he took away their scooter as they were giving Nour rides in the street, he said it was improper but she's only three, when this was pointed out to him, he said I talk like a *roumia* too. This letter comes to you from my brother's house, we can trust him not to read it.' (I blushed to think that Wally's wife was spied on at every turn.) Then came a line that proved this woman could defend herself: 'I am sharpening a pin for your return.'

Reading on, I learned that Wally's father was all but paralyzed with a flare up of arthritis, the half brother wanted the whole house for himself, and had already threatened to evict everyone when the time came. The chaos in the about-to-be-liberated country seeped into the household. Charles liked to imagine the 'Biblical purity' of Wally's origins. And yet the Book of Genesis – how did Charles of all people forget this? – is full of killer rivalries, Cain and Abel, on and on.

Lacking a name for Wally's wife, to myself I called her, as he did, 'Mafemme.' Mafemme was missing in the photos I had seen, an arm, a hip, at the edge of a snapshot of two boys perched, grinning, on a dented wall. Were there other photos somewhere? I did not go hunting for them. Not that I wouldn't stoop so low but I was afraid of what I might find. The face of my betrayal. Wally's too. He betrayed Mafemme with me as later he would betray me with Mafemme. I hated it when he called Mafemme '*ma légitime*' . . . as if he were an ordinary Frenchman, instead of Albert Camus's tragic, dark-hued twin. But perhaps it was just one more way of veiling her given name.

Almost immediately on my return from England, I wrote the Fulbright Committee to say I had decided to interrupt my studies and, while grateful for the opportunity offered, would not be taking advantage of the second year of my two-year scholarship. Nora's opinions weighed with me, despite everything. 'You'll never have an original thought,' was an inescapable verdict, Prof Chiunsi seconded the motion. A new languor chased thinking altogether. To fight it, I returned to the task, abandoned the previous winter, of translating Thucydides's Melian dialogue, but again the work lagged badly. Wally noticed my distraction and scolded gently. When I begged off dancing one Friday night, he sulked for a minute and then said, never mind, we'll invite Davy to eat with us.

On my twenty-second birthday, on line at the bank to deposit my final check from the committee, I fainted dead away and awoke in a large leather arm chair, surrounded by concerned employees, including the bank president, a kindly man with white hair who offered me a drink of the liqueur brewed in the distillery downstairs from Wally's room. Hair of the dog, I thought. A fellow student gave me the name of a doctor who confirmed my fears. Now I had another secret to keep from Wally.

Mafemme wrote again. This time I had no shame about reading the letter. Pregnancy made me practically a member of the family. Would I go home with Wally and become his second wife? What a cruel surprise for Mafemme after her long wait. Mafemme was Penelope, the French army of occupation were the abusive suitors. There was even an olive tree, not in the bedroom, but in the yard, close enough: a beautiful romance when I first heard it, now a torment.

Why didn't Wally notice the change in me? I resented his unflagging good mood. How could he be so cheerful when he knew his brother was harassing his poor wife? Of course he had no choice, he couldn't just pack up and rush home overnight, he had to work, and life at home would be chaotic and dangerous for another six months at least. By then I would be visibly pregnant . . . unless I did something quickly, but what?

I waited three weeks before telling him the news. I was carrying a part of him, unthinkable to propose its destruction. But when I announced my intentions, he agreed at once, nodding sagaciously. Of course it made sense to end the pregnancy, if it could be done safely. But then his true nature won out and eyes flashing merrily he confided, 'If it's a boy we could call him Kamel. That means perfect. If it was a girl, we could call her Leila. That means night. I've always liked that name.'

He made it sound as if we were having twins and it was his prerogative to name them both. It struck me too that he had just given me my first formal Arabic lesson, and that without the prospect of a child, there would have been no lesson, now or later. And the ache returned, almost unbearable, because except for a few odd expressions, factual curiosities, he had withheld Arabic from me till now. It was remote and private knowledge. How do you say dawn and dusk, birth and death, beauty and destruction? He never told me. I never asked.

The naming game was just a passing fancy. He offered me no practical advice, valid for the next thirty years. He didn't say, come home with me, I'll take care of you. He seemed content with my decision or at least, quietly resigned, so quietly it could have passed for male obliviousness.

Charles wrote from war games in the snake-infested bottomland of deep East Texas. I showed Wally the letter. He read and shook his head.

'Which war do they want him for? Korea, Berlin, Indo-china? Any way you look at it, they've got the wrong man for the job. Poor Charles doesn't have a mean bone in his body. You know we owe him a great deal? He introduced us. Without him, we might not have met. Or say we'd met, impulsive and impatient as we are – our chief defect, wouldn't you say – we would have scared each other off somehow. He was the perfect go-between. He gave us time to get acquainted.'

Charles didn't know we were together. He certainly didn't know about Kameleila. What would he have said? I daydreamed for a week about rushing back to the States, asking Charles to marry me and adopt Wally's child as his own. Closing the circle, so to speak. In the end, I sent a friendly neutral letter urging him to watch out for rattlers and copper-heads, and feeling like a snake myself. By the time he read my letter, Kamel was no more.

The day I left for Switzerland, Wally inspected my appearance in the doorway of our room, as if I were on my way to an interview for a fantastic job, one that would make full use of my education and talents. He talked that way, too.

'Fear nothing and no one,' he told me in the doorway. Then he added softly, 'And if it doesn't work out in Geneva, don't panic,' with a steadying hand on my shoulder. 'If it comes to that, my family would always take the kid.'

What an offer, and what timing! I didn't know whether to be grateful or appalled. Did he imagine I would abandon my first-born son? (Kamel had fully eclipsed Leila in my imagination.) But before I could ask Wally what he meant by this decidedly ambiguous offer, he took off in another direction.

'You know, it's very picturesque where we live,' he gave

the word a jokey, half-bitter twist, 'little kids running around half naked, peeing in the corners, the courtyard is just a heap of sand.' His family was poorer and more disorganized than he liked to admit, but he was giving me the whole picture now, so that if, by some remote chance, I showed up in the village with our baby, I would not be shocked by what I found inside the cactus fence. To spare him, I quickly changed the subject.

'Will you send Nour to me later on? When I'm back in the US and have my own place, she can come to me to learn English.'

'Would you do that?'

'Sure, if I can.'

'*Tu es trop bonne*,' Wally fell for my fake optimism or pretended to.

'Well, don't count on it a hundred percent,' I warned him. To plan for Nour's future while plotting Kamel's doom made me dizzy, or maybe it was just morning sickness, a mild nausea I would be rid of soon along with its root cause: the child Wally named in a moment of abandon and then let go.

12

If in Catholic France, as I had lately learned, doctors were afraid to so much as discuss contraception with their patients for fear of prosecution under current law, a few miles away in the Protestant cantons of Switzerland, abortion, although illegal, was in fact rationed by a hierarchy of experts in matters of women's health and well being. The composition of the hierarchy, the likelihood of its granting access to this controversial form of relief from the consequences of one's carelessness varied from one place to the next. In Geneva, I had heard, what you needed was a doctor whose opinion carried weight with the colleague appointed to serve as a sort of judge of last resort. Women didn't even have the vote in Switzerland in 1962. In some cantons they did, but not at the federal level. The doctors, mostly male, knew each other's reputations, history, and susceptibilities. They had friends and associates to whom they owed the courtesy of a favorable ruling now and then. Politics in other words: you had to play the system. I had no idea of this when I arrived in town, dazzled by the visible prosperity of Switzerland, after church-mouse Cularo. France, as Uncle Max warned me ages ago, had been at war since 1939.

The disparities in wealth between here and there made it feel like extortion. You consulted with one Geneva doctor who certified, for a fee, that you were pregnant; with a second who could confirm, for a larger fee, that your health was in danger. The 'tribunal' extracted a third fee, for its ruling. It all added up. I found a cheap place to stay, a boarding school on a hill, near the United Nations compound, with funereal grounds, vast empty lawns and wintry dark pines, in the local style. The students had already left for the year.

I shared a room in the dorm with a woman on her own sad errand. A mother of five with an alcoholic husband, she had come all the way from Brussels looking for a doctor willing to sterilize her. There too, there were rules and pre-requisites she listed for me. The woman must be over forty, married at least ten years, with four or more children, all living. Although my roommate met these qualifications, she had been turned down once already, the year before. She said it was because she was a foreigner. The Swiss did not want to become known as the European destination for women in trouble.

Men had power over our lives. We accepted that. The system, with its hostile, even punitive assumptions, was right and we were wrong. When the judge ruled against us, we did not rebel or draft petitions. We slunk away, disappointed and slightly mystified, beat back our panic, and looked for ways to outwit those we could not overrule. Our alliances were surreptitious, shamefaced, and sly.

I arrived in Geneva on a Thursday night. The tribunal sat on Friday afternoon. That morning I managed to see an obstetrician who confirmed my pregnancy in writing, as required. He offered to refer me to a psychiatrist for the next step of the process. That meant another week of dread uncertainty. I decided to take my chances, and show up that afternoon, without the requisite certification of my fragile mental state.

The tribunal was just a doctor's office on a broad boulevard lined with tall sturdy plane trees that made Cularo's crop look rachitic and neglected. The doctor sat as his desk in an unaccountably large office. Outside the handsome bay windows, the traffic streamed by. To the doctor's right sat a woman assistant.

'You say he's married with three children,' the doctor replied to my timid explanations. There was pity in his smile, not for me, but for my story. 'I doubt that sincerely. No, Mademoiselle, he's just a student like yourself. Isn't that so?'

'But why would I lie to you?' I demanded.

'That's obvious, isn't it? So I'll feel sorry for you. I don't feel a bit sorry for you and your privileged boyfriend. That is not to be expected.'

I had never in my life met anyone so smug, self righteous and judgmental.

'But . . .' I spluttered, dumb-founded.

'I'm sorry, you'll just have to marry your young man. It's all for the best you know. Some day you'll thank me.'

Nora's brand of malice was barely recognizable; it was erratic, passionate, and grounded in her own bitter frustrations. I would never not feel sorry for Nora, even at her cruelest. This was something very different: the cool, bureaucratic malice of an office holder. From the height of his tribunal, the doctor/judge enjoyed watching me squirm. I did a lot more than squirm. I sat down on the floor and kicked my heels in a temper tantrum, not a very diplomatic response, but since the case was hopeless anyway, I vented my rage while the assistant joined forces with her boss and dragged me by my arms to the door of the office. I

107

sprang up and ran out into the street. They let me go without complaint. Their fee was collected in advance.

At the time I was ashamed of my tantrum, but in retrospect I wasn't sorry I upset the dignity of a bogus court. Say what you want about Mediterranean misogyny, that Swiss doctor was the worst case I had ever seen. A case so blatant even I, half terrorized by my predicament, recognized it and rebelled. I was so addled and angry, I stopped thinking straight. I totally forgot essential facts like Kamel and Leila, either/or, or maybe both, what if it was twins? I thought only of outsmarting that chill, smug doctor.

My roommate brought good news that night. She had heard that in the next canton, a fifteen-minute train ride up the lake, there lived a physician who actually liked women. I would need an introduction, but that was easily obtained, through a colleague of his, a kindly woman doctor. Next morning I took the train up to Lausanne, found a bed in the youth hostel, went for a long walk along the lake, sent Wally a postcard, and on Monday afternoon went to meet Dr Vidal.

He was a tall, gangly man in corduroy pants. With his blond drooping *Gaulois* moustache, he looked like a direct descendant of Vercingetorix. In fact, he had just returned from a trip to Red China. A sheaf of Chinese magazines, printed in English for the export trade, lay on his coffee table, in an upstairs office not far from the train station of a small town half way between Lausanne and Geneva. His office had a shiny wood floor, a few straight-backed chairs, and a battered settee. A denim worker's cap with its telltale red star hung from a corner hat rack.

First things first, I blurted out the story of my Geneva debacle.

'They turned you down across the way?' He smiled at my

108

lack of guile. I realized only then that I had blabbed incau-
tiously. But it was clear he found my naivety endearing.

'And you're American, you emigrated, or your grand-
parents, where from?'

When I told him they were Russian Jews, his face
clouded. He appeared to be in physical pain.

'We Swiss didn't do nearly enough for the Jews during
the war,' he said, as if that were an imperative reason for
helping me now.

'But I wasn't in Europe during the war, I was in the US,
All we had was sugar rationing,' I protested.

'Never mind,' he said. 'You're Jewish, that's what counts.
And your friend?'

'Algerian.'

He broke into a broad smile under his *nos ancêtres les
Gaulois* moustache.

'So, a Jew AND an Algerian.' Two oppressed races for
the price of one, he was clearly in his element, this kindly
Red. 'And what's he doing here, your Algerian?'

'He works in a factory and sends his paycheck home to
his extended family.'

'I see,' with more gravity. And he really did see, bless
him, this sympathetic Vaudois.

'All right, Louisette,' he had already adopted me under
a nickname of his own devising. 'We'll do it like this. You
go see my pal Gagnon in Lausanne, he's a Socialist, but a
good man, he'll guide you through the dull formalities.
Then next Friday you come back here early morning, on
an empty stomach, and I'll take care of you. You'll have to
spend the night in the local hospital, as a precaution, and
they'll charge you for the room, but for the rest you needn't
worry. My fee won't be a burden, I don't think.'

'What is your fee?'

'Is five francs all right?'

I laughed. Later I learned the good doctor charged everyone the same low fee for his services, on principle. A wealthy patient who protested had been famously reproved, 'You're no better than anyone else, you'll pay the same rate.'

So Kamel would be killed with kindness. I took the train back to Cularo and gave Wally the news. He nodded gravely. If he suppressed a sigh, I didn't hear it. He offered to miss work and make the trip with me next time. But I had studied his paycheck. I knew about the *prime d'assiduité*, the bonus for perfect attendance, that counted heavily in the computation of his monthly earnings. I said I would expect him in Lausanne on Saturday night. Till then, he was not to worry, I was in good hands.

Dr Gagnon's deep-set eyes gave him the look of a sly Alpine fox. He chain-smoked furiously, so that his comments issued forth from a great cloud, like the utterings, half hissed, half whispered, of an oracle responding not to things seen on earth, but to some inner vision that could not be gainsaid.

'You're scared stiff, little girl, men terrify you.'

'No they don't,' I talked back to the oracle, who emitted a self-contented grunt or sustained hum. His information came from higher sources, the little humming sound implied.

If he wanted to think he knew me better than I knew myself, all right. I needed his introduction to the judge at the new tribunal.

Then it was out of my hands; I was a patient, in need of treatment; the judge had ruled accordingly. I went under the knife, as scheduled, under general anesthesia. The last thing I heard before I blacked out, was Dr Vidal's cheerful greeting, from somewhere overhead, '*Bonjour Louison, tu nous apportes le soleil!*'

110

The following day, a Saturday, at approximately four p.m., Wally was arrested at the border and placed in a holding cell on the Swiss side, a complicated case, he told me later, still shook up from his close call with a punitive bureaucracy. His papers were not in order. His French ID card was no longer valid since he was clearly an Algerian. Nor did he deny it. Unless, since he had no other papers to present, he was simply stateless. As an African from a country that was two months old and on the verge of civil war, he could not afford to sit down on the floor and kick his heels. He had to play it cool – both hands on the table, no smoking, no phone calls – and answer questions. What was his business in Switzerland? What faction did he belong to? Was he a rebel or a terrorist? When was the fighting down there going to end? Wasn't seven years of war enough?

He told the truth, that he was on his way to meet a woman friend. When they asked if she were Swiss he lied and said yes, thinking they might take pity on a fellow citizen – a grave miscalculation, he realized at once. His innocent fib seemed only to stiffen the phlegmatic ire of these stolid pale-eyed *Fremdenpolizei*. Sexual jealousy? Hard to say. Their ugly blue-gray uniforms covered a multitude of petty grievances. But in the end his fate was not theirs to decide. They telephoned to Bern for instructions. He would just have to sit tight and wait for the reply.

What an irony. He had outrun the French police, the French army, the FLN, the OAS, the harkis, and the Bachaga Boualem, only to be taken prisoner by the world's oldest democracy. While waiting in his cell, if one could call it that, he read the newspapers from front to back. The news from home was sickening – the war that seemed destined to go on forever, as rival armies battled for control of

111

the new state. There were brutal reprisals against the hapless thousands France had recruited to fight on her side and then abandoned and shameful squabbling over the spoils of war – the abandoned assets of nearly a million Europeans who had fled the country in panic. Better a prisoner in Switzerland than a free man in the new Algeria of greed and power grabs? The question shamed him, but the answer was out of his hands.

At six o'clock the police brought him a cup of coffee and a ham sandwich. He ate the bread, drank the coffee, and thought about Kamel, who had made a quick entry into life and a quick exit. Amen. For the hundredth time he replayed the scene in his mind: he's home and reunited with his family at last, when I show up, with Kamel in my arms. Wally's wife is in the courtyard, shelling peas into a bowl on her lap. She looks up and knows everything at once. His sons learn to hate him. No matter how lofty, stoic, and resigned his wife appears, she teaches her sons to hate their father. The future rots on the vine.

It was midnight by the time word came from Bern. The gray uniforms released him just in time to catch the last train to Lausanne, a rattling local with hard wooden seats that stopped in tiny hamlets with strange names. Avoriaz, Avessieux. Large farm implements, mechanized harrows and hay balers, cast eery shadows on the quays. The train sped swaying through rich farm country. In the dark he could mistake it for the fertile plain below the village where he lived till his twelfth year, when the mayor caught him stealing a handful of dried apricots and chased him round the main square with a pruning hook and his father, in despair, sent him to live with his uncle in Oran. His own sons, Wally thought, would be spared such humiliations. His spirits lifted at the thought. The long cruel war would

112

be forgotten, there would be work, dignity, and God willing, years of peace.

All this I heard later or figured out for myself. That night, I paced the sidewalk in my nightgown, like *La Folle de Chaillot*, ready to leap out at him. He dropped his small valise and embraced me under the street lamp. Then he asked me gently to release him, so he could pay the cab driver.

He wasn't worried for himself, he told me, in the room I'd rented sight unseen, from a classified ad for *hotel garni* – chintz curtains, a portable bidet, a sagging double bed – a basement boudoir meant for transients like us. While in police custody, he wasn't worried for himself, Wally assured me, but feared I might conclude that he was not a man of his word. I assured him I could never, ever think that.

'What did you imagine?' he asked.

'I was afraid of a train wreck,' I said. He laughed and hugged me.

'*Ma pauvre Louise*. Are you glad to see me? I'm glad to see you, I swear to you.' He filled that shabby room with his reassuring presence. Inspecting the corridor, he discovered a washroom and took a quick shower. Then he sat down on the bed and had me sit beside him.

'What next?' he asked. My week of crying jags in public-toilet stalls and hospital stairwells no longer seemed worth mentioning.

'Hold me till we fall asleep,' I said.

'Hold you how?' he asked. The speckled boudoir mirrors mocked at our dilemma, but they were wrong. We lay down together, I summoned my courage, dived beneath the sheets, and wreaked sweet vengeance on the source of all our woes.

13

It seemed like a smart move, a mature act of self-preservation, Nora would have said, to stay put where I landed. Wally was going to be returning home soon. It was destined. I had to break the habit of sleeping in the shadow of a man with banded eyes, like Cupid, or like a candidate for execution. In Lausanne, I rented a less tawdry room, and found work with a trio of American lawyers in need of English-speaking help.

The preemptive separation didn't work. We wrote each other every day and fumed with impatience. On Fridays after work I ran to catch the train to Cularo. On Sundays I couldn't tear myself away but often slept another night in Wally's bed, in Wally's room. The republic was tottering but not yet fallen, although it meant missing Monday morning at the office. Such nonchalance was unheard of even at a firm like ours.

'*Qui trop embrasse, manque le train,*' Charlotte, our office manager, left a teasing note for me to find when I sneaked in one Monday afternoon. All eyes swerved toward me. Preoccupied with memories, I forgot to blush.

Brigitte was German, slender, fair-haired, sharp-nosed, and in love with Mr Wiley, the firm's accountant, who flirted with her while waiting for his wife to arrive from Peoria and set up housekeeping. During my first week on the job, Brigitte invited me for coffee to size me up and see what good could come of me. Her slyness puzzled me. I would have given her anything she asked for outright, except maybe the right to make fun of Wally, whom she had never met and never would. In good faith, which she promptly betrayed, I told Brigitte about the constraints of seeing him on weekends only.

'*Liebe auf Rate?*' she laughed in my face. 'That means love on the installment plan,' she said and laughed again. People were cruel to me that first year on my own, outside the protectorate of Wally. Dr Vidal was a sterling exception. I knew that Europe was recovering from war. I didn't know that war is just the ordinary human nastiness, intensified and armed to the teeth.

'*Wir assen Gras,*' Brigitte tried to impress me with tales of German wartime starvation. We ate grass. I was duly impressed, although even I realized that no one was starving in Lausanne in 1962. The main street, a procession of lavish bakeries and dainty tearooms, ended in a glass-walled café where I hung out after work, following Aunt Nora's instructions to the letter. I sat reading the newspaper till someone interrupted. My new friends were a flyweight boxer from Singapore, a gangly Swiss who dressed like Marcel Proust, in morning coat and spats, a whole crew of Hungarians, young heroes of the '56 uprising down on their luck after five dull (they said) grim (they said) years in prosperous Lausanne, and a French army deserter who stole frozen steaks from the supermarket on Marxist principles. I met refugees, heiresses, self-made millionaires (Venezuelan oil, Persian carpets), and lacquered finishing school graduates in search of sugar daddies. Their projects and agendas fitted together like the pieces of a giant kaleidoscopic puzzle I gradually learned to read, but only as an outsider, a misfit among the dreamers, schemers, and young playboys cruising with their Papas (Peruvian admirals, Saudi sheikhs) among the local beauties.

One Friday night in early spring, I caught the train to Cularo. It was dark when I reached Wally's room. Davy was sitting at three chessboards, Sasha dozed beneath the bed, and a Spaniard named Firmin, a Protestant with no future in Franco Spain, strummed a guitar. This was my home, but not for long. That Sunday afternoon, our time for spacious conversation, Wally gave me a little sermon on WHY IT CANNOT BE.

I already knew it could not be, I had no expectations. He could have spared me his rationales. Some were vague and abstract: we could not build our happiness on others' misery. Others were silly: he was too old for me, when I was nearing forty he'd be an old man, incapable of giving me what I required. Women in their forties needed a great deal of love. I wished he wouldn't talk like a dumbed-down version of Colette.

Finally he came out with the simple urgent truth. His wife had written to say that people in the village made fun of her. Was her husband ever coming home?

'In that case you must leave at once,' I said, in a panic, as it hit me for the first time, that Mafemme was a real person and felt real pain.

Yet it was July by the time we set out on our first and last trip together. We took the train to Port Bou and crossed into Spain. We sat on a stony beach. The waves crashed on the shores of Europe and Africa. Once there was no gap between them; the two continents were one, within their mother Gaia. That time was long past. We ate authentic sardines *en escabeche*. Spain was a foretaste of Wally's Africa: he exclaimed with joy over the light, the heat, the domino players in the cafés.

In the little seaside restaurant where we ate one night, disgruntled Germans muttered mutinously over their plates. Wally urged me to step in and interpret for the restaurant's owner, a harassed-looking woman who ran the place with two young sons.

'Why should she put up with such arrogance?' I asked. 'Let them go eat somewhere else.'

He corrected me, 'She can't afford to lose a customer, much less a whole crowd like this. She's probably under contract with an agency for the entire season.'

So I spoke to the tourists from Stuttgart, who wanted their sole fried in butter, not swimming in olive oil. I relayed this message to the cook, who was nonplussed at being asked to skimp on oil, like a cheapskate. Then Wally sat down with the Germans, and, with me translating, explained that in Spain they could ask for less oil, perhaps but not for no oil at all.

That was the first law of the Mediterranean, valid on the near and the far shore. And then, because I knew Germans were trained to respect the old Greeks, I dragged in the legend of the divine contest for the hearts of the Athenians. Poseidon and Athena, the horse and the olive. You know who won, I reminded them. Athena of the sea-gray eyes.

'Some day I'll show you our olive trees, we have some that are a thousand years old,' Wally told me in the street that night.

'When will that be?' I asked.

'You know how it is,' he said, and took my hand and dropped it again. Franco's *guardia civil* suppressed every public display of affection, no matter how chaste and tenuous.

117

In Barcelona he admired the old men in the Ramblas, gossiping in their endless *tertulias*. That too was just like home, he said, or had been before the war, men standing in tight groups under the open sky, talking, talking, as if they had already found the solution to the world's problems and were just working out the fine points. The solution, Wally said astutely, was in the waiting. While men talked they were not pursuing old feuds. Enmities cooled, bloodshed was postponed indefinitely.

We did not make farewell speeches. It all went without saying. He was going to write to me and I was going to write to him and educate his daughters, when they were old enough to leave home on their own. That was the deal. We had Mouloudji's word for it: '*Un jour tu verras.*' Someday by some stroke of luck or fate, we would meet again. As if to certify that promise, in Perpignan the ferry crews went out on strike, delaying Wally's departure by three whole days. We made the most of them. Being is shot through with Non-being: that week I discovered the ontological ache in its purest form.

When the time came, we went to the station and boarded the train together. A man of pliant strength, slender, and compact, Wally stood alongside my seat without impeding the traffic in the aisle of the northbound train. He stood as close as possible without actually touching, fiercely attentive to the last, as if to guard me from whatever danger lay ahead, in straight allegiance. Then the train lurched into motion, he jumped out through the open door and I knew I'd never see him again.

He was true to me in his fashion. He sent me letters, photographs, even, to my surprise and delight, a book wrapped in brown paper and tied with string. I found it in the office mailbox one Monday morning, a soft-cover edition of some mildly racy stories from the court of Louis XVth, count-esses in wigs and décolleté, soft-core pornography of no redeeming social value whatsoever. I hid it in the bottom drawer of my office desk, where every so often I could stroke the pleasantly rough surface of the wrapping paper with the palm of my right hand and study his beloved sig-nature, with its forward slope and rising curves. It was as if the letters spelled out not merely the address on rue du Bourg where I toiled for Mr Arnold (who did not value me at my full worth, Wally said) but some alchemist's for-mula that could whiz me across the seas, to where my lover stood on line in his small town post office, waiting to have his package weighed, stamped, and sent abroad, by ship of course. I stood on line behind him and caught the warmth that emanated from his back, his shoulders, I grew dizzy with longing, soon his errand would be done, he would turn toward me, his eyes would slide across my face and come to rest dead center, and he would chide me gently, *Sacrée Louise, qu-est ce que tu fais là*? You should learn to be more patient, you'll have your book in a few days, I'm just mailing it. You see, I told you I would remember you no matter what, I hope that you remember me as well, I swear to you, that even if I wanted to, I couldn't forget you or what you did for me, your generosity. You told me I was talkative, you called me a human parrot, but then you listened while I told you where I'd been since I left home. I had nothing else to give you but my 'life in chapters' as you called it. I thought maybe now you'd like a real book for a change, with all those funny pictures, so *vieille France*. You can't imagine all the flotsam here, if I hadn't rescued this book from the heap it might have wound up in a bonfire, a book burning, there have been too many of those lately. You know the OAS bombed the Algiers

119

library, burned it to the ground, sixty thousand volumes reduced to ash, there, there, don't cry, it's only paper, it can be replaced, some things are irreplaceable. You and I know what those are.

14

Like in a French farce where doors keep opening and shutting, Wally wasn't gone two weeks when my mother arrived on her first – and last – trip to Europe. From the moment she walked in, she began to scold after her fashion, making up for lost time.

'Everyone keeps asking me, what is she doing over there? Working for an international law firm, I tell them, with all her languages. For her it's a snap, German, French, Italian, you know my Louise. Jake's sister Dora remembers you from when you were little, how hard you cried that time Tom's dog Queenie got run over and had to be put down, and I said yes but now she's all grown up, she graduated with honors, she studied ancient Greek, and your Aunt Frieda said, "My niece is so smart, she's stupid, know what I mean?"

'She doesn't really think you're stupid, but she knows how I worry about you. When people ask, I say, "She'll come home when she's good and ready." We all thought by now you'd have had enough of Europe. Your father told me to just pop you in my suitcase and throw away the key.'

It took real courage for my mother to come see me. She

was not the traveling kind. Afraid to fly, she crossed the Atlantic in a great-many-tiered ocean liner. She did not enjoy the voyage out, not for a minute. And then Aunt Nora in London was a tremendous disappointment.

'I don't know what's happened to her,' my mother complained. 'She used to be so bright and funny. She was a fantastic mimic; she had us all in stitches. She's turned into a rabid Tory. We took a cab across town from Victoria station, she lives in a very out-of-the-way neighborhood, and the whole time she was railing against the Irish, I thought the cabbie would dump us in the street. I remember when Nora was a raving Commie, tearing up the Trotskyite brochures and burning them in the trash can out back at Frieda's farm.'

'What year was that? Was I alive?'

'Oh, that was before your time. Nora wants you to go live with her, you know. She told me to order you to pack your bags and get going. I told her you don't take orders from anyone. Least of all your parents.'

'But you'd like me to go?'

'And live with her? You'd be out of your mind. Her husband deserves a medal for putting up with her.'

'And what about you? You're the one who really deserves a medal,' I said. I was slicing zucchini for a ratatouille the way Wally taught me, and by force of love, I transmuted the slice in my hand to solid gold and tried to pin it to my mother's blouse. She pulled away; she feared a stain.

'I have my children,' she said, 'that makes up for everything.' The tears swam inside her eyelids but did not fall. People call my mother cold. She's not cold, but she keeps her feelings hidden lest they reduce her to helplessness.

I was grateful to her for coming to see me, my brother

was at a summer science camp, my father had finally ditched his unspeakable Washington cronies and found work as a proofreader at some labor union's in-house rag. I didn't dare ask where my mother found the money for her trip; it was probably from Uncle Sid. I owed him, I owed them all, a letter.

'I don't know why you go to so much trouble, other people just dump all the vegetables into one pan and it comes out fine.'

'Someone showed me how to do it this way. It was a real feat, we, I mean he, had one hotplate and one frying pan and he washed it between eggplant, pepper, and zucchini.'

'Was he some sort of chef?'

'No, he once washed dishes in a really good restaurant. Later they made him a prep cook for a few months.'

'Where is he now?' my mother asked, unlike her. She was not a great questioner. Unless the news was rock solid good, she would rather not hear it.

'He went back to his tribe in Africa,' I said.

'Just as well,' my mother said.

No point in arguing with her. Before she left, however, she bought the *New York Times* and the *Trib*, to read about the march on Washington. A great occasion, she exclaimed. She read me passages from Martin Luther King's reprinted speech. It didn't register with me. My mind was elsewhere.

Wally's son, and mine, was probably conceived on our last night together. As if Kamel wouldn't take no for an answer, but came knocking at the gate of ivory again. By the time my mother left I knew for sure that I was pregnant. I didn't tell her, that was not what she had come to hear. To me, at first, it was good news. It meant Wally hadn't left me after all. For the next nine months at least, we were still inseparable, bound in blood.

At the expat law office, the hired help worked in one big open room. To deflect my co-workers' prying eyes, I bought new clothes, shorter skirts, and taller boots. Capes were in style that year. Mine was dark plaid with passementerie down the front, I wore it all day in the underheated office. As a spoiled eccentric American, I got away with it. To complete the look, I wore a tam o'shanter in the same plaid as the cape. At five-thirty p.m., when the workday was over, I went home alone and writhed with longing for my absent lover.

I never loved Wally more than in those months, when he was out of reach and I was forced to conjure him from his letters and the gentle steady process we had set in motion without trying. Crabby Mr Arnold, Alan Arnold, Esquire as he insisted on being identified on every document that left the office, was astounded by the unprecedented spike in my efficiency. Perfectly typed letters in sextuplicate. The baby, the thought of the baby – as long as you can't see it, it's just a thought, a gift of the imagination – fed me confidence, sadly wasted on that thin-lipped lawyer's timid correspondence with powerful men for whom he, in his Swiss self-exile, was at best a polite afterthought. When I asked him for a raise that fall, he accused me of disloyalty. If I had asked for maternity leave, he would probably have called me a traitor to the nation and fired me on the spot.

My plan, my mad idea was that the baby would lure Wally back to Europe for a passionate reunion. I knew I could count on him to do right by any child of his. But as the months passed complications arose. A Kansas manufacturer of small airplanes wanted to open a branch in Switzerland, for tax evasion purposes. As usual I calculated the advantage – it wasn't even algebra, just simple arithmetic – and prepared a chart. Next day Mr Arnold informed me, giggling, that the visitor had noticed me, and asked if I was pregnant or misshapen? Prudish Mr Arnold took offense and defended my honor (and the firm's) to this prospective client. What would he say when he learned the truth?

My Aunt Nora sent another diatribe. With her wicked intuition, she guessed, by something I had said, or failed to, in my letters, that I was down, and pounced. After several pages of family history seething with contempt for her mis-married sisters, their lumpish husbands and unrewarding offspring, she turned on me. She had meant to write me ever since my mother's stay in London. In fact, she had written many times, and torn up every draft. Till finally my uncle told her, just mail the damn thing, get it out of the house, and then let's take a trip somewhere, so by the time I read her letter, she informed me, she would be in Cornwall in the vicinity of Virginia Woolf's lighthouse. Virginia Woolf, surely I knew this, worshipped her mother, whom she lost at an early age, unlike some people who took their aging mothers entirely for granted, allowed them to live the life of drudges in big city slums, while their ungrateful daughters went off and did as they damn pleased with anyone they pleased, like a common prostitute but worse because prostitutes at least get paid for lying down, and . . . well you know . . . my aunt reverted coyly to non-U British slang, 'removing their knickers.' If I had any self-respect, at all, she warned me, I would return home at once and arrange to marry a rich man who could be relied on to provide for my poor mother in old age.

The only possible excuse for not taking this course of action, she went on, single-spaced for three more pages, was Italy. No one can call himself civilized who has not lived in Italy. There my search for a rich husband would have to be delayed of course, my aunt was thinking out loud here, as I had often heard her do, weighing possibilities, unable to decide among them. In Italy – severely impoverished by two world wars – American heiresses were in high demand, but a woman of no means, no matter if she knew Latin and Greek, the dates of Caesar's major battles, and Dante and Petrarch by heart, was of no interest as a marriage partner. *Peccato*, but there it is.

Had my mother confessed something to her sister that she hid from me, I wondered with mounting dread. An incurable disease? I was relieved to read, 'Of course your mother is strong as a horse and will probably outlive us all, but that's precisely why you must think now about providing for her in her later years, even, should the need arise, after you yourself are gone. Such things are possible.

'Your Uncle James has read this letter in its entirety and ratifies the contents, with one small proviso, he says to warn you that the best is often the enemy of the good, whatever that means. I think what he means to say is that the man need not be madly affluent, but solvent. Good manners and good nature will do, but not Italian, in that case, as merely solvent Italians tend to want large families, which is not fun for their wives.

'Write to us from Venice, Rome, or Florence. Do not write to us from where you are. At the moment, you are precisely nowhere. Do not disappoint your loving aunt and uncle,' signed Nora and James. QED added underneath in James's neat broad strokes, a schoolboy joke, like a dab of witch hazel, to reduce the sting?

That letter flattened me. If Wally had been by my side, I might have rallied, but he wasn't there, although he continued to write increasingly non-committal letters. I hadn't informed him yet of Kamel's return. Nora's premises were cuckoo but her conclusion was accurate. I had no idea what I was doing.

One Saturday late that fall, I took the train to Bern, the federal capital, for the first time. I don't know what I thought I'd find there. Some answer to my dilemma. I stopped to look into the *Baerengraben*, the enormous concrete pit in the heart of the city, with a family of brown bears in residence, the wild power of the mountains brought to the lowland as spoils of war, entrapped, and disempowered. I thought of jumping into the pit, as a test of the kind they performed on witches, not so long ago. If the bears befriended or ignored me, I would trust my judgment. If they mauled me, I would know that I was on the wrong path but it wouldn't matter because most likely I'd be dead.

There was no way of getting at the bears. The fence was high and a policeman patrolled the adjacent sidewalk. So I walked on till I came to a Catholic church. I slipped into a rear pew that promised me an hour of blessed invisibility. Frau Tischer may have been trolling for lost souls; she was waiting for me on the front steps. She spoke some kind words and invited me to tea in the nearest café. It didn't take her long to learn that I was a foreigner adrift, in need of help. She was not patronizing. She did not press me for details of my predicament. Instead, canny woman, she talked about herself.

Frau Tischer longed to be ordained a priest, with all attendant powers. In another century or two her goal might be achievable, but in her lifetime? Out of the question. The new Pope was democratic and farsighted but even he would not alter fundamental church doctrine. So she did the next best thing; she took advanced degrees in theology and then sought an enlightened parish priest willing to share his duties with her, as a near equal. Understanding that 'near' meant 'far.' She could recite the Mass; she could not perform the sacraments. A woman simply could not be the conduit for the miracle of transubstantiation. Superstitious nonsense, Frau Tischer said. On a par with the legend that a menstruating woman can't produce a decent mayonnaise.

To be excluded from performing the sacrament of baptism was especially hard on women, Frau Tischer, married but without children of her own, confided, a month later, when we had become, not friends, but debating partners. She did not moralize. She did not try to convert me. But she had her own heroic streak. Like Dr Vidal, she saw me as a victim to be rescued, and not just me: she would rescue Wally and the baby too, by a well-timed diplomatic intervention.

I accepted her urgent invitation, quit my job, and went to live in a large apartment in a new building on the wooded edge of a German-speaking city in eastern Switzerland, with other young women in my same predicament. We were Frau Tischer's wards for the duration. The church ran a number of homes for fallen women in those days. This one was meant to be pleasant and respectful, in keeping with the new dispensation emerging from Rome under Vatican II. The word sin was never uttered. When Frau Tischer told us, with tears in her eyes, how Pope John XXIII, the first in many generations, left the Vatican City within days of his election, to visit the inmates at nearby Regina Coeli prison, how could I doubt her goodness, which seemed to flow directly from his?

Unlike Nora, Frau Tischer didn't rant and rave, or practice inept subterfuge. If she had, I might have rebelled outright and avoided much grief later on. Frau Tischer was an educated woman with a steady, disciplined mind. She set out to discipline mine. When the other guests, as we were euphemistically called, had gone to bed, Frau Tischer kept me up late, sipping wine, which I mostly refused, and talking quietly but purposefully, citing unimpeachable authorities, not doctors of the church, but anthropologists, historians, and novelists.

'Children need a stable, unified environment,' she insisted. 'In that tribal Arab world of which you know very little — how could you guess what it's like, from your experience of one expatriate who is in fact, haven't you told me, a pariah in his home milieu? — in that world, any child of yours, known to be yours, would create dissension and disturbance in his father's family, with possibly disastrous results.

'You who are a classical scholar,' in the pursuit of her goal, Frau Tischer resorted to crude flattery, 'you know the story of the House of Atreus: feuds that simmer for generations, skimming off the most promising males, are known throughout the Mediterranean basin.'

Oh dear! Cannibalism, infanticide? Perhaps Frau Tischer was not too different from Aunt Nora after all. She could pursue an argument to absurd extremes.

'But if the child remained with me? If his father never knew . . .' I protested, but the question was already moot, because of course Wally knew, I had written him and he had written back, to say *mine de rien*, *salaud*, that as always in the past, he would be guided by my wishes.

'Oh my dear, you know I have seen many such cases. The passionate attachment to ones offspring, the philo-progenitive strain in tribal societies is beautiful but also dangerous. Say you raised the child by yourself, there would come a time, three, four, or seven years from now, when his father would assert his claim against you. No matter how enlightened, progressive, and Europeanized the father may seem . . . and in fact be,' she quickly added, seeing me frown. 'But we'll talk about it again. There's still time for you to see the light.'

'You've said it yourself,' Frau Tischer reminded me, after I signed the papers that settled Kamel's future.

'Your friend will be a mother AND a father to this child.' I wished I had never shown her the photograph Wally sent me soon after his return home. He's sitting on one of those beautiful Algerian beaches he used to talk about, with Nour, a four-year-old beauty, nestled in his shadow. With her great mop of reddish hair, her bare chest, and child's underpants, she looks like innocence itself, infinitely protected.

15

Our son was born in a public hospital in that Swiss German city. I was under sedation from the start of labor, nine hours of fog, and fifteen minutes of intense pain and joy. It was Kamel, come to reclaim his name. I recognized him right away. I'd had him to myself for a nine whole months, held a running conversation with the unseen snippet anchored in my flesh. I had only those nine months to tell him the whole truth. That his parents loved him, that they loved each other, that they met at the wrong time and place, that I would come to him in dreams, and later on, in waking life. I would not abandon him, I swore it, and I meant it. Just as well prenatal memory's a myth. If he'd held on to those promises, he might have become bitter.

In those days they kept you in hospital for ten whole days. I tried to make them count. I raised a row and won the right to keep him with me round the clock. I nursed him non-stop, he gained weight fast, and he could hold his head up from the start. His skin was preternaturally pale, his genitals were outsize in proportion to his tiny body. That's how it is with newborn males. A perfect fleshy orchid, mauve in color.

Men have all the power in this world and yet here was this tiny male creature, whom I could have destroyed with a quick stab of a scissors. The thought terrified me. I clamped him to my breast and let him feed. He was insatiable. I tried to live in the moment, not mourning him ahead of time. That would have been unfair. I thought, if need be, let him live, and let me die. While Kamel slept on my breast we rode backward in time together, we were still physically joined, we need never separate. Birth was an illusion.

Dr Vidal, my best friend on the European continent, sauntered into the room, took out his stethoscope, listened to the baby's heart and smiled. To see his big hands close around those tiny limbs was both reassuring and unbearable. He pronounced him a fine specimen and a credit to his race, the Semitic race, the Arabo-Judaeic, the Judaeo-Arabic race, which, for all its ups and downs, he did not doubt would learn to harmonize its warring elements in time.

Then while the baby slept, he led me to a remote terrace, full of vents, fans, and broken lounge chairs, a sort of no man's land within the hospital, within Switzerland itself, and quizzed me closely. How had it all transpired? Had I been coerced into giving up the child? Would I like to rescind my decision, negotiate a more human arrangement, some kind of joint custody? I could go live in Algeria, had I considered it? They were desperately short of teachers. A new career in a new country. But he was talking to someone else: a heroine, a militant, a woman who could take a stand.

I had figured out Frau Tischer by then. I worked it out during the long twilight hours of labor under semi-sedation. She was a bureaucrat, with a bigoted sense of order: Muslims had their place, on their side of the Mediterranean.

I could have upset her applecart, with pleasure, just as I had enjoyed provoking the bourgeoisie in France. What were the French to me? My own family was a different story. My aunts and uncles weren't racist, I don't think, but they were ambitious for their children. With Wally, I had sinned against the immigrant creed of upward mobility. The family tribunal sat inside my head.

Uncle Bud's lubricious scorn: 'Two years in Europe, on scholarship and that's all you achieved? You could have done that right here in the Village, without even crossing the street.'

Uncle Max: 'An African, eh? Fine people, the salt of the earth, but they often treat their women badly, it's a sad fact of life in some of the former colonies. The scars of imperialism won't heal overnight. Remember, you can always come to me for help.'

Uncle Sid: no words, just a cosmic shrug of disappointment.

Uncle James: paraphrasing Montesquieu, *'Comment peut-on être Algérien?'*

Aunt Nora: 'If that's what you want to do with your life, fine, but really, how boringly predictable of you. And you can forget about Italy now, for the next twenty years. Pity.'

My mother: 'Just don't let your brother know where babies come from.'

My father's cold contempt: 'Change the poor kid's name for God's sake, they'll rag him in the schoolyard. Or would his father object? I assume he has a father somewhere around?'

To save Kamel from those cruel voices – no, to save myself – I let him go.

When Dr Vidal saw it was no use, he tried to paint a rosy picture for my sake.

'You'll stay in touch, you'll be the *oncle d'Amérique,*

everyone in this world needs an American aunt or uncle. This is a good time for a kid to start his life down there, a new country with new schools, new laws, free medical care, authentic ground-breaking African socialism, and national, ethnic, and racial pride. In the US your *petit bonhomme* would be just another colored man, at the mercy of those Alabama sheriffs.'

I couldn't speak.

'You still love the guy, don't you?' Dr Vidal switched his tack. '*Quel drame.* Even after all he put you through?'

'It's not easy for him either,' I defended Wally. I defended him on all occasions, even when I was furious with him, as I had been, intermittently since he left me. Left us.

'He'll probably catch it from his wife,' Dr Vidal saw the humor in the situation. To him it was a good French farce, but with some foreign accents here and there, since the main players were foreigners. Nor did he hold that against them. It simply meant they needed his protection.

It was not an adoption, Frau Tischer acknowledged, but would be treated as one, and not just for bureaucratic reasons: no contact between birth mother and the receiving party. That was harsh and counterintuitive somehow, but in my catatonic state I acquiesced. When I could bear to think about it, I imagined two stout older women in white dresses and a young male escort, sent to collect Kamel. I was not keen to meet them.

Dr Vidal was appalled when he learned of this punitive arrangement and took steps to sabotage the protocol. And so on the eve of the transfer as it was called, under cover of darkness, Wally and I met again, in the good doctor's car, parked on a side street a few blocks from the hospital. Dr Vidal announced he was going for a beer and would return in half an hour.

It took us that long to churn through our fears and resentments so that when the doctor returned he found what he expected, a couple locked in silent, tearful embrace that in fact marked a truce of despair, after hostilities that left us both feeling defeated.

Wally had apparently been forewarned and was ready with a speech about the beautiful gift I was bestowing on his family, how grateful they were, and how it would be treasured. I was floored. I looked at him, and thought, who is this stranger mouthing pieties? I looked again and saw the weary traveler. Leaner, darker, as if winnowed by a harsh wind, harried by the complications of his taxing journey. I realized he was terrified I'd change my mind at the last minute, and send him home empty handed.

And he was right to worry. The last week had put a new thought in my mind. A warm infant tugging for dear life will have that effect. The word I wanted to hear from Wally that night was *maternelle*. That's what they call those schools in France that take children from the age of two years so that their mothers, even unwed mothers, *mères célibataires*, can return to work. Everyone says they are extremely well run, a model for other countries that still haven't caught up forty years later. Kamel could have gone into the *maternelle* somewhere in southern France, and I would find work and earn enough to keep us, and Wally would have come to see us now and then, a commuting marriage and in between his visits, I would dream of him and be the one to remind our boy, as needed, 'You are not from here.' We could go on that way for quite a while.

The dissonances were so strong that even when Wally kissed me I suspected his motives. He kissed me and mussed my hair, which was messy to begin with. I nuzzled his shoulder, reaching for the old reality. My breasts mistook

135

their cue and spurted milk, imposing the new reality. Wally pulled away from me, for the first time ever.

'We won't abuse the doctor's hospitality.'

He always had that strong sense of propriety. I would give him another chance.

'Take off your jacket,' I told him.

He did as he was told, humoring the madwoman? So be it. He allowed me to stroke his forearm. The tattoo was right where I remembered it, the ink-dark line of grease injected by some machine he was learning to handle, his first year in the factory.

'I claim this island in the name of our son, whom you have come to remove from me, isn't that so?'

'You sent for me,' Wally said, which was true, but heartless.

'This is hell,' I said. 'Vidal owes us an apology.'

'*Sacrée Louise*,' Wally said, the way he had a hundred times before, when he meant it as a tribute to my irreverence and insouciance. Now my volatility alarmed him. I found him self-protective and remote. Case closed? Too soon, too soon.

'I have filled eight bottles with mother's milk. It has been frozen for future use. Make sure they give it to you.' Reassured that I was not going to play havoc with the plan, Wally relaxed.

'This is not the end,' he said with some of the old urgency. 'I'll write you, I'll tell you what's going on down there. Things you wouldn't believe.'

'Tell me now,' I said and kissed his hand, his cheek, his moustache. He slipped a grudging arm around me and kissed me briefly, once, on best behavior.

'There isn't time,' he said with rueful simplicity. I wondered about the shocks and stresses of his life *là-bas*. The man who met me with that swollen speech was a product of the new Algeria. The republic of Wally, our privileged, isolate realm, was history.

Dr Vidal, an incurable romantic, tapped discreetly on the window, a warning to the star-crossed lovers that it was time to move on.

When I got back to the hospital, the crib was empty, stripped of its bedding. I went up and down the hall looking for an explanation till a nurse came and accompanied me back to my room. She shut the door, motioned for me to sit down, sat next to me, took my hands in hers, and said, 'That meddling doctor, I know what he's been up to, he just made it harder for you in the end. Some girls don't even want to see the baby once it's out. They deliver and walk out the next day. We call it flying blind. Here, if you're having a hard time these next few weeks, you can call this number.'

She handed me a business card. The name embossed, red on white, was that of Frau Tischer.

Wally wrote me, true to his word. But the news was oddly censored. I never learned what name they gave my son, or what he looked like as a child or a grown man, or if he ever heard of me, and by now so much time has gone by it's foolish and self-indulgent even to wonder. I thought our son would be a bond between us. He became a barrier instead.

16

Ten-Minute Cigarette Break

Aissa

'But if I've told you all of this, it was for a good reason. It has taken me till now but I am going to make amends, break down the walls, or die trying,' Louise rested her case.

What an afternoon. Did Tariq know what he had set me up for?

'Don't cry,' I told Louise. 'It's far too late for tears,' I rapped out harshly. Scolding a woman my mother's age? I had better let her be. I told her I was stepping outside for a cigarette. She nodded and flashed a weak smile, waving me toward the door of the establishment. For once the New York City ban on smoking in public spaces worked in my favor.

The rain had stopped. From the pavement rose a tonic coolness. I lit up and inhaled my favorite poison. I was not alone in front of the tall building a few blocks from the UN. Two young women chatted happily while puffing on their smokes. When they had finished, they stowed the butts in a small steel ashtray with a hinged lid, so as not to soil the public thoroughfare. Oh, you careful conscientious

Americans. What kind of woman abandons her infant son to his indigent father in a chaotic newborn country teeming with war orphans? Hard to imagine. Louise deported her own son. Back to Africa, where you belong.

What could I possibly say to her? It's all right, don't fret, you missed your son's first forty years, you missed the life of his country, two decades of misguided optimism, a decade of galloping corruption and escalating crises, followed by a decade – it wasn't really over yet – of bloody civil war. Let me bring you up to speed, and we'll take it from there?

'Make sure you get your facts straight first.' I knew that voice. My friend Said clung to the nearest lamppost, frail but upright, rainwater dripping from his shock of straight black hair, a man of fifty with the look of a bright schoolboy. Last time I saw him was at his funeral in Algiers in '93. Algiers that year was like Baghdad now, car bombs, midnight raids, and targeted assassinations of increasing viciousness. Said wrote a column, a quick graceful riff on the day's headlines, for one of the newspapers the regime had not yet shut down. We read him with our morning coffee. After our terror-stricken nights, his wistful tone, sweet reasonableness, and skeptic's jibes were meant to help us through the day. They shot him on his lunch hour, two bullets to the head, in a pizza joint across the street from the paper. After his death, a lot of us gave up and left the country. Without his tutorials – he taught us how to live with fear – we didn't think we'd make it.

Even I, a lowly accountant at the paper he edited, looked to him as a big brother, for advice.

'What are you doing here?' I asked him, hoping he would not vanish before I'd had the chance to reconnect. New York was full of lures, snares, and desert mirages.

They travelled with me. I couldn't shake them, I couldn't embrace them. Cruel city.

'Gathering material for my next column,' he said, but he was kidding. 'Really, I'm just looking for a cigarette. Let me have one, it's been years.'

'And here I thought you'd come to help me.'

'You don't need my help. This is not a complicated case.'

'It's not?' I wanted details, not deathless concision. But he spoke with irresistible authority: he knew life from both sides of the grave.

'Life is short, life is hard, give the dame a break.' And he was gone in a puff of borrowed smoke. I got the message, I'd heard him scolding cub reporters about letting the facts speak for themselves.

The facts in this case pointed to a mutual betrayal.

In Ahmed Ouali's patriarchal household, another male child could easily slip into the pack of barelegged urchins destined to become the first generation of doctors, engineers, and architects of their new country. So her lover led Louise to believe. But more likely, a distant cousin was found who would welcome a male heir, despite his obscure origins, left deliberately obscure for good reason. Ahmed Ouali's wife would forgive the offense because, mother of three, quite soon to be four children, she had no choice, and because immediately on his return from Switzerland, her husband, perhaps unbeknownst to her, or perhaps not, delivered the small bundle of blankets and towels containing maybe ten pounds of dazed and somnolent infant male flesh to a childless older couple in a distant hamlet the war had halfway spared. The couple would offer to cover the expenses of his trip to 'the big city orphanage.' He would refuse any such payment. The adoptive parents would not insist, aware of the unspoken intricacies of the transaction.

140

A man who has given you his newborn son does not want money in return.

What does he want? Visiting rights, discreetly exercised? Possibly. But what if Ahmed Ouali got fed up with the ragging and bickering over small stakes in the village he had escaped many years before, and decided to set up for himself with wife and kids in the nearest city, like the godless *roumi* his brothers accused him of having become in France. Half the country moved to the cities in the years after independence. We're still getting settled. His wife would welcome such a move, although it meant another separation from nearest and dearest, shared daily routines, the endlessly reknitted chains of gossip. Gossip that circled back too often to the 'orphan' child, adopted by those distant cousins she was glad to leave behind once and for all, since the scandal touched her too, by association. She would no longer have to taste the bitter fillip every time the boy crossed their doorstep and her husband's eyes fixed on a pair of sturdy legs and feet in plastic sandals.

SHAME before her own kin, a shame so deep she couldn't name it forty years after the fact, drove Louise to abandon her infant son. SHAME – *horma*, *aib*, *hashuma* – it's our natural element – made Ahmed Ouali drop his offspring, like a magpie, in a borrowed nest. Trouble was kept at a safe distance, outside the immediate family circle. Any rumor of disorder was attached to a foreign temptress, a well-known hazard of the exile years. Let the sin be on her unnamed head.

I tossed my cigarette into the rain-washed gutter. Halfway down the block the Korean grocer's Guatemalan stock boy was reordering a Technicolor raft of flowers ruffled by the recent squall.

'What are those for?' Louise protested when I laid a sheaf

of orange tulips on the table. Her hand shot out and stroked them, as if they were a dormant animal, a sleeping child.

'It was wartime. You were trapped, an innocent. It's nothing new.'

'It wasn't like that, believe me. I could have asked the universe to budge an inch or two. There were alternatives, offers of help. I spurned them all.'

17

Louise

The helper was Irene. Her name meant peace and she offered me a truce, but neither of us knew how to make it stick. I met her in a bookstore in the town where I was hiding out, waiting for the baby to be born. I gave up reading when Wally left me. I ran from libraries and bookstores as a rule. But that day it was raining and when I stepped inside, I saw a slender gray-haired woman looking for a title on a bottom shelf. I dropped to my knees, landing heavily, and found her book, the poems of Christian Morgenstern, and handed it to her.

'Here, let me help you,' she insisted, but she lacked the strength, and instead of her lifting me, I pulled her down, and we wound up on the floor in a tangled heap. I apologized of course, but neither her person nor her dignity was injured. She was up again before I was, springing nimbly to her feet.

She invited me home for coffee. I accepted. I had few friends in Europe at that point. And this woman looked honest and straightforward. Her eyes were gray-green, the color of the sea, a good omen in a landlocked country.

She lived alone in a ground-floor apartment at the

bottom of a steep hill. She wasn't used to living by herself, she added, not self-pitying, just factual. Her husband, who had died the year before, was a lively, witty man, who wrote radio plays and adaptations of everything from *Gone with the Wind*, in ten half-hour segments, to *The Magic Mountain*, in forty. When he died his friends and colleagues dropped her overnight. She was not complaining, she had her widow's pension, and occasional fees for her translations from the English. More than enough for a woman of simple tastes with no heirs.

She talked nonstop, which was fine with me as I was not eager to be questioned.

'My husband used to say the trouble with Germans is that when they see the police stop someone in the street, they at once assume he's guilty.'

'My husband used to say Germany will be divided, the border will run from the Elbe to the Oder.'

'Your husband must have had a lot to say. You quote him often,' I said.

'While my husband lived I never said a word, he had so much to say, and it was all so witty and profound. My sons say I'm making up now for lost time, I have to fit thirty years of stifled talk into the next ten, God willing. It has made me a garrulous old woman.'

Cruel sons, I thought and resolved to listen respectfully to this keen-eyed woman whom life had overlooked. Even her husband, she told me later, was not secretly, but quite openly, in love with another woman for most of his life. Irene kept house for the three of them for many years. After listening for weeks I began to think of Irene as a minor undiscovered saint, wrapped in a saving legend. Jewish, German-born Irene and her German anti-Nazi husband reached the Swiss border with Italy in December

144

1943, after a series of improbable and sometimes tragic assists from priests, hairdressers, Communist couriers, and the courageous nuns in a Tuscan convent. But at the border it was Irene who took charge, threatening to kill herself on the spot, if the Swiss refused sanctuary to her stateless, formerly German husband.

A year later, released from a Swiss internment camp, they moved to the little apartment at the foot of the hill, and Irene's husband went back to writing odes to the love of his life, his former mistress, who had vanished in the war.

'Would you like to see the rest of my small lodgings?' Irene asked on my third visit. Sitting at the dining table in the front room we looked into the alcove with her husband's desk, his craggy typewriter, and his mammoth wooden filing cabinets. At the back there was a large shady bedroom with a balcony overlooking a narrow strip of grass edged by tall dark pines that looked transplanted from the high Alps.

'That's all I have to offer, I'm afraid. But if you get tired of your current situation, you could stay here for a while. I'd give you this room and take the daybed in my husband's office.'

'That's too kind,' I said. But I doubted I would make a move, I had accepted a whole string of prohibitions, sought them eagerly in fact, as a hedge against the panic that set in when I actually focused – for a few minutes at a time – on 'my situation.'

On my next visit I found Irene playing checkers with the neighbors' son, a plump, pasty-faced boy of eight, with dark, promising eyes. She sent him home when I arrived. By now I was eight months gone. She insisted I sit with my feet on a hassock and waited on me happily, the way she must have waited on her husband all their married life.

That day she spoke of her two sons, whom she saw only rarely, as they lived in the US.

'We sent them away in 1936 to relatives in New York. If they had stayed in Italy with us, they would have had to fight in Mussolini's army, in Africa, or Greece, or Russia. You know they sent Italian boys to Russia without boots or winter coats. Motherhood is full of pitfalls,' she sighed mightily.

What was her word for motherhood? I don't remember. We spoke German with bits of French and English mixed in. Not a word of Arabic, alas.

'We sent them away for their own good, but they have not forgiven us. The older son teases me, "Why didn't you come away with us in 1936, and spare yourselves all that excitement later on? Why didn't you leave Europe after 1918? Wasn't one world war enough for you? Did you have to stick around for two? You didn't have to remain German all your lives. I didn't."

'He has changed his name, you know. That's fine. None of that matters. But he won't give up.

'"Why do you stay on in this boring little country, why don't you return to Italy? In Italy you were twice the woman you are here. And father was twice the man." I don't know where he gets that from. It's a kind of mourning for his interrupted childhood. Whenever he comes to see me, by the third day he feels ill, he says he can't breathe, he blames it on the weather, the landlocked Swiss dampness, and I wind up urging him to leave for his sake, as well as mine.'

Her confession unsettled me. Maybe I was making a mistake too, hanging on in Switzerland. What was there to stop me from returning home, even in my current state, so obviously pregnant that in the trolley now, old men offered me their seat at once. As if reading my mind Irene said, 'I have a suggestion to make. We need to talk about it. Convents have their uses. But we are not in wartime now. There's no one you have to hide from, your life is not in danger, unless I have misread the situation? Why don't you and your child come live with me? I'll give you the big room and I'll sleep in my husband's office; I often wind up on his daybed, when I can't sleep at night. You can stay for as long as you like. I have no grandchildren of my own, it's past hope now, my sons have left a trail of broken hearts across the United States. Perhaps if we had kept them close to us till they were older, but we had no choice. What do you think? I haven't asked you any questions and I'm not asking any now. I leave it up to you. Do you think you could stand the company of a talkative old woman?'

'Arrangements have been made. I can't undo them,' I said, harsh and dismissive, because I knew that if I began to talk, I would unravel completely.

Irene nodded, suppressing any sign of disappointment, her thin lips pressed together for a second, a diplomat until the bitter end. Did I thank her for her wildly generous offer? I don't recall. I was about as gracious as a hyena in those days.

'I won't ask again, but if you change your mind, do say so, we can find solutions, even last-minute solutions.'

One afternoon her next-door neighbor looked in, a large blowzy woman with two small blond children clinging to her sturdy legs, one child to each leg. From the way she cocked a hairy eyebrow at Irene, I could see they had discussed me in my absence, and I was glad I had refused to join their club. Frau R. was a widow of the mountains, she told me. Her husband was a mountain man, at under four thousand meters he felt unwell. He was in the Grisons that month, training for a second go at Everest.

147

'This is a house of women, one way and another,' Frau R. said.

'Women and children,' Irene corrected her.

'By the way,' said Frau R., 'I have some clothes these two have outgrown. Boy and girl clothes, I have both, would you like to take a look?'

'I'm superstitious,' I said, only half lying. 'I won't look at clothes until my son is born,' I said, admitting out loud for the first time what was obvious for all to see. But now these strangers had it from my mouth as well. If I was not careful, their kindness would entrap me.

'I have to leave now, I have to catch my bus,' I said. The two brats had detached themselves from mummy's legs, and were grabbing cookies from the table and crushing them in their small fists. The girl held out a hand and offered me a crumbly portion. I thanked her carefully and fled, before those pudgy, square-faced kids sabotaged my set resistance.

I didn't mention Irene's invitation to my cellmates, afraid they would prod me to accept. I was astonished by her kindness, her easy, no questions asked humanity. She made me feel petty and suspicious by comparison. Was that what her teasing son meant when he said that in Italy she was twice the woman? Perhaps he had miscalculated, and she was twice the woman still. She put me to shame, and all my kin, and maybe Wally too, whose name she never heard from me.

And what about Kamel in all of this? But I didn't think of him, I thought of my own safety, that I was loathe to step beyond the lines Frau Tischer had drawn, the geometry that held me upright. Postponing responsibility, I made a game of it, a gamble. If something fell a certain way, a coin, a shadow; if a café waiter took my order last of all the patrons in the house, as often happened as unescorted women, even in cafés, were suspect in those days; if in the

148

park the gingko held its golden leaves in a strong wind, or if it knocked them loose – these were fateful signs. If a bird sang overhead, while I climbed the last hill from the trolley landing to Irene's ugly concrete esplanade . . .

On summer nights in Cularo with Wally, in the weeks before we split, we lay awake past midnight and listened to the nightingale – the liquid trill, the eery expectant silence, followed by another burst of song. His nest was in the army barracks down the street. Wally, trusted scout, always knew that kind of thing. The nightingale, he added, sang only in high summer and migrated southward in the fall.

'Like you,' I said and leaned into him. Nothing stays.

But now in German Switzerland a blackbird cawed a warning in the pollarded plane tree by the trolley tracks. Beyond the squat apartment houses clustered at the bottom of the hill the bourgeois mansions loomed, engulfed in an obscene profusion of bougainvillea and roses. Since property is theft, I plucked a single bloom from someone's overhanging sheaf of winter roses and gave it to Irene, essential anarchist. She fixed it neatly in a buttonhole.

'Since nothing blooms at your end of the hill,' I told her. Only apartment houses with bare concrete stairs up front, ugly and functional. The Swiss equivalent of slums, I thought, for minor state employees and grounded mountaineers, and widows with small pensions.

'I have nothing and I want nothing,' Irene took my arm and we skipped up the hill, the three of us, Irene, Kamel in his blind perch, and me. She was not telling the truth. She badly wanted sons and grandsons, her own or someone else's, at that point it no longer mattered.

In the reign of the blackbird, I bought a bunch of long-stemmed roses at the florist by the trolley tracks. After paying for them I had nothing left, not even the trolley

149

fare for the return to the apartment-jail, but it was all downhill, I could walk it easily. No matter what she said, I would never take Irene's bedroom from her, I had decided, but might, just possibly might, accept her husband's alcove-shrine, with the sagging daybed and the massive typewriter on which he pounded out nine novels, eighty radio plays, hundreds of sketches, the lyrics to three operettas, and two unpublished memoirs Irene wanted me to read.

'Are those for me?' A tall man answered the door. He spoke English with a heavy Middle European accent. Was this the teasing son who rarely visited? Or the sulking son who never visited at all? But in that case, what was he doing here?

'Mama, you have company.' Irene came out of the kitchen. A heavy dark green poplin apron, like body armor, like a curse, shielded her satiny silk blouse and knitted skirt. She brushed the hair back from her forehead with one wrist, and said, 'This is my son, Mischa, we have not seen each other since 1954.' To him she said, 'Put these in a vase, I'm just flouring the cutlets. Set a place for Louise.'

'Dorothea will be back with the salad any minute,' the sulker reminded his mother. And then, true to his nickname, he added, 'We hoped to have you to ourselves, Mama. We've come all the way from California for your birthday, don't you think it's right and proper?'

'I've already eaten and I have to go, I just stopped by to bring you these,' I told Irene.

'Stay and talk to Mischa while I finish in the kitchen,' she pleaded, as if afraid that if she left him for a minute, he might get bored and disappear again for years on end. Then she rushed away and shut the kitchen door behind her, to spare him the irritating sight of woman's toil.

Mischa poured us both a glass of sherry.

'Sit down for a moment, what's the rush, the tram runs every fifteen minutes. You can set your watch by it. You know California?'

'Not yet,' I said. 'Maybe someday.'

'Too bad, I was hoping you'd help me persuade my mother that's where she belongs.'

'You mean Irene?'

'She is my mother.'

'Oh, I know that, she talks about you all the time.'

'I'll bet she talks a lot more about my father, hmm? See, I knew it. Never mind, once she gets to Carmel, she won't want to budge. You mean you've never seen the Pacific?' His accent thickened, he sounded like an SS man in a comic skit, Vee haff vays of making you talk . . .

'I've only just discovered the Mediterranean,' I said, with private melancholy.

'I guess I'll go say goodbye, then.' I ran to the kitchen. Irene was busy at the stove. I tapped her on the shoulder. I could not embrace her, my big belly got in the way. She smiled ruefully.

'You'll forgive me for today. They arrived unannounced last night, they're still settling in,' she exclaimed, with almost abject gratitude. 'Ten years since I last saw him, hard to believe, and yet it's as if we've never been apart. You'll keep me posted, won't you? You'll be fine. We'll talk soon. No foolishness?' she cocked her head, coquettish and cajoling.

'Of course not,' I said. But I already knew that I was never coming back.

The prodigal son had vanished from sight, but his wife was coming up the front steps as I flew down.

'*Grüss Gott*,' I faked a Swiss greeting. She waved her fingertips at me.

'So long, kiddo,' she breezed by me. The game was up.

18

After Wally took his son away, I packed up and returned to where I came from, Lausanne, a furnished room, and an office job. Mr Arnold offered me a few weeks' work, glad to have me back, until I tried to kill myself. One evening late I swallowed sleeping pills, washed them down with whiskey, and then I vomited, they didn't even have to pump my stomach at the hospital.

Dr Gagnon came to see me on the ward where I remained 'under observation,' for an entire week. He stood at my bedside like the avenging angel, and said enough was enough, he would make time for me in his schedule and I must expect to remain under his care for at least two years. So while Kamel learned to walk and talk with no help from me, I was infantilized, '*en traitement,*' was the term in use. I was given to understand that there were people who knew me better than I knew myself and I was bound to study with them till I too saw the light. It was like living in a cult or closed sect – the Moonies, say – or doing heavy drugs. My years of bondage.

I wanted to undo the harm. On Saturdays I'd wake up thinking, that's it, I can't take this any more, I'm going down to get my boy. I canvassed the travel agencies, the city had a dozen, they all knew me, I took pages of notes, trains, planes, ships, and backwater busses, when I could find a schedule. Then I skipped back to my room, wildly happy, redemption within reach; I'd write a letter to my boss, explaining why I wasn't ever coming back to work again, all sealed and ready to deliver en route to the train station.

And then, Monday, Tuesday following, I'd phone the consulate about a visa. Each time a new voice opened the interrogation.

'Hello, can you help me? How do I get a visa? How do I transfer funds?'

'Who is this? Who are you? What business are you with? Are you affiliated with some governmental agency? Which government? Which agency? You can't just go roaming about our country at will. Not under present conditions. How do you spell your name? What nationality are you? You're an American, you say, then why do you speak French?'

I hung up and caught my breath. That whiff of incipient police state was enough to kill my nerve.

I saw children in the street, toddlers Kamel's age. I had to run and hide from them. Hide and seek, but no one ever came to search for me. Most of my friends were like me, unmarried, uncommitted, dangling, dancing partners, we danced to the Beatles, religiously. In this way a couple of Hungarian refugees met, married, and produced twin boys, Attila and Choba. I showered them with gifts, till their parents ordered me to stop. I never sent a single gift to Kamel. Wally had told me it was pointless, it would only be stolen in transit. I never sent a money order. I had no money, most of what I earned went to pay for the *traitement*. In Dr Gagnon's view my son's birth was an unfortunate episode,

153

a hit-and-run accident. I would eventually emerge unscathed or rather, healed.

'Get your head straight and then you can help others, till then you'll only do more harm than good.'

'How much longer?' I would ask.

'You'll know when the time comes,' he was always cagey. But I was tired of the life in moral quarantine.

What saved me in the end, was that I had to earn a living, I had to live somewhere, and in the back offices and the rooming houses of Lausanne, I met refugees from Hungary and Palestine and Nasser's Egypt, whose lives had shattered worse than mine and been rebuilt, catch as catch can. What saved me was Irene.

Thanks to the literary widow's diligence, her husband's Weimar feuilletons were still reprinted now and then in small town Swiss newspapers. Two years later, I chanced to read one at the dentist's. Her name was in the phone book, or rather, her husband's name, left there for editors to find. Had California disappointed after all? I phoned and found her in. She invited me to visit the following weekend.

'Come in, sit down! How are you? I owe you an apology. But you saw how it was. My son was with me for ten days, and then we had a terrible row. Plates were broken. Also glasses. Not by me. I panicked and took refuge with the neighbors. That was an unforgivable mistake. He felt shamed. He sat up all night typing an indictment of his father on his father's old typewriter. Cataloguing our failures. As parents, as human beings, as citizens – of what country? Of Germany? For many years we were stateless; millions were. And then we were German again, a passport, nothing more. I found that awful letter in the typewriter next morning. He fled in the night. No goodbyes. I sent him to the US in 1936, a moody, kind young man. He returned after the war full of rancor against us, against the world. As if everything that happened was our fault, and not Hitler's or Goebbels's. What if he was right? I was in despair. Frau R. came and sat with me, or sent the children. With them I revived, slowly. But by the time I was myself again, you had moved on. Were you angry with me? You had every right. I failed you completely.'

Not angry, I thought, but relieved, that no heroic effort would be asked of me.

'I phoned the hospitals, you know, around the time . . . but no one would talk to me, since I was not a family member. I could have lied and said I was your aunt, your mother even. How were they to know? My son is right. Not Mischa, the other one, who says that Switzerland has made a stupid honest bourgeois out of me. I no longer know how to cope with real life. An Italian would have lied with a clear conscience, but I stumbled over misplaced scruples.'

'Let's drop it,' I cut her apologies short. She owed me nothing, except the right to change the subject quickly.

'Do you still do translations?' I asked. 'Did they promote you from Agatha Christie to Conan Doyle or Chesterton?'

The publishers had let her go, she told me sadly. Her German was outmoded for the sixties and she labored too long over each text.

'They wanted a younger person, I can't blame them.'

To make ends meet she now rented out her bedroom by the month. The current tenant was a Thai economist, 'A fascinating woman in her thirties, not at all what you'd expect.' Irene had moved into her husband's tiny office, in between the shelves of Goethe–Schiller in matched sets, and the Art Deco cabinets crammed with dated, unsalable manuscripts.

155

On Sunday we took a long walk up the hill, past the Schreber garden plots, and gorged on cherries from low-lying branches. Whose branches were they? Whose trees? It didn't matter. *Mundraub*, helping yourself to a mouthful from another's fruit tree as you passed by, was an accepted practice in the German-speaking lands from ancient times. Even in Switzerland, Irene added, daintily spitting another cherry pit into a lace-edged handkerchief.

'Do you ever feel homesick?' I asked.

'I miss Italy,' she sighed. 'The years before our sons were forced to leave was the best time.'

'It didn't last long, did it?'

'From 1930 to 1936, five years. My dear, do you realize what five years are in the scheme of things? Sorry, I shouldn't burden you with what my teasing son calls my *Lebensweisheiten*. Each of us has to find his own way. There, how's that for a banality?'

That night we drank pear brandy; I let down my guard, and showed Irene a photograph I'd just received from Wally. His youngest daughter, Kamel's younger sister (by a difference of months) sat on his lap next to a table littered with bicycle parts – a wheel, a set of handlebars. In her pudgy fists she held a wrench and a screwdriver. He's wearing a striped shirt Davy gave him. His pipe lies near to hand. A whole iconography of plus and minus. The minus was Kamel. Although Wally continued to write me as promised, no pictures of Kamel were ever sent. No news of him either. A few euphemistic references, as though the mail was censored. That was all.

'So he's the culprit?'

'Is that what he is?'

'Of course, my dear, a married man with children, much older than you . . .'

'How do you know that?'

'He looks his age, don't you think? He has nice lively eyes. Of course from my perspective thirty, thirty-five is still quite young. My husband was fifty before he came to his senses. He was always falling for some actress or a *chanteuse*, once. I was his confidante, he spared me none of the details. He was a writer, writers need to worship from afar. They summon words to fill the gap. Goethe fell in love for the last time at eighty, with a girl of nineteen. It was a boy, was it?' She snuck in that question, but I asked for it, showing her the photograph from Wally. Bad idea. I nodded.

'You don't have to tell me anything,' Irene said. The pear pickled in brandy resembled a small pale fetus in a bottle. 'But if I may say so, that was not *Mundraub*, what happened between you two. In this case, I would say, the tree was stripped completely,' she went on talking to herself in a way that I was bound to overhear.

'Trees bloom anew each year, however.' Then, as if it followed logically from what preceded, she sprang the question.

'Why don't you go home? You've been away, how long is it, three years?'

'Nearly five.'

'Your poor mother. She has no idea, does she?'

'None at all. She'd sooner see me dead.'

'Are you quite sure of that?'

'I can't return home empty-handed.' Without Kamel I was forever empty-handed. Loss defined me. 'I don't want to put an ocean in between us, don't you see?'

'But if the child was as good as stolen from you?'

'No, that's not the way it was, I swear to you. Don't make his father out to be a thief.'

'Who said thief? Fatuous, maybe, or charmingly vain. Also lonely, homesick, war weary, hounded and insulted in the streets by the police and ordinary citizens, we know what went on in those years (she made them sound eons away). You were kind to him, he was kind to you, according to his lights. His lights were a bit dim, if you ask me.'

'I didn't come here to consult the oracle,' I said rudely, but Irene didn't take offense. She laughed and asked, matter of fact,

'Do I sound like an old crone? Oh dear, I think I need a good cigar about now.'

She slipped away and returned with a flat box of small, gnarled cigars, like twigs from a fruit tree.

'These are called Toscani. Would you like to try one? I acquired the habit in Italy. It's all I have left from those years. My anti-Fascist years. We haven't settled anything, have we? Here, I'll light it for you, it's a bit scratchy in the throat, if you're not used to it.'

I inhaled the good strong smoke. Irene laughed,

'Look at us, like a couple of old peasants, with our brandy and cigars. Let's go sit on the balcony, the moon is full tonight.'

And there it was, waiting for us, a fat red golden baby-faced moon, lolling just above the bushes bordering the small backyard where Kamel would have learned to walk, if it was meant to be. If it was written.

'What you are, is a fatalist,' I told Irene after a few more puffs and the beginning of a headache.

The moon had gone behind a cloud. We sat together in the dark, she on a straight-backed chair and I at her feet, like a disciple.

'No, I am an optimist,' Irene corrected me. 'My husband used to say, things will go wrong without our help, no need to anticipate.' The rising moon slid into view again, a small chill wizened face, increasingly distant.

158

The next day Irene led me to the Goethe–Schiller book-case and told me to help myself. To keep, or to return to her, some day. She filled my arms with storytellers, Keller, Storm, Adalbert Stifter, whom Kafka loved. I stopped read-ing after Wally left. Books led me back to myself and finally back home, where I returned the borrowed books to Irene's teasing son, who had read them as a child, in the same editions, with the same faded bindings. His handprint was all over them.

AISSA'S GROUND ZERO

Her tale was ended. The tulips lay untouched.

'There, it's closing time. But you haven't told me anything about yourself,' she said.

'You have not actually asked,' I said.

'And I won't start now, don't worry. But you looked so sad when you came in this afternoon. It almost stopped me cold. What were you thinking about just then?'

'My wife,' I said without thinking. It wasn't even true, except in a general way. She was never not on my mind.

'You lost her in the war?' Anyone might think that from reading my book.

'A traffic accident in France, a country road in morning fog. I was driving. I no longer drive.'

'I am very sorry for your loss,' she recited woodenly, as people – even educated, widely traveled, multilingual people – often do. They are sincere, they feel your loss, they're not monsters, but they are embarrassed, so they blurt it out in a rush to get it over with. But then she asked, daring of her, 'Were you together long?'

'Ten years – we met first year at university. I was just getting to know her.'

'I know what you mean. I've been married thirty years to a complete cipher.'

'I'm not speaking metaphorically,' I said. I told her a good deal more.

'There was an autopsy. After the traffic accident. They found a ruptured spleen. And a pregnancy, third month.'

Louise covered her mouth with her hand, as if to stifle a cry.

'Had you picked out a name already?' she finally asked.

'No, we hadn't got that far. I didn't know about the child, I had not been told.'

'And you are forced to wonder why. It must torment you, not knowing. Not having known. But it could just be – I speak from experience – that your wife, your late wife, didn't know that she was pregnant.'

'Impossible!'

'Why? Sometimes you can't tell what's going on. Or maybe she was superstitious, and didn't want to tell yet, in case things went wrong. Which they did.' And again she said how sorry she was, and this time I thanked her.

'God knows what you were thinking, while I went on and on all afternoon. Did they tell you the sex? That would have made it worse.'

'It seems I lost a son I didn't know I had until I'd lost him.'

The luncheonette was closing. Up front they were pulling down the blinds. We shook hands and parted, exhausted by our long wrangle with the past.

Tariq phoned to ask how I'd like to spend my last night in New York.

'I may go for a walk, if the rain lets up. I have a lot on my mind just now,' I told him.

161

'You intellectuals,' he moaned. 'Can't you let up on yourself for a minute?'

'See you tomorrow,' I said. He did not insist.

I stood for a long time looking out the window of my hotel room at New York by night. From the twenty-fifth floor I couldn't see the sidewalk. Said might still be standing by the lamppost a few blocks away. What was he doing so far from home? Restless and burdened like Hamlet's father's ghost.

What if I ran into him again and he cried out for vengeance. What would I do, knowing that for both of us, vengeance equals truth?

Truth was, he hired me the week the paper opened in spring 1989.

'What title would you like,' he asked, his pencil poised above the *organigramme*.

'Numbers man, algebrist, that's a good Arab root,' I said.

'How about Chief Financial Officer?'

'You know that my last job was at a sock factory?'

'Their loss, our gain,' he said, his bonhomie not inspired by any quality of mine, but by the extraordinary moment we were privileged to share: the birth of a free press from the loins of an aging, scared dictatorship.

By the spring of '96 Said was three years gone, an Islamist car bomb had demolished our offices, and a servile judge had just sent our brilliant young cartoonist to jail for offending the national flag. As long as the paper was under attack from its enemies on all sides, I was determined to resist. But that spring, the attack came from another quarter.

The day our cartoonist was sentenced, a tall, gaunt woman followed us out into the street. I recognized her, one of a group of women who seemed to live at the courthouse. With their voluminous headscarves and sweeping skirts, they looked as if they'd come to the big city from the back of beyond with a live hen or two tucked about them somewhere, to bribe the court clerk, who surely had fancier tastes. In fact, one knew they came from the city's poorest neighborhoods, frequent target of police raids unreported in our paper. One of the many open secrets of those years: the hundreds, some said thousands of young men who had been disappeared in the course of the civil war. These women were their mothers.

Their representative spoke to us from behind a hand covering her mouth, from timidity. But she spoke, she didn't let us get away.

'We're sorry for your young man. He doesn't belong in jail. We haven't seen our sons in years. Why don't you put them in your paper? Names and photographs. Someone might recognize a face. Even over in France, since they claim our children left the country long ago.'

'Excellent idea. I'll run it by the editor in chief,' an embittered colleague said. The poor woman invoked God's blessing on us all and let us go.

That night I told my wife about the woman who spoke from behind the closed gate of her fingers.

'She wasn't fooled. She expected nothing from us, she expects nothing from the courts. Why did she ask?'

My wife knew the answer.

'If she stopped asking, she'd be giving up the search. You gave her a few days' reprieve.'

'We gave her an illusion,' I said. Our newspaper was an illusion: we printed only what the regime permitted us to print. The alternative was to join the roster of papers that had been shut down for the duration.

'What would Said do now?' I asked my wife.

She said, 'He lived in different times.' We used to say that

163

each year of our civil war was like a century. That night I banged my head against the wall. My wife was not alarmed. Head–banging was a sign of life.

She didn't protest when I finally quit the paper six months later. But she fought me about leaving the country. She taught English in an Algiers *lycée*; she was unwilling to abandon her students, entering their teens in grim times.

I won that argument by promising to return home as soon as the state of siege was lifted. It's still in force today.

The woman who conquered her fear to confront us outside the courthouse, and Louise, voluble, confident (pretending to be a reporter to waylay me), and free with intimate details, were worlds apart. Pondering the difference between them, between the iron blade of fate and the curlicues of an ambivalent adulterous relationship, could lead straight to despair.

I remembered Said's dark mood on his return from a quick trip to Amsterdam, a few months before his death by an assassin's bullet.

'Who decided that Dutch children and Algerian children should lead such different lives?' he asked in the doorway. The answer lay buried under a thousand years of stone and rubble. Our Sisyphus hung up his jacket and got back to work.

Louise's suffering was real, as Said's ghost reminded me. So, surely was Ahmed Ouali's. (The name Wally irked me, a bad joke, a bad beginning, from which the rest was almost bound to follow.) But, oh, mothers of the world, why do you besiege me? There is nothing I can do to help you. I myself am tainted by egregious failure.

My last admission in the darkened luncheonette shocked Louise. She tried to lighten the mood with an Italian saying she had learned on her travels. It was just a saying, she conceded, she wasn't actually sure what it meant, but she said it anyway. American nature abhors a vacuum.

164

'*Chiodo scaccia chiodo*. One nail drives out the next.' I was nonplussed. What new trouble did she wish on me?

Tariq was eager to show me ground zero my last morning in town. He couldn't believe I hadn't made the pilgrimage on my own.

'I'm not boycotting ground zero,' I told him. 'I have a prior engagement.' He tactfully withdrew. I phoned Naima and asked her to meet me at the hotel at noon.

I had met her in the subway five days earlier. A Honduran guitarist was playing tepid ballads on the downtown platform of the 81st Street station. I stopped to listen, so did she. The guy was selling a CD from his guitar case, I bought a copy quickly and offered it to her. She didn't take offense but thanked me graciously and asked, 'Are you Colombian by any chance? You look a lot like Juan Valdez,' she laughed. 'All that's missing is the moustache.'

'I'll get right to work on it,' I said, and then I asked her, 'Who is Juan Valdez?' I thought a famous bandit, or a nineteenth-century patriot. When she told me he was an actor in a well-known advertisement for Colombian coffee, I was delighted. How different from the Paris Métro where people pitied or loathed me on sight, depending on their father's history of military service in Algeria forty years ago.

This subway beauty was only vaguely Colombian herself, she told me. She had an irresistible Arabic first name bequeathed her by a Lebanese emigrant great-grandmother: Naima. Naima was studying fashion design. On Wednesday we met briefly outside the school on Seventh Avenue, a regular bazaar, the vendors, including many Africans, line the sidewalk like our *trabendistes,* our petty smugglers, at home. She accepted the tribute of a scarf,

165

a pair of sunglasses, and a subway map of Paris as a souvenir of meeting me. She knew the film *Pépé le Moko* starring Jean Gabin. Otherwise Algeria was a closed book to her. What a relief. She doesn't know that I was married. It did not come up. She called me Juan Valdez again and admired the faint outline of a moustache shadowing my upper lip. Me a Colombian, why not? This is the land of opportunity. Let freedom ring.

On Thursday Naima had exams. She agreed to lunch on Friday, before I took my plane. When I suggested we meet at my hotel, the well-fed beauty showed up with a paper bag containing two enormous sandwiches, some New York combination of cold meats and cheeses with all the trimmings. Our first kiss tasted of half sour pickles, after that it was pure honey and acceptance in the midday glare, and when I asked her please, to keep her eyes open so that I could look into them, like in a dream where you are both actor and observer, she complied.

She was terrifyingly compliant, I thought, reliving the encounter late that night, on the flight home. Like Louise with her Wally at the start. Her Wally, who, with all his faults (I could not resist comparing) behaved better than I did in the end. He lied when cornered, I lied from habit, for the fun of it. Before we parted, in a farewell flourish, I gave Naima my correct Paris address. Who doesn't want a friend in Paris? Then I added in a rueful rush, that I lived there with my fiancée, who couldn't make up her mind whether to marry or to separate. Pure invention. Naima asked no questions, although she may have had her doubts. That was all right too. Better for her to dismiss me as untrustworthy: it was all part of a well-oiled exit strategy.

I didn't used to employ such shabby tactics. The very idea of tactics would have repelled me at one time. But then my life changed. As long as I thought of myself as a suicide manqué, a death-row inmate, a man living on borrowed time, I viewed every romantic adventure as a sort of 'last meal,' a quick entitlement. I was like that cold fish Julien Sorel in *Le Rouge et le Noir* at his least admirable, concluding that as the son of poor peasants, it's his right, indeed his duty, to seduce the daughter of the marquis, his benefactor.

Louise with her melancholy revelations, her Stendhal obsession, showed me what I had become in the years without my wife – a self-protective (because wounded, but who has not been wounded?), manipulative cynic with a light touch.

Speaking of manipulations, what to make of Tariq and his brand of white magic? He had me well in hand. He let me roam the city on a long leash, meanwhile recruiting – an apparent case of sidewalk serendipity – earnest, oblivious Louise to rein me in and then, still unwitting, confront me with my failings.

That Kurdish Francophone ambulance driver knew more than met the eye. He didn't like my book, he told me so en route to the airport.

Tactful as always, he said, 'That sort of thing does well in France, but you and I know better. You had to shake the mud from your sandals. Next time you'll aim higher.'

Was he my spirit guide, sent to prod me on the road to enlightenment and right behavior? Who believes in such things? Where were the spirit guides during our civil war? Three generations back our country produced many men revered for holiness, erudition, and a special grace. Jealous of their moral authority, the French killed or exiled them. Now we do the job ourselves.

167

Naima was lovely, I left her with some caressing memories but who was I kidding? The minute the door closed behind her, I was myself again, no coffee baron, just a loner on the lam. While shaving off the three-days growth of Latin lover moustache, I avoided looking in the mirror.

Part Two

Louise

Wally wrote me for the last time in the fall of '68. A French firm had recruited him to help run a powdered milk plant in Algeria. They were sending him back to the Charente for six weeks' training in maintenance of the machinery, pipes, and boilers, a sort of engineer without diploma. He was too proud to ask me to drop everything and meet him in Poitiers, but he must have hoped.

By the time his letter arrived, I was three months pregnant and about to marry Irene's teasing son. A few years younger than my Uncle Max, Walt had served in the Pacific theatre but unlike Uncle Max he had been sent into combat, and had been badly wounded in the Philippines in 1945. That near-death experience left him with a sense of entitlement I could not share, but was willing to serve. The war destroyed most of his hearing in both ears. I learned to speak up, to enunciate, to interpret between him and the world, between him and our three children. People some-times claimed he had selective hearing, tuning out whatever bored or distressed him. If so, that was his right. This man had paid his dues, he could have sat out the war as division

171

artist, painting portraits of National Guard colonels in Indiana, but demanded to be sent into combat with the infantry instead.

'Those poor boys from the Kentucky hills, in my division, had no idea what they were dying for. I at least knew,' he told me once. 'I was defending the remnant of my mother's family. But then I didn't die. A lot of them did.'

I loved him for the way he remembered his fallen comrades. He was more diffident than Wally, if I didn't ask, he didn't tell, but what I learned revealed a man of true feeling. His deafness made intimate conversation, whispered confessions impossible. How could I tell him about Kamel? It wasn't something to declare across the dinner table, in a loud clear voice. Perhaps I could have written out a signed confession. I refrained, for all kinds of valid reasons.

Irene was adamant, 'You haven't told him, have you? I thought not. Neither have I. That's as it should be. We won't betray each others' secrets. Please don't hurt my son. After what he went through in the war, he can't take another wounding.'

I wrote Wally the briefest note, telling him I was about to marry. He never wrote me again. At least I don't think he did. He was a man who knew how to cut his losses. Maybe by now he was beguiling another woman with the stories he told me our first winter in Cularo. From my secure vantage point, as a soon-to-be-respectable married woman, I could afford to take a jaded look at what had been. But where did that leave Kamel?

The next spring, with our infant son, we made our first trip to Ecuador. We wandered into a mountain paradise, a

172

colonial backwater of great beauty and rank ancient injustice, beyond reach of the US postal service, the Internal Revenue Service, and the *New York Times* announcing the start of the Nixon era. A lot of us went into glamorous exile in those years, the years of Vietnamization in Indochina. '*La lejanía*,' distance, a globe-trotting Mexican poet identified the lure of poor shabby Santa Prisca for a group of rapt exiles – another name for sheer escapism.

If you wanted to keep a secret, you would go far away, but if the one person you wanted to keep it from, shared your bed? Difficult. *La lejanía* made things both better and worse. I had already lived my life. Marriage to Walt was an undeserved second chance. No complaining.

When women asked, 'How did you meet your husband?' what they meant was HOW did he wind up with you, this handsome, well-spoken painter – dashing, romantic and broke most of the time? We went to Ecuador because the life was cheap and since we never made any money, we just stayed on, doing without TV, radio, books, and running water for a while. I did a lot of household chores, like boiling water for baths in tin tubs twice a week, and cooking meals in clay pots on a charcoal stove. At dark on winter nights the neighborhood smelled of pinesap from the drenched twigs used to light the little stoves fashioned out of scrapped lard cans. The lady two doors down sold bread fresh from her ovens, after dark. She baked it into little shapes with impossibly poetic names like *hojarasca* and counted them out into large flat baskets, carried off to remote *barrios* by old barefoot women in black dresses. Someday, I thought, I will be one of them.

Our fifth year out, we met young refugees from Pinochet's Chile. Whenever possible, I wrote down what I heard from them. If they saw me taking notes they

173

clammed up right away. So I memorized their words and waited to take notes until they'd gone. I was not working for the CIA, just keeping track of news I'd never read, and still haven't, but wanted to make known somehow, someday. Later we met refugees from Argentina and Uruguay. They spoke of torture, disappearances. The French military had exported their techniques and strategies from Algeria directly into Latin America. The Americans were busy gobetweens. In Uruguay the sons of American missionaries wound up in radical resistance groups. They lost many friends. A Guatemalan came to visit and organized a soccer match where the ball was an outsize papier mâché head of Kissinger. The children and I modeled the head and Walt painted the features. The refugees were on stopover, hiding out in the highlands while waiting for visas for longterm exile in Sweden, Britain, or France. We outstayed them all. We already spoke French and German, we learned Spanish together. Walt, twenty years my senior, was a generation ahead of me in his experience of the expatriate life. He taught me the ironic sympathetic-passive viewpoint of the outsider who will never be an insider, but doesn't care. He painted three hundred paintings in those years. They were shipped back to New York on a banana boat from Guayaquil. My visual memories are not of churches and mountains silhouetted against the setting sun, but of empty lots, unused unloved spaces where weeds with tiny orange flowers grew, and rain turned the mud to clay so you had to stop every few steps to scrape the bottoms of your shoes. If you had shoes.

By the time we left Santa Prisca some of our neighbors were emigrating to the US. If they could do it, so could we. Our kids hit the US and their teens in the eighties. They learned to care about money and possessions and everything we never gave them in *la lejanía*. We set them up for it: our laxness taught them to be strivers.

Ours was an arranged marriage, we arranged it, but it was not a love match the way they say. It took a few years for us to find each other. I sometimes felt like giving up. The starch of Irene's blessing and her character, held us upright and together. And the children.

What I love about Walt, I've said this already, is that he doesn't ask questions. If something is wrong he waits for it to go away. I haven't decided yet if that's a sign of wisdom or indifference; the two may be related. When Uncle James said, 'Marry someone who will let you alone,' he could have had Walt in mind.

The powdered milk plant was first nationalized and then allowed to fail. In Algeria as in France, Wally would always be one of the hired hands. Already in summer 1965, he had named – so soon! – his bitter disappointment with the new Algeria. It was no different than the old, he said. He must have meant the coup that brought in the military cliques still running the country today.

I carried that letter in my purse for years, like a membership card in the human race. It was linked in my mind with the Ferré song Wally introduced us to in his room in winter 1961. '*Paname, si on te battait, je prendrais des armes.*' I was ready to take up arms against the colonels who hijacked Wally's dream republic. Meanwhile, however, he had stopped writing to me.

A bi-monthly magazine, published by a church-related NGO doing good works abroad for the past eighty years, has agreed to send me to Algeria, to report on recovery from the recent civil war. The magazine has only a small staff. In fact the editor, art director, and chief reporter are all the same person, a young man in his twenties with a BA in anthropology. Never mind, he seemed impressed by my credentials. Middle-aged wisdom, fluent French, an extended family living in Algeria (I hinted without naming names), and close acquaintance with the country's leading exiled pamphleteer. (Forgive me Aissa, I dropped your name, no harm done, it didn't register.) Under cover of this admittedly ill-paid assignment (but they WILL cover my expenses), I plan to search for Kamel and present my husband with a small *fait accompli*, an after-the-fact narrative of a belated family reunion, which he will accept because I will lay it before him on my safe return from Algeria, when any warnings or misgivings he may have, about my safety, or God help me, my loyalty, will be moot. I'll be home free.

In preparation for the trip, last week I consulted Prof L., who teaches at a small Catholic college in Rockland County.

'Wonderful people Algerians, tough, skeptical, and cynical, with good reason. Not easy to know, in fact I'd say they're generally downright suspicious, again with good reason. But once you've won their trust, once they accept you, and mind you it can take a while, no one makes a better friend than an Algerian. They adopt you. You become part of the family. For life.'

'For life,' I nodded. 'Were you there on the day the country became independent?' I asked him.

'No, were you?'

'I was in France,' I told him. 'I celebrated with some friends. Expectations were so high back then, too high I guess.'

5 July 1962, Algerian Independence Day, fell on a

Thursday. Wally left for work as usual at six a.m. While he was gone, I stitched together the flag of his new nation, in scraps of red, white, and green cloth I'd been collecting for this day. Small scraps: this would not be a regulation flag to fly in parades. It would be no bigger than a handkerchief, for personal use only.

Wally returned at six p.m. with his haversack slung over his shoulder, like a modest Sinbad. When he saw the flag, his face lit up, but then he examined my handiwork closely, and said, 'The star is out of place. The crescent moon is a bit lumpy. You don't mind my saying so? Here, let me wash my hands and I'll show you.' Ablutions before handling the flag, I took note. While sewing and snipping he told a story I'd never heard before, dating from the first year of the long war, when he left home, for reasons that now became quite clear.

October 1954, a young cousin entered the French primary school. Children started late, back then, age seven, or eight. There was always a shortage of places for Arab boys. One day in mid November, the teacher handed out paper and pencils and invited the little boys – the schools were segregated in those days – to draw whatever came into their heads. Wally's cousin drew a picture of the star and crescent emblem on the banned Algerian flag. The teacher, walking round the classroom, stopped to ask the boy where he'd seen that motif before.

'My father keeps it at the bottom of the wooden chest.'

That night the gendarmes arrested Wally's uncle, took him to headquarters in the next town and gave him the bathtub treatment, Wally said, *la baignoire*. I didn't ask for details and he didn't offer any, but by now it's common knowledge, that water-boarding is a form of torture where the victim's head is plunged into a toilet, or a pail of soap

177

suds, or a mixture of water, and say, kerosene, till he's drowning.

This went on intermittently for three weeks, till they were satisfied that Wally's uncle had no more idea than they did who was responsible for the synchronized bombing of police and military targets around the country on 1 November, which marked the start of what the French called 'the events in Algeria.' The Algerians, absurdly hopeful, called it 'the revolution.' The gendarmes held Wally's uncle for another week, and then they let him go, with a warning to keep quiet.

A week later a stroke felled this strong man in his forties. He regained his speech in time, but not the use of his right arm. And Wally left for France, because he knew it was only a matter of time till they hauled him in for questioning. And because hard times were coming and the entire family would need his help.

'And your little cousin, what became of him?' I asked Wally.

'He went back to school the next year, and learned to keep his mouth shut.'

'But did teachers really spy on their own pupils?'

Before Wally could answer, his pal Larbi walked in on us. When he saw the flag, his dour, squarish face relaxed into a large, unprecedented smile.

'Louise made it,' Wally boasted and pushed Larbi to accept a glass of wine.

'Just this once,' the friend agreed. After the second glass, he started talking about his plans for when he returned home. He was going to open a paint and body shop, he had the place picked out. He promised Wally free service, when he got a car of his own, that is. I remember thinking that a war had been fought so poor Larbi could knock the dents out of old cars. A senseless, stupid war, by now everyone agrees.

'The age of socialist utopias is over,' the professor said and then he wrote me off completely.

'Algeria? What do you want to go there for? The place is a shambles. Why don't you go to Cairo for a couple of weeks? Egypt is the mother country, the cradle of humanity, it's called.'

'I thought the worst of the violence was over in Algeria by now.'

'The cities are safe enough but you never know. For a reporter it's a can of worms. Deep grudges, shifting alliances. To sort it out, you need ANTENNAS,' he warned. 'Tell me, do you think you have antennas?'

I made a quick exit. I was afraid I might begin to twitter like a bug.

I read lately that pregnant women keep some fetal cells forever. Male cells turn up decades later in the livers of women who have borne sons, or even miscarried, or aborted sons. Kamel has colonized my liver. I am going to liberate us both. That professor will be shocked to learn.

Something is bothering Walt. No mystery there: he doesn't want me going to Algeria without him. And he doesn't want to go with me. He's made that clear. He's engaged in a high-intensity campaign of dissuasion.

'Running off to unknown countries to report, is something you do when you're twenty-five, not sixty,' he warns me. 'You're too old for this game.'

'That's why I have to go right now, before I lose my memory completely.'

179

'You suffer from *Gedankenflucht*,' he piles it on. He means I'm scatterbrained.

'Latin America maybe,' he continues, 'at least you've lived there, you know your way around.'

'Please let's not fight,' I say.

'But you don't even speak the language. Speaking French to Algerians is like speaking English to Pakistanis,' he tells me. 'It's a colonial holdover.'

It's late afternoon, the long slanting rays of the not-yet-setting sun enter his small studio. He should be sitting quietly before his canvas, capturing the soul of a great heap of rotting fruits and vegetables, a variegated indoor land-scape, made richly baroque by the twirls and wisps of the plastic bags in which the vegetables came from the mark-down shelf at the local discount grocery store. Instead he's pacing and haranguing me.

'You act like a rich woman who can go anywhere when-ever she wants.'

'You're not a visual person. You'll miss the story, like you did in Ecuador for all those years.' Cruel man.

I forgive him.

'You'll be a Jewish-American in an Arab country. You won't be welcome. At least if the Israeli situation were resolved . . .'

'That might take another generation,' I remind him gently.

Never mind, he's found another argument.

'How much is this going to cost?'

'Very little,' this is one charge I can answer. 'The maga-zine is paying for the trip, and I'll stay in a cheap hotel.'

'And get yourself kidnapped. I've never even heard of this magazine,' he grumbles. I don't answer this charge because I share his Groucho Marx misgivings, that any magazine that would hire me is a questionable operation.

180

He picks up his brush. The steady scratching sound of stiff bristle on canvas pursues me across the room. Painting is like automatic writing for him. It emerges from the unconscious. His conscious mind meanwhile churns out debating points.

'Anyone you might want to interview is likely to be in jail or in exile, isn't that so?'

'Or dead,' I say. 'A lot of people are dead.' Including Kamel's father, probably. *The masquerade is over*: that song turned up on the flip side of one of Wally's stack of 45s.

My husband says nothing for a moment. Then he lets loose again.

'You can't interview the dead. Stay here and read their posthumous memoirs, isn't that more sensible?'

'But there's a younger generation coming up, over half the country is under thirty. I'm just going to ask questions, modestly, and record the answers,' I say, with wholly spurious assurance.

'You don't know how to operate in a police state. You'll get other people in trouble.'

'Have some faith in me, please,' I plead. I'm not talking to a wall, exactly, but to the blank side of the canvas. He's painting on the other side. The stretched painting hides him, seated at his easel, almost completely. The scratchy sound accelerates, then stops.

'I've been gathering pointers from experts. They see no obstacle,' I fib.

He retaliates with a real stinger. 'American ignorance masquerading as know-how. You're no better than George Bush.'

That did it. His taunt achieved what years of offhand kindness failed to. In a rage, I spilled the whole story, start to finish, I flooded him with facts and feelings, I spared him nothing. My husband now knows I have a son in Algeria whom I intend to see before I die. He took it like a prince, or let's say, since we are not royalists, like a man.

I did not name Kamel to him, as I'm not sure it's the name he goes by, and because it has a foreign ring to it that might confuse the issue. I simply said 'a son.' Everyone knows what that means.

'Hmm, I suspected it, you know. From something my mother said, before she died.' Irene died in her sleep of a heart attack, in 1985, she was ninety-two years old. I had known her twenty years by then. There was no one I loved more.

'Oh, what was that?'

'Nothing, she just said we were both war wounded.'

'Odd way to put it. You suspected, but you never asked me? Weren't you curious?'

'Actually, I preferred not knowing. And you seemed to prefer not telling. I respected that.' Oh dear, what a strange moratorium our marriage was turning out to be.

'I see. Are you sorry that I told you now? I really told you, didn't I?'

'Oh well, at least I understand what's going on. Why this sudden obsession with Algeria. I thought it had to do with 9/11 somehow.'

'Anyway,' he concluded briskly. That word was his broom for sweeping away troubles that could not be helped. 'Anyway' for him was a complete declarative sentence.

'It happens in the best of families,' he said (another German proverb, he's been falling back on those a lot lately). He did agree, when I persisted, that a gesture on my part toward this lost branch of our family – he actually said 'our family,' which touched me deeply – was long overdue.

182

'But don't ask me to go with you, I'm too old for such adventures,' he concluded. Which saddened me, as ten years ago he would not have said that. Or maybe he was being overly discreet, afraid it was the father, not the son I longed to see again. Something troubled him, clearly, because he asked, 'Couldn't you have had an abortion?'

'It was too late for that,' I said. Then I asked him, 'Would you have married me if you had known, when we first met?'

My husband is a man of deep feeling but little surface display thereof. This sort of open, candid exchange was highly unusual. So much between us has been left unsaid from the outset. Even now, I hesitated to ask this question – and I had to repeat it twice more, till he heard.

'Probably not.'

'Why not?' I asked.

'I'd have worried you might leave me for your other family. Are you going to leave me now?'

'Of course not!' I said. How can he doubt my loyalty? We've been together for thirty-five years. I planted a quick kiss on his bald pate, to reassure him. His right arm continued to run the brush back and forth across the upper right hand corner of the canvas.

Once I told my husband, I had to tell the children too. That was easier. My older daughter is an environmental lawyer, a woman of the world, known on her beat, which includes most of the Americas, as a 'tough cookie.' Which you have to be to sue the major oil companies and win. She began at once to take a deposition.

'My mom . . . hmm . . . Any more secrets you've been hiding from me all these years? Do you have a picture of this long-lost brother? Is he cute?

183

'Don't worry, if we ever meet, I'll tell him he lucked out, he was spared the ordeal of growing up in our totally dysfunctional family. He gets to meet us as adults, fully recovered from our erratic upbringing.' She talks a tough game but really she's all heart, a secret softie.

Years ago she hung out for months in a vest pocket park she was trying to protect from a rapacious developer in a rapidly gentrifying Seattle neighborhood. One day she told me that in order to be a good activist, you have to love the people whose rights you defend. Everyone in the park asked her out, even the junkies who had no place to go, and nothing to offer but opinions. My beacon child hides her light under a bushel as heavy as the Vatican dome. I don't know if the metaphor works: where my children are concerned, I quickly lose all sense of proportion. Sometimes when I look at her I feel as if I had given birth to some stronger, smarter breed than mine, a wild colt, perhaps, or a raccoon, or a cross between the two. Her teasing was on the mark. In whatever ways I failed Kamel, I also failed my other children. He forces my eyes open now – his vengeance perhaps?

The *Goldkind*, Irene used to call our son, in her dotage, when she reverted to the sentimental language of her childhood: our golden boy, quiet, reliable, good natured, and generous. When I told him about Kamel, he pressed his lips together and dipped his head sideways as if I'd thrown something small, hard, and sharp in his direction. Then, to my surprise, tears welled in his eyes and he turned away in embarrassment.

'What is it?' I cried, alarmed. But I knew without asking. My tenderhearted boy, a new father himself, felt wrenching pity for the infant his own mother had abandoned.

184

Or maybe it was as if all at once, the grievances he'd left unvoiced for thirty years, out of self-effacing modesty or gallantry or shame, had arrived in a great horde to demand redress. I thought to myself, why go chasing to right imaginary wrongs, when real need stands exposed before you. And I put out my hand and patted his head, the way I did when he was little and suffering from one of those bellyaches he used to get when we lived at ten thousand feet above sea level. He never adjusted to the altitude. If I hadn't known he loved his wife and told her his troubles, my resolve would have crumbled right there. It did give way a little, I admit. I began to worry. Maybe my obsession with Kamel was a luxury indulged at the expense of my other kids, who, from the moment they were born, never had my full attention.

My son did not view Kamel as a rival, but as a secret sharer, hidden, and vulnerable. And since he'd been our only son till now, and always wanted company, he began to think of Kamel as a kid brother in need of help and guidance. We all did, somehow. Yet why should we think of him as small, dark, and needy? He might be big, strapping and successful, another Zinedine Zidane for all we knew. Or he might be a minor provincial satrap, although I doubted that. No son of Wally's could grow up to be a satrap, no matter who raised him. No more than a gnarled olive tree could morph into a rhinoceros.

A week later my son announced, out of the blue, 'If you need plane fare, I could probably help out. I've always got a pair of frequent flyer tickets due me from somewhere.'

'You are a prince among men,' I told him. 'Maybe some-day we'll have a family reunion?'

185

'In Algeria? No thanks. But keep me posted. So I'm not your first-born son after all?' he added. He had been pondering the ramifications.

'No, you're not,' I admitted 'But you know—'

'That's OK, first-born sons are the ones they always go after, like in Egypt under the Pharaohs. This is actually reassuring news, you realize, Mom,' he said. He never calls me Mom these days, except in jest.

My breasts were still gorged with milk when I found the postcard in the mailbox, with a view of Mont Blanc seen from the Swiss side. I decided Wally wrote it in advance, reassuring me that everyone had arrived home in good order. He thanked me, again, on the back of this postcard, for the 'beau cadeau' I had bestowed on his family. His family! So that was the plan. Kamel belonged not to his birth parents, but to an entire clan that was closing ranks against me. Wally was of the tribe but also apart from it, or we would never have met. He was telling me, as gently as possible, that our son had got away from us both. It was after deciphering this message, that I ran out and bought the sleeping pills.

Waiting for the visa is like waiting to give birth; a long gestation monitored by anxious family, plagued by sleepless nights. The children sympathize. They fret and bring me gifts.

My younger daughter is the timid one. Childhood nightmares sent her running to our bed. She often slept with us for safety's sake.

At four she dreamed she was pursued by monsters.

'Why didn't you call me in your dream? I would have chased them away.'

186

'In the dream I was a grown up,' she wailed. Or did she mean 'groan up,' to her it was the same word.

9/11 has brought on a regression of sorts. She's afraid she won't live to marry the man she loves, who's playing hard to get; won't live to move up to first violin or solo work.

'Is my brother a terrorist?' she asked me the other day.

'Which brother do you mean?' I said.

'You know, the one I'm going to meet someday. What if he hates everything we stand for?'

'Now you sound like Bush.'

'I'm sorry,' she was always quick with an apology, 'but you hear so much now about what can go wrong. They hiked up the alert to orange yesterday again. I can't help it, it scares me. But I shouldn't have asked that. Do you forgive me?'

'Of course I do, my sweet. It's my fault for creating this odd situation. When you meet him, you'll see for yourself. Who knows, maybe he'll be musical and you can play duets.'

That sounded rather Pollyannaish but on the other hand, why shouldn't what began in sorrow end in harmony? When Wally wrote me from home, he called Kamel '*le beau cadeau,*' to avoid writing his name, out of discretion but mainly because names can hurt, and he wished to spare me and himself fresh pain. *Le beau cadeau* could be a – *tout finit par des chansons* – light-hearted, euphemistic Francophone translation of an Algerian disaster. That light heartedness of Wally's that so moved me when we first met, but that I distrusted later on.

'I made a CD for my brother,' Anna announced yesterday. She mentions him tentatively, as if to do so might give offense. Timidly polite, despite her proven talent and tenacity

187

in pursuit of her goals: a violinist with the City Opera orchestra.

'There's a Rimsky-Korsakov suite with a sort of oriental lilt to it which I thought he might enjoy. The rest is just Bach and Mozart, is that all right?'

'That's wonderful, thank you so much, did Isaac get to you?'

'No,' she's miffed and has a right to be, 'it was my own idea. I'm a human being too, you know. My friend Polo is in there too, on cello. When I told him he volunteered at once, isn't that sweet?'

'You told someone else, just like that?'

'Oh dear, I didn't think you'd mind. Polo is a good friend, he's from Morocco, his family left in 1960, some went to Israel, some to Paris. Anyway we recorded this for . . . you didn't tell me his name. Do you not know it? I mean, that's all right, no reason you should know it, or maybe you don't want to tell me, that's all right too, I understand how hard it must have been . . . You're not mad at me, are you?'

'Of course not, how can you think that?'

'The Bach piece is a trio, we left out one voice, so if he plays the violin, he can sit in with us, a virtual performance. That's done all the time now. If not, he can just listen. Whatever works for him, you know?'

'I'm sure he'll be thrilled,' I say. 'I'll bring you a letter from him. Maybe a CD.'

What is this fairy tale I'm spinning? I'm in my third month of waiting for the visa that may never come.

But why not be optimistic? Look how well things have worked out for my children's generation. The sons and daughters of refugees from Nazism and the Indian partition, living well in the US, their hard work rewarded with money, prestige, and tax cuts.

188

If there was ever a time to include Kamel in our own brand of tribal solidarity, it's now.

'What if he doesn't own a CD player?' Anna asks.

'If not, I'll buy him one, how's that?

'This is all so weird,' she blurts out. 'Immature impulse control,' a social worker diagnosed when she was in third grade. The label stuck, a family joke. Thank goodness someone says what's on their mind sometimes, is how I feel.

'What if you encounter some hostility, at the outset? No offense, but you know what I mean. Will you be able to handle it?'

'I'll have your CD as an ice breaker,' I told her.

'That was sort of the idea. I'm glad you agree. Look, I'm sorry, but I have to run, rehearsal starts in half an hour. Will you be all right?'

Why do my children talk to me as if I were a halfwit or an invalid? As if I hadn't taught high school Spanish for twenty years, inculcating into thousands of students the essential difference between *ser* and *estar*. Two of my star pupils are language instructors for the Peace Corps, one brilliant young woman has translated Martí's best-loved poems. I'm credited in the acknowledgements, first paragraph, third sentence. Who dares call me an underachiever? Or let them call me that, but only I know what it means.

'Uh oh, Mom is spacing out again, earth to Mom, earth to Mom, do you read me?' The kids used to tease good-naturedly. Or sometimes, wounded: 'Never mind, I'll talk to you when you can pay attention.' I was an island apart from the main, Algeria means the islands, in Arabic, Aissa told me that. I will write to him when there is news, good news. He's had far too much bad news in his life.

189

'Of course I'll be all right.' And to prove to Anna that she has my full attention, to step up to my obligations, I tell her, finally, 'Your brother's name, the name we talked about, is Kamel.'

'Oh, like in *Amahl and the Night Visitors*. I mean, it almost rhymes.'

'It means perfect,' I add.

'There you are,' she kisses me and runs off, scarves, curls, and ruffles trailing. She'll tie up her loose ends before she takes her instrument in hand.

'If it's a girl we could call her Leila. That means night,' Wally was quick to stake his claim on my belly. I liked the sudden closeness, the inclusiveness, as if now at last, he was free to show strong feelings, but I remember wondering, why Night? Who calls their daughter Night? Then I remembered *The Thousand and One Nights*, the evening tales as they are called. Leila was a product of our story-telling sessions. Or was Night a name for a dark-haired beauty, perhaps a temptress, a woman (but first an infant and then a girl child) outside convention and propriety. As in 'ladies of the night'?

And then I forgot all about it, because I was sure I was carrying a son. I'm talking now about the baby I aborted, and damned if I didn't have to fight for the right to remove that shameful burden from my gut. In those days they scraped it loose with a spoon; metal on flesh. First they dilated your cervix with a chilly metal cone. It would have hurt like hell if you were awake, but you slept right through it, under general anesthesia administered by the surgeon himself, or was I already confused when Dr Vidal smiled and spoke to me on the verge of sleep, from above, '*Tu nous apportes le soleil.*' You have brought back the sun.

190

Aristotle taught that women's role in reproduction was negligible, she was a mere vessel for the homunculus implanted by the male. I thought more or less along those lines. I was invisible along with all my sex. I could not conceive the thought that Kamel, my perfect boy, might have been a girl. Losing her, I lost a part of myself. And that part perished without a murmur of complaint. If I could only learn to complain, my daughters, I would have something to tell you.

I was a good mother, conscientious and playful. I invented songs, rhymes, and games, to entertain and educate my children. But I am a terrible grandmother because the sight of Nisha causes me pain. I look at her and see Leila. Greedy of me to want her now, and idiotic, after all these years, but that's the way it is. I look at my granddaughter, a beauty by the way, with auburn hair and big brown eyes, and feel bereft, cast off, and secretive. I pray I may outgrow this numbing sadness. Meanwhile I mask it with more songs. Nisha is a quick study. Her repertoire is growing all the time.

My older daughter is the only one of my three, no four, children, given to deep speculation about the meaning of life. She is the most articulate and demanding: she asks me to bare my inmost thoughts and feelings, so she can sift them for some larger pattern in things.

Now that I've finally leveled with her, she is besieged with worries.

'Did you ever stop to think that all these years affected not only this son of yours – do you even know his name? – but the rest of us as well? I'm not just talking about your tendency to tune out in the middle of a conversation, but something more basic. Do you see what I mean? I think I understand what happened to you. You sacrificed my brother to some kind of ambition, as if you were meant for greater things, but when you lost him so to speak, you lost your ambition too . . . so that your daughters have to start from scratch. We were left with the mystery of your, I don't know, generalized abdication from the exercise of your talents? That sounds harsh, I know, but I'm just trying to get it all straight in my own head. No, but really, why did you wait so long?'

'Better late than never,' I reply. She needs a steady hand in these moments of deep self-doubt. It took me years to see that. In the meantime, it was hard on both of us.

'Well, we forgive you for keeping secrets from us for so long. But you should realize that it may make it difficult for us to trust you in future. What other deep dark secrets are you hiding? Were you ever in the Congo? Just kidding. Anyway, here's your chance to come clean,' she concluded, half joking, half in earnest. The most earnest of my children, too, it showed in her shuddering sighs as an infant at the breast. She took things to heart; her heart expanded to make room for all of it. ('To be a good lawyer you have to love your clients.')

'No, but really, why did you wait so long? Ashamed? Or did you think Dad would be jealous? He's terribly jealous, just put yourself in his place, you would be too. Of course he's too quiet, too permanently sheepish to make a scene. But I'm not. So, tell me, whom do you miss more, the son you scarcely knew or the father you were madly in love with, apparently, although you have offered very few details? That's all right, it's your prerogative. But I wonder if you yourself are clear in your own mind about all this. Maybe you are having a belated mid-life crisis and this old flame represents the quickest way

192

back to your vanished youth? You know what I mean? I mean if you kept it secret for so long, why tell us now? Hmm?'

'Would you rather not have known at all?' I asked my passionate truth seeker.

'I'm not sure,' she replied after a pause, with almost fatuous gravity. 'It is a kind of bombshell. I'm still getting used to it. I have to go back over everything and fit this in. For instance, there was that time in '86, right after Irene died, when you and Dad were fighting, we thought you might be going to get a divorce. Did it have something to do with this?'

'I don't remember what that was about. Probably not.'

'So you're not longing for old days of *La Vie en Rose*. Was that your song back then?'

'That one was already dated by the sixties.'

'You don't seem to realize,' my daughter had worked herself into a crescendo of indignation, 'if I had known I had an older brother in North Africa, I would have lived my whole life differently.'

'In what way?' I asked. I was about as sad as I could be by then, but I kept a straight face. Two simultaneous meltdowns would do us no good.

'I would have gone to see him, that time I was in Morocco, when I was eighteen. I can't believe, I spent the whole time shopping for a pair of *babouches*. Remember them? Russet silk with gold trim? I wish I still had them. Does he even speak English? How will we communicate?'

'I could help,' I said. The prospect took my breath away. All my children seated around one table, in lively conversation, with me as the interpreter. The first round of peace talks, with more to come.

'I'm really curious, you know,' my daughter admitted,

with a squeal of glee. That was the way with my little grand inquisitor; she would scratch and dig till she had found what she was looking for, some shard of reassurance, and suddenly her mood would lighten and she would relent. Life could go on after all.

'I might even offer to represent him, if he wants to sue you for neglect,' she added. 'Just kidding, don't look so worried. Besides, you have no assets worth going after. But you haven't answered my question. Or, maybe you have. There are some things you still won't talk about. Which suggests . . . hmm . . .' she let out a melodramatic sigh.

'You obviously have feelings for the guy in spite of everything. Poor Dad. He hasn't been himself lately, you may not have noticed, but I have. So, in conclusion, I've been thinking, maybe you should let your children take the lead in this search. Your American children, that is. It makes more sense from every point of view. We're his contemporaries after all, we don't have the history you do . . . sorry, but that's just the way it is. You know what I mean?'

'I know exactly what you mean,' now it was my turn to sigh, measuredly. 'Of course this is all hypothetical until I've actually found him,' I reminded her, to carve myself a little breathing space.

'You really need to go online, the web is a whole universe, an encyclopedia of everyone who's ever been alive, at least since 1983. How old would he have been? Eighteen? Nineteen? I can't believe you're not computer literate. Why doesn't Isaac just buy you a computer, have you talked to him? If you don't, I will. What are you waiting for?'

She didn't wait for a reply but brainstormed right ahead.

'Of course he could have made an effort too, by now. Is

194

that what you were hoping? A perfectly legitimate response. Where is he anyway, our mystery man? What's keeping him? Why doesn't he get off his duff and try to find US?

One Sunday late last year, when she was tired, but otherwise in good health, as far as I could see, my mother told me not to mourn for her when the time came. She would be glad to go, she said. There was so much she disliked about the world today. For example, 'I hate the *New York Times*, all those real estate ads, mansions, Park Avenue apartments, those heavy special supplements. And the colored pages, now, I fold them back so I won't have to look at them. I hate computers and everything about them. They drive people apart. Even you who used to write me letters.'

'But we live in the same city . . .'

'I guess . . . you used to go away.'

'I'll go away and write to you,' I promised her. I had mentioned my Algerian fugue in vague terms.

'I know what you're planning, Miss. Does Walt know? I hope you don't intend to drag him along at his age, that's all he needs.'

'Oh, I'll spare him this adventure. And I'll be quick, two weeks, in and out and done, maybe forever.'

'Well, I won't try to dissuade you because I know it won't work. But what are you trying to prove, I'd like to know? It's not as if you were the State Department, with funds to distribute. It's not as if you're Condi Rice,' she giggles, and so do I.

'Or Madeleine Albright,' I add, 'or Hillary. I'm just your daughter.'

'I know you are. I know it better than you do. I'll bet

195

you don't remember when you were in third grade, you brought those girls home to lunch because you wanted them to have my pea soup with frankfurters. You felt sorry for them with their soggy jelly sandwiches.'

'I made you extra work.'

'I didn't mind. Pea soup stretches easily, you just add milk. That one girl, what was her name, Irish, beautiful red ringlets, she had had TB. For her I added cream. She cleaned her plate and asked for more. What can you accomplish in just two weeks, I'd like to know?'

'I hadn't thought of it like that. There are things I need to see for myself . . .'

'Not good enough,' my mother shook her head. She wears her hair the way she wore it at thirteen, she's never varied, straight hair, bowl cut, bangs, the only straight hair in the family, some kind of throwback, but to whom? First generation born in the US, self created. Father died when she was twelve.

'You can't go there as just a tourist. I remember how you lived in Ecuador. That was different, you were younger, you had small children, they took all your concentration and Walt took the rest. You need a project, a purpose . . .'

'I have one,' I said.

'Yes?'

'I'll tell you when it's farther along,' I was coy, as if we had all the time in the world. Three weeks later she died in her sleep. Curled in a relaxed fetal position, her usual, with the radio blaring. She always slept with the radio on. First I turned off the baseball game. Then I pulled the sheet over her face – that was the hardest thing I've ever had to do. I would have crept under the sheet with her but I restrained myself. Then I phoned my brother in Chicago. He came next day with his wife and they

196

took charge of the formalities, seemly mourning in a rented space. No, it was the second hardest thing I ever did.

My husband's father fought for Germany in the First World War, my husband fought against Germany in the Second World War. Our son was born in New York during the Vietnam War.

'A boy, eh? Another one for Uncle Sam,' the Jamaican orderly waltzed his mop around the room.

'Not if we can help it,' we vowed, and left the country while he was a babe in arms.

Back in the US, after 1980, as the arms race intensified, we feared he might live to fight in the Third World War, when it began at the border between the two Germanies.

We never dreamed he would become a twenty-first-century war profiteer. Neither did he, to be sure. He founded the company in his college dorm room, his senior year of engineering school. His aim was to make a fortune by designing video games that were less violent and sexist than the run of what was being marketed to nine year olds at the time. He designed a game where the goal was to coax frogs of endangered species back into a restored habitat. I suggested he call the game 'Froggy went a courtin'.' He said that wouldn't sell.

The next year he rented a small office on lower Broadway overlooking an airshaft, and hired a recent Brazilian immigrant with a cartoon style so baroque as to be almost illegible, to draw the characters involved in the frog rescue. My son's job would be to design software for the visual/computational interface. When my son told me he soaked up languages like a sponge, he meant computer languages. He spoke only English.

197

He all but moved into that dingy office, surviving on stale pizza and lukewarm sodas (no beer for these abstemious young men). At the end of six months he had nothing to show for their all-nighters, but new code writing skills in demand from several large accounting firms. This work paid the rent, but it eventually sabotaged the original project. The cartoonist lost patience and took his gifts to Hollywood. That was the end of Froggy. The engineering grad continued to design software for the growing field of data management.

Then a Silicon Valley giant made him an offer he couldn't refuse. So he changed the logo on the door, bought some office furniture and replaced the old torn window shades with Venetian blinds. He hired a full-time receptionist. After 9/11, the California company sold their software to a data-mining firm under contract with the Department of Homeland Security. My son has benefitted from the enormous windfall budget of the war on terror.

Success has not spoiled Isaac. He's the same down-to-earth young man he ever was. A bit straight laced, like his namesake, a German Jewish great grandfather who owned a bristle brush factory in Dresden before the First World War and put his life's savings in German war bonds and lost it all. Isaac Kirstein, Irene's father, was a straight arrow, a tall, stooped, kindly, reserved Jewish gentleman, with one passion in life besides his family − Roman history, although hating travel; he visited Rome only once in his entire life.

I'm beginning to think my son has a secret passion, too, his missing brother. What does Kamel represent to him? The part of himself he hid from sight in a household of teasing sisters? The ideal recipient for his philanthropy?

Isaac likes looking after people. Even in grade school he befriended the kids in the class who needed protection, a half-blind boy in fifth grade, who was always picking fights to prove he was one of the guys, a sly shoplifter in junior high, whose father had disowned him.

'I should have told you about Kamel sooner,' I said to him lately. His reply was telling.

'If you'd told me sooner I'd have been too busy to respond, you remember the twenty-hour days I put in on Froggy. When I wound up in the hospital with that liver malfunction, it was from nothing but lack of sleep, they told me. Now I'm in a position where I can really do something for a new member of the family, even if we can't communicate.'

The Bible is full of feuding brothers. Cain and Abel, Isaac and Ishmael, Jacob and Esau. That doesn't frighten my son. Genesis was just required reading in his college humanities course, one week's assignment out of many. Biblical pessimism has no meaning for him. His favorite movie (I like it too) is *Close Encounters of the Third Kind*. Kamel is his intergalactic soul buddy, waiting for him out there in the Arabic-speaking beyond.

What excitement when I finally received a small flat package in the mail from the Algerian Embassy in Washington. I held it and kissed it the way I kissed Wally's letters from *là-bas* eons ago. But when I looked inside, there was my passport all by its lonesome, the pages blank and forlorn. No visa had been stamped therein. Apparently, the Algerian regime shares the motto of the late British Empire: 'Never apologize, never explain.' I went for a walk to steady myself and then phoned Isaac from a phone booth and told him the news.

'I'll be over on Saturday afternoon. Don't fret meanwhile.

Things will work out. They usually do. We'll just have to engage plan B.'

'Considering the role computers have played in my life, it's time for you to learn something about them,' Isaac announced when he arrived on Saturday. 'Now you can perform a virtual search,' he wrestled open the big package that contained my first computer, a bright orange laptop shaped like a gargantuan clamshell. The colors on the screen twinkled softly, as if under clear water. A through-the-looking-glass world at my fingertips. By the time the cable company man arrived, Isaac had drilled the holes and strung the wires needed for a quick hookup. He began his brilliant career as a high-tech plumber, threading networks through ceiling crawl spaces where no one had ventured in decades. Poisonous spiders, generations of asbestos and allergenic dust, it was all part of a day's work to him.

After he went to all that trouble, I had to learn to surf the web. Do people still say that? The internet is one big memory lane with endless side roads, dead ends, and detours. Kamel Ouali has a thousand namesakes, and I don't know how to tell them apart from the real item. Farmers, economists, soccer stars, even a terrorist killed in an ambush in the mountains of western Algeria in 1996.

Kamel Ouali was blessedly missing from the published lists of massacre victims in Algeria's recent civil war. Those lists laboriously compiled by embattled human rights groups are notoriously incomplete. Kamel's absence from them was scant comfort. In the end, I invented a saving story: I pictured my son well out of harm's way, sitting in a room somewhere, playing the guitar. In Patagonia or Saskatchewan or even Brooklyn.

'How's it going?' my son phoned from work.

'Not so hot. What if he's a poor shepherd in the mountains somewhere?' I had just stumbled on a UN website, where it said ten million Algerians subsisted on 'the equivalent of two dollars a day.'

'In that case, we'll get him an air-conditioned barn. A Toyota truck, whatever. We'll let him decide. Have you begun to narrow it down?'

'It's hard,' I said. 'There are so many sites. I get sidetracked easily.' I didn't want to hurt his feelings, so I kept mine to myself. I found doing computer searches was like playing solitaire. They erased your time and emptied your brain. After two weeks online my list of favorites ran to five hundred sites. Favorites was the wrong word, call them grim reminders. It was as if the unprecedented powers of the internet had arrived just in time to keep track of an unprecedented multiplication of global misery. Either that, or I was reading the wrong sites. In order to keep pace, you had to spend your waking hours online, with no time left to help an actual individual human being, or even hear his plea for help.

'That's actually not the case,' my son corrected me in his polite but firm way. 'The internet allows us to hear cries for help that would never reach us otherwise.'

'Hear?' I said. 'I haven't heard a single voice so far, except robotic ones.'

'If you want live audio, that can be arranged. But it sounds like you're already suffering from information overload.'

'Is that what it's called?'

'Happens to everyone in the beginning. The cure is simple.'

'What is it?'

'Give it a rest for a few days. Pull the plug. I'll be there on Saturday. It's waited this long . . .'

201

I was ashamed to tell him that he couldn't help. What I wanted the computer couldn't give me. I wanted Kamel as a boy of ten, not a sullen bearded man of forty with strong opinions and an ingrown chip on his shoulder. Kamel at ten broke my heart, Kamel at forty scared me. He was older than his father, the day we conceived him in a cheap hotel in Perpignan. Wally went out early to the pier and learned his ship's departure was postponed, due to a wildcat strike. So we went back to bed, to celebrate this last-minute reprieve that lasted three whole days, time enough for Kamel to insinuate himself between us, as in the saying, '*Jamais deux sans trois*.'

Isaac came by to see for himself what we were doing with our new machine.

'What's this grit on the keyboard? You can't even read the letters.'

'I was wearing a kind of heavy mascara called kohl and I must have teared up and it ran on the board. Don't worry, I'll restore it to its pristine state before you take it away.'

'Is that what you really want?' my son was disappointed. But he recovered fast.

'Whatever. In that case, I'll take over the search for the missing party, from here on out. I should have done it long ago. It's my line of expertise after all: high-tech detective work. We just get a major contract from, oops, I'm not supposed to say.'

Wally called Kamel '*le beau cadeau*' to avoid naming him on paper. A dodge, a euphemism. We were not fooled. But what if Kamel really is a *beau cadeau*, mine to my American children. In the midst of wars, war on terror, war in Iraq, war in Afghanistan, Somalia, Kashmir, the Congo, here is their chance to know the meaning of the word *fraternité*. The kids, not just mine, are starved for some good news.

202

For this reason and for others I'm less eager to contemplate – their embarrassment over the revelation of my disorderly early life, their fear for the stability of their parents' marriage (my husband keeps referring to Wally as 'your sardine man'); the children have all jumped on the bandwagon and run with it. My little Swiss Family Robinson was raised in relative isolation in the Andes. I home-schooled my children for years, reading the classics aloud each afternoon. One day in a noisy thunderstorm I told them the story of a little boy who lived in such a dry climate that when rain fell everyone stopped work and ran to watch the puddles form. Thanks to Kamel in fact, my children seem to have recovered their early castaway solidarity, a family pride or loyalty that resurfaced in the letter they drafted last weekend after dinner at our apartment, laughing, teasing, and invoking the name of the absent one as if he were about to walk through the door.

Now my secret is out I think about other people's secrets too, all the stories Walt has never told me. Given the difference in our ages, there are bound to be a few. It's not that he doesn't communicate, but he has an abstract, speculative, maybe resigned is the word I'm looking for, or philosophical, way of looking at the past, that makes me wonder. Do all his feelings go into his paintings? Is there nothing left inside to gnaw at him? I need to draw him out and listen harder, figure out what's really going on. After thirty-five years together, it's time to dig out some core truths.

I asked him today, while he was painting, since painting engages only his subconscious, leaving his conscious mind free to roam through time and space,

'Did anyone ever break your heart?'

His reply came so quickly and easily, it sounded like a cover-up. But this time, for a change, I listened intently for sub-tones of old grief.

'Three days before we went into battle, Irma wrote to say she had met someone else.'

I knew the names and dates. Irma was his fiancée in 1945. ('You were in kindergarten,' he reminds me when her name comes up.) She was in New York City, that year, he had just landed in the Philippines, the colonel's right-hand man during the landing on Luzon.

'Is that why you were so badly wounded right away? Did you throw yourself into the line of fire?'

'No, no, the general had been there earlier that day and said we had to take more casualties. "Give out some medals," he told the colonel. We were in a tough position, the Japanese were dug in on that hill. Boys I'd been with all along were killed that night. I was out of ammunition, about to attack with my bayonet when he shot me first . . .'

Impossible to imagine Walt in combat, but I'd leave that insoluble conundrum for another day. Right now we were talking about love.

'But you got over her?'

'Once I was shot – they expected me to die, they put me in that sealed tent to let me die in peace – I concentrated on staying alive, it took all my energy. I liked talking with the nurse in the New Guinea field hospital, she was the daughter of a senator, she'd been written up in *LIFE* magazine. There were not many people you could talk to in the army.'

He was just getting started when I let him get away again. At that point, as so often, and despite my best inten-

204

tions, I lost my focus, I veered off on to a tangent. The tangent was named Aissa.

'So if someone were in mourning, the best way to get over it, would be to have a near-death experience . . .?'

'Or to fall in love again . . .' He doesn't mean with me, of course, I came along much later in the story.

'But what if . . .'

'If you like women, you are always meeting women. It's not difficult. Finding someone to marry, that's difficult.'

'You managed,' I said, angling for compliments.

'I had my mother's help, although I must say, ordinarily that would have worked against us.' He means worked against 'you,' that is, me, but his innate delicacy leads him to switch pronouns in my favor.

'Why all the questions, hmm?' His tone is affectionate but distracted. The painter in a race with darkness, with the waning light, has to keep a steady pace, perhaps accelerate it slightly. Steady, steady, almost there. Tomorrow is another day.

'I'm thinking of someone I know.' I haven't told Walt how I poured my heart out to a stranger, who turned out to be Aissa. If they meet some day, that will be different. Meanwhile I wonder to myself, Does Aissa have a mother to worry over him? I tried to recall what little he told me. If only I hadn't talked so much that day.

Aissa

A year has gone by since that brief trip to New York. Just as well I went then, before the Iraq invasion. Many around me now say they'll boycott the US until the troops leave

Baghdad and Guantanamo is shut down and what else? Oh yes, till they abolish the hateful practice of taking our fingerprints as we enter the country. Welcome, suspects. Enjoy your stay.

As for me, I would like a moratorium on odious comparisons, on American commanders in Iraq studying the published works of French war criminals like Colonel Trinquier and General Aussaresses – and even minor field commanders like that two-bit lieutenant David Galula, now hailed as a great theorist of counter-insurgency warfare by American generals with Ph.D.s in history – perhaps because he, Galula, was a guest at Harvard in 1962. Galula claims, in his recently republished war diaries, that he won the hearts and minds of war weary rural Algerians in 1956, by his friendly, culturally aware approach, and yet it's obvious to me – as it would be to any Algerian of mine or my father's generation – that the man was a smug, self-deluding fool, and probably a downright liar as well. But it's not surprising some powerful Americans respect him. He talks like they do. Secretary of Defense Rumsfeld trivializing torture (I stand at my desk eight hours a day) sounds exactly like Lieutenant Galula, pulling a pair of overalls over his uniform and climbing cheerfully into the freestanding bread oven, where his prisoners under interrogation are threatened with the possibility of being baked alive.

So, a moratorium on stupidity, if possible. But I don't believe in boycotts. I believe in the law of unintended consequences, which can only come into play when people mix it up and take risks. That week in New York had an unpredictable impact. Since my return, I have spent a quiet, ingrown, introspective year, trying to read my own shifting thoughts. Why for example, has Ahmed Ouali, Louise's

206

Wally, stayed with me? He's not the kind of man I would have wanted to spend time with, glib extrovert, seducer, gossip, and yet I don't seem to have the choice, as he keeps turning up in my dreams.

Last week I dreamed he was playing dominos with Sayyid Qutb in a small town café, deep in western Algeria. Of course I knew, my waking mind knew, that Qutb spent his last decade in Nasser's jails, tortured and then hanged. In prison he wrote the books that are said to be required reading for al Qaeda.

In my dream he grumbled that dominos are a game of chance, hence *haram* – forbidden – and a huge waste of time as well.

Ahmed Ouali tried to soothe him.

'For an accomplished player like yourself, dear sir, dominos are a game of skill, not chance.'

Qutb won the round. As he shuffled the tiles, Ahmed Ouali saw his mutilated fingers. (In my dream I saw them too.)

'Uncle, what did they do to you?' he asked aghast.

Qutb's reply was brief and to the point, 'Shut up and take your turn.'

Ahmed Ouali has planted himself in my unconscious as a sort of symbol, an Algerian everyman, modest, good humored, and accepting, who makes the horrific violence of our civil war seem like an aberration. It WAS an aberration, not a civil war, we learned to say, but a war against civilians. It must be a sign of my desperation that he of all people has become a faint beacon – an old kerosene lamp, primitive but still functional – in the gathering darkness. This is a metaphor. I am thinking of Baghdad where the lights went out this week under the bombardment.

I am thinking of my own narrow predicament. The other day on the RER a wreck of an old man slept on the seat behind me. I heard his heavy breathing. It continued after the train reached its suburban destination. I took a bill from my wallet and on my way out of the train, tapped the poor fellow on the shoulder lightly. He shuddered, sat up and addressed me, '*Sale arabe.*'

Such crude attacks are rare these days. Perhaps the fellow noticed me as he was falling asleep and took an instant dislike. That happens. Our two countries have a history. Or perhaps I humiliated him without meaning to.

When Ahmed Ouali tenderly reassured his young sons, '*Vous n'êtes pas d'ici,*' he was making them a promise: real life would begin at home in Algeria. For me, banished from Algeria, and not wildly welcome in France either – as I had just been reminded – where and when does real life begin?

In New York I spoke to Said's ghost. In Paris this week, I spoke to his widow at a memorial on the tenth anniversary of his death by assassin's bullet. I dislike these occasions where we all pile into a room somewhere on a low-ceilinged second floor in the nineteenth arrondissement; the place seems so full of suppressed grief you feel as if the building might collapse, fall flat on its face. If it did, none of us would lift a finger to rescue his neighbor from the rubble. The lack of solidarity among us exiles is our saddest trait.

And why did I make the mistake of mentioning that I saw Said last year on East 31st Street in Manhattan? Cloying pity seeped from the women present who knew the story of my Uncle Amar, the brilliant linguist who wound up sleeping under bridges with the beggars in the Latin

208

Quarter in the fifties. The women suspect I'm heading in the same direction.

An angry ex-colleague asked why I thought I rated the posthumous attentions of a man, who, while he lived, was barely aware of my existence. After he and all the rest had gone, Said's widow led me over to a window. Between us we managed to yank it open.

Against a background of late afternoon traffic noise she assured me that her husband was fond of me. She wanted me to know that. Then ironic-sympathetic, she challenged me.

'So you saw him in New York? Tell me something, was he bitter?'

'Bitter? Not at all, in fact HE urged ME to judge others less harshly.'

'I'm glad to hear that. I have not been honored by any such visitations. It's probably my fault, our two children are now in their teens and take all my time and focus. They will be full citizens of two countries, God willing.'

'Were they here this afternoon? I would like to have met them.'

'They're rehearsing a play at school. That seemed more important than another act of public piety. But tell me, what else have you been up to lately?'

She meant besides talking to ghosts. A strong, unsentimental, unsparing woman. She reminded me of my late wife. She deserved a better answer than the one I gave her.

'I've had some interesting dreams,' I said.

'That's good, glad to hear it, dreams are often the start of something new, my family in Bejaia used to say.'

'Bejaia,' I said. Our beautiful city of ninety-nine saints.

A note from Louise at last. Poor woman, I feel sorry for her, and for the people whose lives she is about to disrupt.

209

I feel sorry for myself too, as she proposes to drag me into the fray.

April 2003

Dear friend,

My children are on the case and promise quick results. I don't think I can do this without help from a neutral third party. When they find Kamel, will you be the *raqqas*? I love that word that means dancer but also – according to my Arabic teacher – one who steps back and forth between two points, a spy, a courier, a messenger, a lookout, a commuter, a go-between, a matchmaker. Does that sound right to you? I'm learning Arabic for Kamel's sake. French can sound so snobbish in some contexts. I'm not sure exactly what your role of *raqqas* will entail. I would not let it become onerous.

Did you know that from *raqqas* derives the Italian *ragazzo*? One of the Arabic language's many hidden gifts (a kind of poetic time bomb) to the other shore of the Mediterranean.

I lie awake nights and obsess. The other day I came across this line from the French philosopher Levinas, do you know him?

'To recognize another is to recognize a hunger.'

That's exactly how it was in Wally's room, the day of our first visit. Granted, we had our agendas and preconceptions. He had his as well. He was an Algerian entertaining strangers from halfway around the world. Algeria could hold up its head among the nations. He was learning something, proving

210

something, and maybe that lively, dark-eyed girl who turned up unexpectedly would sleep with him some time, if he hadn't forgotten how to get close to a woman. But before all that, transcending that, for an hour or two – or maybe it can't be timed by the clock, maybe different states of mind and heart can coexist – there was hospitality, the openness to others, the offer of disinterested friendship all around.

I wrote and told Louise I'd be glad to help in any way I could.

Part Three

1

Louise

Aissa brought me those orange tulips, why orange? Because
New York was gray that day, it had been raining. He laid
them on this table, as if upon a tomb; it was a sign, he was
preparing me for the news he would deliver a year later. He
called me a week ago, out of breath, he was just back from
Grenoble, where he spoke to Wally's daughter, he didn't
want to let another minute pass between the hearing and the
telling, my faithful messenger, a gallant, careful man. I wish
I'd never met him, life would have been easier without
him. I was ignorant and powerless, now I have knowledge
but no power. Is that the human condition? Am I more
human now than I was before his call? Don't give yourself
airs.

I came back to the luncheonette this afternoon, because
it's where we talked a year ago, and because sitting in a
confined public space, I can keep a grip on myself. The
streets are different, in the streets, the tears start every five
minutes, the way they did right after 9/11 with all those
flyers flapping on the lampposts, like iron stelae scattered
through the city . . . *O xein aggelein lakedaimoniois ote tede.*
Oh stranger, tell the Lacedaimonians that we lie here . . .

I forget the rest of that speech from beyond the grave. The grave.

Aissa said that only men were required to bring the body to the cemetery, to witness the burial. He said women are 'exempt.' The sight is thought to be too bitter for them to bear. He said Amina was in a rage at having to abandon her brother to that crowd of boys who barely knew him, or if they knew him once, forgot him till he achieved the celebrity of martyrdom. The October martyrs.

Amina said the sight was too bitter for those boys to bear, she called them boys, although they were in their twenties like Karim. And when the civil war began, she knows some who joined the Islamist hotheads, attacking police stations and army posts, driven not by theology or ideology, but disgust over murder left unpunished and unmourned, except on that October day, when Amina stood inside her uncle's yard, clawing at the splintery gate that may even have been locked shut from the outside.

'Would they do a thing like that?' I asked Aissa.

He said it was not impossible.

All over the country in those weeks, the last weeks of 1988, boys the age of Karim, my Karim, dare I call him that? No, that's an arrogation, all over the country boys in their teens and twenties saw their friends and schoolmates carried out, wrapped in those green blankets with white lettering, billboard-size calligraphy. I'll ask Bechir what words were written on the blankets, a prayer maybe? I couldn't want a better teacher than this subtle, tactful, young man. He actually apologized for asking me to read the word *tabout*, meaning coffin, when it turned up in the Arabic for beginners workbook. I don't want to shock him with my morbid curiosity, but I need to know every last detail.

And then I will have to go to see the cemetery in the village near Tiaret. Bechir says church groups organize tours all the time, to the birthplace of St Augustine, Souk Ahras, near the Tunisian border. He suggests I travel with one of those groups and slip off on my own once we arrive, it's quite a distance, east to west, but he knows people who would help me. I must learn to be proactive, we are a nation at war, this is wartime, we have a war president, people are dying every day, I hate the men in suits with their opinions. Aissa stutters when he is excited, he gets hung up on the letter 'd,' maybe Bechir can explain that too, is there some word beginning with the letter 'd' that stymies Francophones especially? Aissa who stutters is worth a hundred of those soft, fleshy pundits on TV from whom the words flow like perfumed water, an expensive bubble bath. Bathtub warriors. Don't cry. Don't cry.

Aissa told me we would meet in France someday.

'Amina will come round,' he said. How does he know? Does he have influence? Perhaps that's what he was trying to suggest, ever so discreetly. They sat up talking for an entire night in the lab she manages for some hotshot bio-chemist in Grenoble. That sounded like a prestigious job. I thought Wally would be pleased to know, he wanted his daughters to go as far as anyone, a vindication of the house-bound generations, we talked about it often, *Je te le jure*, Louise, I swear to you. But Aissa said no, Wally's daughter, born to his lawful wedded wife (*ma légitime*) three months after Karim in the Swiss hospital – that makes her what, late thirties now – was just a glorified secretary taking orders

217

from a brilliant, charming but overbearing man who had no idea what she left behind when she emigrated, or of what she took with her. She and the half-million others who fled the country, beginning that year.

When will Algerians be able to stay home at peace in their own country? Bechir told me the story of Djeha, hero of a thousand trickster tales, who sold his house, all except a single rusty nail and with that nail as a bargaining point, he repossessed the house in time. May you live to repossess your house, dear Aissa, who insisted on telling me over and over that Karim was not alone, that history or destiny decided, that I could not possibly in a hundred years (but in a thousand maybe?) have saved him from his fate.

Karim was twenty-four, do the arithmetic, I will and I have, but it's hard. If I had known ten or even fifteen years ago what I know now, I could not have raised my children – my other children. If the news had hit me fresh, in '88, the children and poor innocent Walt would have paid the price. Who says they didn't anyway, or won't again, in some horrible unforeseen way, once they hear the truth? Isaac is already showing signs of mid-life crisis, this will send him right over the edge.

Hey kids, you had a brother, but he was shot dead in the street in Sidi Bel Abbes early on the morning of Friday 7 October 1988. It might have been a stray bullet. From whose gun? The army was sent in to restore order during the riots but there were no investigations in the aftermath, and later they declared a blanket amnesty for everyone, murderers, torturers, and boys throwing stones at the cops.

'Was Karim out there with the rioters?' I asked.

'Amina says no. He was a musician, a guitarist, he wasn't one of those guys who just hung out in the streets waiting for their turn to live. He inherited his father's drive,' she said. She meant her own father's. Why did she call him? Not Wally. To Aissa she said 'My father' and sometimes, forgetting herself 'Baba,' Dad.

I came here to figure things out in my mind, some people go to church to think straight, I came to this lunch-eonette. The pies on their pie stands are like saints on pedestals in Roman churches, just the sight of them is reas-suring.

But the learning curve is too steep. I can't climb it. What do these expressions mean, 'on the ground,' 'at the end of the day,' 'for the duration?' Everyone wants to sound like they're in Iraq with the troops, 'taking it on the chin,' that's another one of those expressions. Wally never talked like that, his father was a soldier but he escaped that tainted vocabulary, he was steeped in music hall, instead, '*la môme piaffe.*'

Wally – Aissa did not volunteer this information, I had to ask for it specifically – Wally lived just long enough to bury his youngest son. Two years later he was gone too. Lung cancer. Once I heard that, I stopped asking questions. I had reached my limit, Aissa knew it, hence his reticence. I owe him a great deal.

I will order another cup of coffee, black, no sugar, and drink to Wally's memory, and ask his forgiveness, *quand-même.*

Dear Wally, I am not a serious person, I tried to warn you from the start, but you rejected the word 'phony,' it infringed your dignity, you couldn't know that I was talk-ing about myself, a suspicion you rejected first to last, since as I have now learned, even many years later, when you could have changed your mind, you defended an absurdly noble, not to say quixotic view of things. Of me.

I should have taken notes when Aissa phoned, I was in

no condition to. Grief in the mind: I have to get it straight so I can tell the kids, the other kids. First things first, your brother's name is not Kamel but Karim. Is or was? I'll start with is.

2

Why did Aissa phone me in the middle of the night? He was too deeply shaken by the news to keep it to himself a minute longer. When he apologized for waking me, I said, 'Of course you had to call at once,' and thanked him for taking on the burden.

A pause and then he said, 'Now you are one of us.'

That nearly knocked me out. I held the phone away so he wouldn't hear the sob struggling to break loose. Where do sobs originate, in the back of the throat like the Arabic letters *kha* and *rha*? I brought the phone back into speaking range and thanked him for accepting me into the club. He said it was a dubious honor, given the recent history.

'Well, I will try to be worthy of it all the same,' I said and thought about Bechir and Souk Ahras. Maybe he would come with me as my guide and interpreter. Tunisians look upon Algeria with horror and pity. Algerians think Tunisians are sissies, they couldn't take the pain Algerians endured to win their independence from France.

To deprive the rebels of popular support, the French drove two million Algerians out of their villages and into what they blandly called 'relocation' camps, behind barbed wire, where children died of hunger and dysentery, and the army delivered social services and torture in the same tightly controlled space. It's no wonder Karim's adoptive mother, entering her teens, failed to thrive in the camps, but when it turned out, later on, that she could not have children, her husband Hamid might still have divorced her or taken a second wife, Aissa said. She would have been thrust into the bitter background. By abdicating and allowing her to raise my son from tender infancy as if he were her own, I had – unwittingly of course – saved her marriage and allowed her to know the joys of motherhood for a few years, at any rate, because she died young. Karim was fifteen when she succumbed to stomach cancer. She was not yet forty.

Did Aissa mean to tell me I was the woman's benefactor?

'You are one of us,' entitled me to hear many bitter truths that night, although he struggled valiantly to coat the pill.

Aissa was speaking to a group of senior citizens in Grenoble, in fulfillment of a commitment made a year ago, at the height of his short-lived celebrity. Amina arrived late and sat in the last row, planning to take a quick look and slip out without speaking to him. What changed her mind, she later admitted, was an incident for which Aissa claimed no credit. After he had finished his talk, a heavy-set man in late middle age came up to Aissa. He was missing his right arm, except for a stump joined to his shoulder, which he used as a sort of clamp to carry things. That night he offered an envelope he retrieved clumsily with his functional left hand to Aissa, who did not recoil but accepted this strange offering in a relatively relaxed and friendly way, and thanked the old vet politely. His age, his mutilated

222

limb, no question, the guy was clearly a vet of what the French used to call the 'events in Algeria,' hard to believe they sent more than a million kids into the meat grinder, most of them draftees.

Which proved, as Amina's father used to say, how little regard France had for its own children. Aissa was pleased to hear Amina quote her father earnestly and without irony, because French friends sometimes made fun of him for doing just that. An inordinate respect for paternal sayings – he didn't deny it – was tangled in his mind with memories of old men in the cafés, swapping proverbs by the hour, the creaky patriarchal wisdom of the race. In short, there was a fair patch of common ground for them to explore that night.

To begin with, however, Amina was more than reluctant, she was downright hostile. She showed Aissa a small packet that had reached her from New York, a clutch of photographs, a classical music CD, and a brief note from self-effacing Isaac. He mentioned having heard of Aissa as someone who could vouch for his good faith.

Why didn't Isaac include me in this venture? Did he hope to spare me the pain of a brush-off? Was he waiting to spring the good news he dug out of the data stream for my benefit? Or was he protecting secret sources in that unsettling new way of his?

Amina for her part, had seen Aissa's name around, she didn't take him for a plant, exactly, a spy for the Algerian regime or its post 9/11 ally, the CIA. It was my authenticity and hence that of my entire family she seriously doubted. With good reason, she told Aissa, who was amused by her portentous glare.

'What brought these people blundering into our lives?' she demanded. 'Was it 9/11? Is that what it took to jar their

223

memory? Assuming there are memories and not inventions. And how did you get mixed up in this?'

Aissa told her he would be happy to explain, or if Amina preferred, he was ready, as the proverb says, 'to avoid waking the sleeping flies.' The two of them could shake hands and part then and there. He handed her his business card. He half expected her to crumple it and throw it back at him. Instead she relented.

'No, let's get this over with tonight.' And then she told him she had some work to do and if he didn't mind, she would talk to him between chores at the lab and he said, not at all. Not knowing what lab she meant or what went on there. But content to follow her across town on foot, lagging several steps behind for the pleasure of observing her in motion. She strode into the night with the loose but purposeful gait of a woman whose grandmothers were locked indoors from ages twelve to sixty.

Once Aissa saw her in her starched white coat he understood why she preferred to confront him in the lab, rather than in a café, or under a lamppost (weather?). That gleaming garment was her protective armor. The lab took the place of tribe and family for this woman who seemed to be alone in the world. It also put him in his place, a layman in the presence of a high priestess of science.

Or an acolyte of the high priest, the esteemed professor, who at ten on a Friday night, came out of his office looking for his crackerjack assistant and was surprised to find her in the company of an unknown North African. Amina introduced Aissa to Prof Cellier as 'a cousin from back home.'

Aissa wondered why the comedy and decided she was protecting her privacy, which was understandable. Or was her readiness to lie for his sake, a sign of something more. Desperation? Trust? Aissa couldn't wait for the old guy to vanish so the two putative cousins could get down to brass tacks. The professor obliged but first he admonished Amina to make sure her cousin donned a lab coat. For his own safety and that of the enterprise. Aissa quickly complied.

'You didn't tell me you had guests coming,' the professor pouted in the doorway, on his way out. Two Arabs equals a conspiracy? Or was it male proprietary jealousy? And if so, on what grounds?

'A surprise visit,' Amina said, which was true enough. 'We haven't seen each other in years.' Also true: all the years of their respective lives, in fact. The professor left the two of them alone in that large room full of microscopes and high-end computers and for the next hour she was busy with papers and charts, taking time out only to serve him tea, heated in the microwave, and to open a packet of dates from Bou Saada, accompanied by the standard greeting,

'"*Marhaba*," *comme on dit*,' she served up the word with that ironic qualifier he had often used himself, with French guests.

'Thanks, cousin,' he replied but didn't get a rise.

She continued to ignore him; he bided his time, read the bulletin boards, gazed uncomprehendingly at the equipment, humming noises, occasional high-pitched whistles lasting only a few seconds. None of this alarmed Amina or interested him. He found himself staring at her small shapely head, bent over her work, her dark curls swept back and anchored with a number two yellow pencil. The offhand coquetry of that ornament clearly intrigued him.

Finally she came and stood beside him at the far end of the lab. He was sitting on a high stool, he fetched another for her. She began by apologizing for the burden placed on him by the authors of the letter from New York. Blundering fools, she said again. But then slowly, in the careful vocabulary of a woman who had come of age in a misogynist police state, she began to talk about the recent past. Aissa was careful not to interrupt (unlike me) when Amina broke the news, the awful news. It was not news to her, she pointed out, she had been living with the fact of her brother's death, his murder she amended, for fifteen years, and as for her father's loss . . . But she wanted it understood, that she had no intention of contacting the signer of the letter or any member of his family. She left all that to Aissa, who was free, she conceded, to do as he thought best.

Once she had spoken her little piece, her denegation, she seemed to relax. They moved on from tea to an open bottle of the Bordeaux the professor stocked by the case, for general after-hours use. A man of high standards in both work and relaxation, Aissa told me. He clearly didn't like the guy, called him a 'tired patriarch' nearly as bad, he said, as anything Amina could have been subjected to at home.

Aissa apologized for Amina's angry comments, which he felt duty bound to deliver verbatim. He advised me to take them with a grain of salt. In fact, he said, although she would never admit it, our long distance clash was helpful in its way. At home the social code enjoined a stoic silence, because no matter what you'd been through in the wars, others had seen worse. One did not complain. It was an aesthetic as well as a moral prohibition, reinforced by a heavy dose of state censorship from day one.

But of course people needed to complain and tear their hair (failure to do so, undigested grief, had led to the epi-

226

demic of ulcers in his parents' generation). Isaac's friendly letter freed her to let loose that night. Which, Aissa implied, was not a bad thing in the end.

She began by admitting with infinite sadness, that in her current life and for a long time, there had been no one who knew her brother or anyone like him, no one who could speak to her about his life in the years when it was just his life and not a prelude to martyrdom. Hated word.

'Our lives ran on parallel tracks,' she told Aissa. 'Karim and I were the parallels that meet at infinity. But infinity is a construct, a concept, you understand.'

Aissa translated into a familiar proverb. '*Ghir ejbal li mayat laqawch.*' Only mountains never meet.

'We were not mountains,' Amina said, with a slight tremble in her voice, which Aissa reported, but did not try to analyze. He went on, 'Or you could say they were almost twins. You know she was born all of three months after Karim?' I knew. Wally had sent me that photograph of her seated on his lap, holding in her pudgy fists a wrench and a screwdriver. Her competence foreordained.

Almost twins, but not raised in the same household. She knew Karim as a distant cousin, living eighty miles to the south of her hometown of Bel Abbes, in a dirt-poor village off the main railroad line. His father, his adoptive father, sold herbs and spices in the weekly markets, making the rounds from town to town by bus. Amina's brothers had a cruel nickname for Karim: 'Koro wa boro,' which translated apparently as 'clueless.' They teased him about his footgear, rubber boots, ankle high, shiny black, no socks. How old was he then, six, maybe seven? The boots were too large for him. To keep from losing them he had to point his toes upward while running, which slowed him

227

down. He would have kicked them off but his father couldn't stand to see him running barefoot. From time to time Wally bought him new shoes. They never fitted. Impossible to buy shoes for a growing boy who's not there when you're buying them, because he grows too fast when you're not looking. That's how it was all along the line, Amina said. Her father's concern for Karim was unflagging but ineffectual.

'But what was he like, what did she say?' I demanded, interrupting again. I couldn't get a clear picture.

'As a child or as a man?' Aissa asked.

'But he was so young, barely a man,' I protested.

'That was not how I heard it,' Aissa said, mystifying me. But he did his best to fill in the enormous blanks. Amina recalled one long hot tiring trip to Karim's village, napping with her head against her father's shoulder in the cab of old Fernandez's borrowed truck. And then forgetting hunger, thirst, and crankiness when Karim ran out in the road to meet them. Amina was ten years old, in that precarious pre-sexual limbo, when if she moved quickly she might still be allowed to tag after him, like a kid brother. He had no brothers. He was that rare thing in Algeria, an only child.

They rushed off to the *oued*, the gully, minus their sling shots, because her father lectured them, 'Birds have to eat their weight in food every day, out here in these dry parts, you think that's easy? For them it's Ramadan year round, *ne leur compliquez pas l'existence.*'

He had a store of wry expressions garnered during his years in France, as if he'd memorized those pink pages at the center of the petit Larousse, with sayings from all over. He wasn't showing off his command of the enemy idiom,

228

she added. It was engrained in him, the cast of his adult mind.

Amina remembered that visit because Karim, running well ahead of her, tripped and landed in the embrace of a tall prickly pear cactus. She watched Uncle Hamid dip the hands of a silent Karim in olive oil before extracting a hundred tiny, invisible thorns while Aunt Zohra spooned soup into her son's mouth, and her own father paced nervously, with no way, for once, to make himself useful.

When Karim came to visit them in the city, Amina's brothers made him turn his pockets inside out and for every fennel or cumin seed they found, residue of his father's trade, they punched him in the arm. Cardamom seeds rated double. Amina never understood why Karim couldn't clean his pockets before his father put him on the bus. He did not fight back, he was a mama's boy, her brothers said. They claimed that when Uncle Hamid was away, Karim shared his mother's bed. Amina heard her parents talking. Her mother disapproved. Her father shrugged.

Amina, champion of underdogs, sided with Karim against her brothers from the start, so that their teenage escapade was predetermined in a way.

'Not an escapade,' Aissa corrected himself. 'There was no such thing with us in that time and place, with our mothers watching us like hawks.'

Karim was fifteen, his mother had died that winter 1980. He arrived in Bel Abbes at the start of summer, with his dog-eared schoolbooks, his gaping bell bottoms, so dated, so seventies, and his rustic diction. His pitiless cousins had no use for him, except Amina, who took him under her protection once again, with specific instructions from her father, to teach the boy French spelling and whatever math

229

he could sit still for. This was Karim's homecoming, if they had known the history. None of them did, except for Wally, who hoped to cement the bonds with a week's vacation on the coast, not far from home.

'*Ash ba33ad 3aynee man Hajbee?*' What separates my eye from my eyebrow, he asked and answered himself, 'Very little indeed, à *bon entendeur salut.*' A word to the wise. They pitched their camp above a narrow cove west of Mostaganem.

Somewhere Amina's father found a big tent for the women. The men slept in Fernandez's truck. They bathed in seawater, which made them itchy; they were pickled in brine and polished with olive oil, they glistened like sardines. Wally's dream, his petty bourgeois dream, Amina called it, had been to go into business for himself, and that year, 1980, under the new president, it seemed less outrageous than earlier.

The sea was less polluted then, they bought sardines from a fisherman who passed by every morning. Karim rowed out in a battered relic of a boat, he wooed Amina's mother with fresh sardines, he cleaned them, and she grilled them each day for breakfast. She had an understanding with the boy. Amina was almost jealous. Her older brothers were allowed to roam the beaches till all hours. Karim arrived just in time to take their place, a providential youngest son to baby. Ouarda mended his jeans, bought him new shirts, and nagged Wally to trim his hair. She would have liked to forbid his morning sortie in the old rowboat. Wally claimed Karim was under special protection and promised to teach him to swim.

If Karim ever learned to swim, it had to have been later on, Amina told Aissa, after his expulsion from their sardine paradise.

'It was my fault, it was his fault, it was no one's fault,'

230

Amina began what sounded like the first line of a tale from *The Thousand and One Nights*. 'There was and there was not.'

There was and there was not a long unsupervised afternoon among the wild carob trees of a hidden cove, where she tried to interest her cousin in quadratic equations, but was distracted by a hand encircling her ankle, Karim's hand. She glanced at him, he looked away from sheer timidity. This was no brazen seduction, the two of them were matched in innocence. But it was Amina, she admitted, who leaned over, grabbed Karim's hair, and brought his face alongside hers, so close their vision swam and they had no choice but to close their eyes, kiss, recoil, and start again.

That was the first, the only time but it was enough. Two adolescents feel the tidal pull of instinct and a family is shattered almost beyond repair. Part of our ancestral madness, Amina told Aissa, who knew exactly what she meant. It was probably her older brother fulfilling his time-honored duty as oldest son and guardian of family morals, who ratted them out. But it was Amina's father, the man I knew as Wally, who shipped Karim back to the boonies the next day. She wanted to shout, What happened to the eye and the eyebrow? but held her tongue. Soon there was no one to talk to anyway, her mother fell into a bitter silence after her father announced without prelude that he was leaving for the Kuwait oil fields, he had signed a contract to work as a welder on a new pipeline, work usually done by men half his age. He was gone for two long years.

Before he left the country, Amina's father took her for a long walk on the beach, told her how proud he was of her progress in school, and predicted a great future for her, in medicine or science, and added that he was counting on her to make headway during his absence. And then as if to reinforce his little sermon, he revealed a shocking fact. Karim was not a cousin, but her half-brother.

'You mean you and Aunt Zohra?' she asked in total naivety.

Her father waved his index finger frantically.

'His mother is a woman I had met in France.' Amina had never been to France. She could not imagine what sort of woman. She did not want to be asked to imagine. She thought of Karim, second-class citizen within the republic of the family.

'It's unfair to Karim,' she remembered saying. 'Does he know what you've told me?'

Her father's reply was elusive, 'Hamid is a good man. Let's not stand in his way.'

A long silence on the line.

'Are you still there?' I finally asked Aissa.

'I'm remembering our conversation,' he admitted.

She made an impact on him, it was clear. Why not, after all? I noticed Wally right away. *Coup de foudre* in a furnished room. My whole life flashed before me, simultaneously, not in sequence. It was more than I could carry in my mind. I was afraid my brain might explode, before my heart. I am a brain person, not a heart person, bad luck to my loved ones.

'Will you be talking to Amina any time again, do you think?' I asked Aissa.

'I expect so,' he said.

'Please tell her, then, no you don't have to tell her. It won't matter to her. But it wasn't 9/11 that made the difference. You don't think that, do you? It was seeing my granddaughter, two years ago, newborn with her dark hair slicked down over her forehead like a wet puppy. A moment for rejoicing, the birth of a first grandchild, but I felt only the pain of separation from Karim, as if it was the very day. I'm ashamed to say this: I felt galvanized by grief. Someone, somewhere pulled the switch, and I came to life again. Like a creaky monster in a science fiction movie. I wish I could thank Zohra, for everything she did. That's presumptuous of me, isn't it? I have no standing in this case, none at all.'

Or, as Wally and I used to say in 1962, the year of the ceasefire, '*Ce n'est pas prévu dans les accords.*' The treaty contains no such provision.

Insterstitial was Amina's word for her father's career in the new Algeria. In the great industrial projects of the new nation, there seemed to be no place for him. He was a misfit, a troublemaker. She figured it out in time. If in France, unsolicited suggestions from the factory floor were rarely adopted and never rewarded, in Algeria a display of practical intelligence or native wit provoked resentment, hostility, and fear in the nervous new bureaucracy jockeying for total control.

Her father opted out. For a dozen years he ran a repair shop, in partnership with his old friend Fernandez, the Spanish holdover who had reached North Africa after the fall of Spain in '39 and was waiting for Franco to die, before he returned home. Fernandez had Wally's gift for *bricolage*, his frugal instinct for recycling before the word existed. There was no piece of machinery the two, working in tandem, could not resuscitate. Fernandez, who was present at the violent dissolution of the French colony, in summer '62, salvaged a huge store of obsolete spare parts from the chaos. When he returned to Spain, in '78, he bequeathed the lot to Wally. It included an old guitar that Wally passed

233

on to Karim, handing it to him at the train station, that scorching August morning, a sort of booby prize, before booting him out.

'See what you can do with this,' he said. But he had taken care to give it a new set of strings.

Amina corseted in starched white cotton/polyester had the look not of a caryatid but of its supporting column, by the time she reopened that long-buried episode to Aissa, who relayed it to me. A Spanish guitar and a broken heart, Wally endowed Karim with the tools of his vocation: he was going to be a songwriter. Amina's heart was broken too, although she didn't know it.

'She told you so?' I asked Aissa.

'Not in so many words,' he admitted. 'But I read the signs.'

And betrayed them to me, because he wanted me know that Karim had been loved.

3

Poor Aissa got stuck with a huge phone bill and a sore throat, and how he lasted all that time without a cigarette, unless he quit smoking since I saw him, but I wouldn't let him go. I kept thinking, what if I never hear from him again, we don't actually know each other all that well, he may feel he's done his duty by me and goodbye. With that civil war that's barely ended, he must have made enough condolence calls for one lifetime and he's what, not yet forty, like my son. My sons.

Anyway once I shut up and stopped asking questions Aissa found his groove, told me what he knew I longed to hear, but he was also invested in the tale, he liked talking about Amina the way I liked talking about Wally, and maybe for the same reason, to hold them near.

Four years later Amina was shopping with some friends in Oran, Sidi Blel, the big booming sidewalk bazaar where *trabendistes*, young petty smugglers living by their wits, without benefit of import licenses or uncles in the Ministry of Trade, sold authentic French perfumes, Italian shoes, and Spanish undergarments. Karim was on the sidewalk with the rest of them. She exclaimed, '*3ash man shafek.*' He lives who beholds you.

No sooner had the words slipped out than she began to argue against her feelings. Her father despised this budding merchant class.

'We have become a nation of shopkeepers without shops, just cluttering the sidewalk, pack mules hauling merchandise from here to there.' His sons were diplomaed engineers, among the first graduates of the new Algerian universities. Someday thanks to them and their contemporaries, the made-in-Algeria label would circle the globe. Meanwhile, however, Mo taught remedial math at an overcrowded high school while Ali, hired straight out of university along with ten of his classmates by the famous Bel Abbes television factory, filled his workdays with interminable domino tournaments.

'It's just like grand uncle's café back in the village, except the drinks are no longer on the house,' Ali joked. He didn't care, he was developing his own sideline, selling pirated videos of foreign films.

A wonder Amina had recognized Karim: he was nearly a head taller, with long dark wavy hair, a prominent Adam's apple, and a handsome beaky nose. She felt dizzy, she sat down on the sidewalk, taking care to miss the stacks of tape cassettes that were his stock in trade. Were they pirated? She would not hold that against them. He pretended to mistake her for just another buyer.

'Karim, don't you know who I am? I am your . . .' She caught herself in time. 'I am your cousin, don't you remember when I tried to teach you math. You weren't very good at it. Have you found a career then? Is this it?' Why was she mocking him harshly when she wanted to throw her arms around him and beg his forgiveness for the way her family had expelled him overnight.

This grown-up Karim talked down to her from his new

236

height. The tapes were not pirated, he told her. They were his by right. He worked with a small recording studio that produced the hits of a rising star. She recognized the name but thought he'd moved to Paris that year. Apparently he still went back and forth. Sober in Paris, in Oran he drank, and arrived at the studio too far gone to keep his bearings. Karim, their Karim, had been hired to feed the rising star his lines and sometimes, he claimed, he slipped in something of his own invention. A line or a refrain that he'd been mulling over, or ad libbed on the spot.

'I always wondered why *rai* offers such a random mix of tag lines from old songs, proverbs, prayers, and lovers' quarrels,' Amina needled him.

'A song is not a mathematical theorem,' he replied, to show that he too remembered their disastrous tryst on the gem of a beach, where a sultan of the new order now reigned in solitude behind high walls.

'Still at the top of your class?' he asked her. Alas, yes, she admitted, the boys in her biochem class had just asked her to slow down because she pulled up the curve, making it more difficult for them to earn passing grades. That sounded awful, boasting and holier than thou. She amended, 'I may quit one of these days and go in for basketball instead.'

'I don't advise that,' Karim said. 'Women's sports do not seem to have a great future in this country.' Islamist factions were trying to ban women's sports in the universities. They hadn't had much success yet. And there was plenty of vocal opposition. Karim handed her a bunch of tapes.

'Give these to your father, with my respects.'

'How will I know which lines are yours?' She was determined to conceal the terror she felt in his presence. Terror and defeat. Four dead years.

'Ah, if you'd kept in touch, you wouldn't have to ask,' he

teased. How had Uncle Hamid's clumsy boy been transformed into this self-assured, smooth-talking young man? Later she heard her brothers talking. Karim was rumored to be living with a woman twice his age, he must have met her in that murky *rai* world she had viewed till then with distaste from afar.

Aissa called *rai* liberated Algeria's one original creation. In a country riven by endless feuds and scissions, *rai* was a rare happy FUSION of backcountry Bedouin wedding music, prayers to the wandering Sufi saints, jazz, rock, samba, and whatever else you could pound out on a synthesizer. *Rai's* founding mother was an old woman from the bottom of the heap, nearly as old as Piaf and a lot tougher, with the defiant stage name of Remitti, Algerianized French for 'Fill 'er up.' Freewheeling *rai* was anathema to the regime who banned it from the radio and to the Islamists, who banned it outright, once they got the chance. But it was the lifeblood of those years, circulating unimpeded on cheap cassettes like the ones Karim peddled in the street the day Amina rediscovered him and her feelings in the same bated breath.

That night when everyone was asleep she played a tape he'd given her. The singer wrapped his supple voice around an old saw, '*Khoud errai elli ybakkik, mashi errai elli ydaHkek*' (Take the advice that makes you cry, not the advice that makes you laugh.)

That refrain was pure Uncle Hamid. Did he know his son was peddling his bitter country wisdom on the sidewalks of sin city? Did he care?

Hamid had taken the advice that made him laugh, presumably, when he remarried at sixty. He was now the father of two young daughters, pride of his loins. His remarriage no doubt speeded Karim's emancipation to the city streets.

238

'So you met our merchant of melodies,' her father interrupted the listening session. She turned off the tape recorder.

'So you know where he's landed?'

'I've kept an eye on him, of course.'

'The eye and the eyebrow,' Amina said.

'Precisely,' her father said. But she had been left in the dark.

After their chance meeting in Oran, Karim began to turn up at the apartment in Bel Abbes, always unannounced and on the fly. He ate everything in sight, hit Wally for a small loan, swapped jokes with Ali and left trailing vague excuses.

'I promised to meet someone,' he'd say, or 'I told some friends I'd pass by late,' marking his independence from their little nucleus. They were not his only fans, his cool manner implied. And he had learned – he had been taught – not to rely on so-called family.

She and Karim were not lovers, Aissa said. Neither of them wanted to push into that uncharted territory. They were not even close friends; that would have taken more years than were given them. They were (Aissa had obviously given the term some thought) joking partners. Never quite sure of one another, but ready to surprise each other, as on that great day in Oran.

Fast forward to 1988. Amina was at university, studying organic chemistry, copying out textbooks by hand when none were available, in those years of across the board shortages, and massive unemployment, when high school dropouts and college grads with no prospects, lounged against the walls of the projects, so numerous and consistent there was a friendly comic name for their profession, '*hittistes*.'

239

From *het*, for wall. And a cruel insult: *shattabat*, brooms, dragging through the streets. They got even by heckling the street traffic. Any woman with a destination was a choice target. Outside her neighborhood, Amina traveled a daily gauntlet of jibes, threats, and obscene propositions. It was enough to make her think of leaving home.

Even Karim came at her crosswise, not an intentional saboteur, Aissa said almost paternally. Perhaps Karim thought he was saving her from herself, from her tendency to push herself to the point of exhaustion. *Khoud errai ybakkik.* Take the advice that makes you cry. She worried about him too: street peddler, illusionist, and petty thief. But when he showed up late one night with a gift for her, she did not question its provenance. It was too big and attractive, and unexpected. A mobile basketball hoop on a tall hardened-plastic pole, set on a small square carriage with wheels.

'Where did you get this from?' she asked. He didn't answer.

'If you flunk your exams, here's a backup solution!' As if by magic, out of the darkness he produced a regulation basketball and threw it at her hard and fast.

'Look sharp, holding is a penalty.'

She began to dribble furiously and he to block her discreetly.

NO BODY CONTACT: the rules of the game forbid it, so did their religion, the ferocious ancestors on both sides, aunts, uncles, brothers, cousins unto the nth generation. She scored her first point right over his head. After that he took unchivalrous advantage of her reticence (what if they accidentally collided?) and scored five points in quick succession.

He was a natural, her brother Karim. 'What a waste,'

Amina told Aissa who agreed. 'What a wealth of untapped talent in our generation, we could have filled a hundred brilliant leagues instead of rushing, as we did a few years later, into armed groups, terror cells, self-defense militias, death squads, police, army, ninjas, and emirs, the whole collective suicide of so-called civil war.'

When the game was over the two went back upstairs, quietly so as not to wake the others, Amina gave Karim a towel to dry the sweat, fried him a plate of eggs and peppers, and then they chatted for a while, sweet neutrality, and then he left as always without saying where he was going, or when he'd be around again. A privileged moment.

By next morning word had spread and the entire male population of the project was battling for a turn to strut their stuff. The noise was deafening. Amina shut the windows, despite the heat, and plugged away at her organic chem.

No one was surprised a few days later when the owners sent a pair of strong-arm men to repossess the purloined hoop. They walked right through the game in progress, ignoring the uproar, cut the long stalk loose from the house wall, and threw it into the back of their sleek truck, where it lay crosswise like a giraffe with rigor mortis. They drove off in a hail of small sharp stones, Amina said, a sendoff from the boys thirteen to thirty, whose game they'd interrupted. She remembered the stones afterwards, because one hit her ankle, leaving a small scar, and because it was a harbinger of things to come.

4

How did it start? Not with the Islamists, who came out in force later that week and owned the streets from then on. Not with the underground Communist party, whose leaders were already in jail. But suddenly on the afternoon of Wednesday 5 October 1988, the street of Algiers were full of angry boys, terribly young some of them; Aissa told me he'd seen kids who couldn't have been more than thirteen, juggling brand new Nikes looted from the hated shopping mall/preserve of the hated regime, and shouting, incongruously but with passion, 'We are men.'

'We had no program,' Aissa said. 'No list of demands. After twenty-five years of army rule, we were simply fed up with the squandering of our good will, our oil money, our intelligence, our sunshine, our matchless Mediterranean coastline, our joie de vivre, our soccer skills, our native vernacular, our capacity for tenderness, our fecundity, our masculinity, our dignity, our scrap of honor . . . our . . .' he gasped for air, he was back in the thick of it with his ire intact.

'Were you in the streets that day?' He was.

'Everyone was on our side, the balconies and terraces

were full of women tossing water bottles, sandwiches, and bandages down to the boys. They cheered us with their *youyous*, their thrilling ululations, we answered them with witty chants. A public festival that could have been allowed to run its course.'

'Tell me what you saw? Don't leave anything out.'

He said it was the youngest kids who burned cars and hurled rocks through police station windows, and assaulted the veterans' associations – a truly liberating gesture for a generation raised in guilty awe of the heroic liberation army. That same army was now sent to clear the streets.

On Thursday afternoon the tanks and armored cars rolled in and occupied the intersections, like in a crazy rerun of the Battle of Algiers, the movie version, 'Except it wasn't the French we were fighting this time, it was our own army, the backbone of the nation. Inconceivable. The shock, you have to understand, was like, like 9/11, for New Yorkers, a breaking point. The Israeli army used rubber bullets against the *intifada*, we had seen it on our own state controlled TV. We knew those things could break your bones. In Algiers our troops used live ammunition against unarmed boys. After the first funerals, the riots spread to other cities. There were curfews, mass arrests, and . . .' he hesitated, from shame; I thought, 'mass torture. In some towns they used dum–dum bullets. Criminal madness.'

'But where was Karim in all this?'

'I'm very sorry, by the way, deeply, deeply sorry.' Aissa sounded almost drunk. Was he tippling at his end of the line? He'd been talking for two hours, stalling for my sake. Pity the messenger.

Sidi Bel Abbes remained calm in the first days of rage, the windows of the trains arriving from Oran and Algiers were

243

black with scrawled insults to local manhood. Amina's mother wept and clutched Mo's hands in gratitude because he stayed indoors all week. Ali was in and out, with his camera, waiting for the fireworks to begin. Karim was unaccounted for, they didn't know if he was looting department stores in Oran or in a torture cell in Ain-Taya. That Thursday night when the sirens began to wail and the first gusts of smoke blew through their windows, Amina tore up a shirt and dipped the rags in vinegar, a protection against teargas, and she, Ali, and her father were about to go out to look for their lost brother. Ouarda, all atremble, stopped them cold. The shaking had begun that year. Plates rattled in her hands, soup bowls capsized, her ankles swollen from early morning hours on line waiting to buy bread or oil, from three a.m. appointments with the kitchen faucet after days of drought.

So the men went out to look for Karim while Amina put her mother to bed and tucked her in.

'He never did anyone any harm,' her mother said. 'We always got along so well.' It was unbearable, Amina said, until Karim limped in, on her father's arm and panic ceded to euphoria. His jeans were torn, his knees were gashed and bleeding, his hands were scraped raw where he fell running from the cops, just like the Palestinian kids on nightly TV.

Ali showed up a few minutes later.

'They shot two boys, I didn't see it with my own eyes but I sure as hell heard the machine-gun fire.' He cursed the Turkish beys, the French generals from Bugeaud and Lamoricière to de Gaulle, Salan, Massu, and their criminal Algerian successors.

Amina's father cleaned his son's wounds and wrapped them in the remains of her torn shirt. Finally the sirens quieted and the lethal stink of burning tires began to drift away. Mma rejoined the living and asked Karim if he were hungry. He was. He ate, the others watched. That night was his authentic homecoming, Amina said. 'Tie him down, don't let him get away,' she whispered to her father.

'He's a free man,' Wally quipped. 'But I think he knows when he's well off,' and he gave Karim a look she couldn't describe, although she could still see it, she told Aissa.

They sat up all night in a fervor of incredulity. After such violence, what next? *Où va l'Algérie?*

Ali did most of the talking. They would have to start from scratch and get it right this time, he said. He already had things figured out. His scheme for national salvation, 'the Great Palliative,' he named it, to be put in place at once, involved all-night outdoor movies, screened on the walls of apartment houses, for the guys who didn't have a bed to call their own. The wall boys dying of boredom and neglect. The great film classics (no more *Rambo*!) would teach them patience and subtlety, and prepare them to run the country when our turn came.

After Karim's death, Ali shelved his plans. He said October made it clear our turn was never going to come, that the generals who ran the country would sacrifice our entire generation rather than relinquish their egregious privileges. He was the first in the family to emigrate. The Canadians gave him an easy visa, he lives in Montreal, he gets some kind of unemployment check, he spends his afternoons in rerun movie houses. He has seen *La Strada* twenty times. He sends his sister letters that consist of strings of cryptic proverbs.

'*Ma 3and el mous ma yaddi man khooh?*' What would a knife take from his brother? His letters make Amina cry.

Friday morning early, Karim went out early to buy a loaf of bread. That's when the sniper shot him, a single bullet to the back of the head. There were no witnesses, but by the time the frantic next-door neighbor came pounding on the door of the apartment, a crowd had gathered in the street, mostly men returning from dawn prayers. The imam sat on the sidewalk with Karim sprawled across his knees, his index finger pointed skyward, a sign that the boy died a martyr's death. Or maybe the imam was only pointing at the rooftop down the street where the sniper had been spotted the day before.

'I was going to buy the bread,' Amina's mother wailed, and bit her hands. 'The way I always do, early, before the long chains form, but he said he would go instead and meanwhile if I made a pot of coffee, he would love a cup when he got back. I've got it ready, piping hot. I should have gone. It should have been me,' fingernails raking her cheeks too feebly to draw blood. Amina was terrified of what her father might say or do. But he said nothing, and there was nothing he could do, because the police took possession of Karim's body, and kept it for ten days, for the investigation they said, but there were no investigations; they were simply under orders to delay the funerals till public rage had subsided.

'That rage is never going to go away, what do they think?' Amina asked Aissa, who elaborated for my benefit.

'Karim was not alone. Not an isolated case. You need to know that. Six hundred boys killed in the streets that week, maybe a thousand. We don't have their names, no official list was ever published, there was no public mourning, no apologies. No memorials. Bodies buried in mass graves. Hundreds of young men were tortured, in police stations and secret police headquarters. That's the way the French ruled us, it's how we've ruled ourselves. Call it history or

246

destiny. *Allah yahdina*. Or let's leave God's name out of it. There was nothing you or anyone could do.'

Aissa meant well but he was wrong. Karim did not have to die. With an American mother, aunts and uncles? Now they are gone and I am older, I have a clearer view into their hearts.

Nora would have loved this boy with an intensity bordering on madness.

'Let me look at him, he's no Omar Sharif, is he? But with proper care, feeding, and a British public school education – he'll go to James's school in Gloucestershire on scholarship, James will see to it.'

'He may excel at games, you know, they often do,' James would have seconded her, flippancy masking his passion. 'Steer him toward tennis, that's my advice. Rugby is so rough.'

Uncle Sid would have got it right.

'Arabs and Jews are cousins if not brothers. Someday we'll all relax and get that through our heads. Meanwhile we'll make sure this little precursor wants for nothing. Cute kid by the way. Takes after his father, does he?'

My first mistake was letting Karim go at birth. My second was listening to Irene, noble of spirit, who – once she had grandchildren of her own – turned narrowly dynastic. For every child I produced that bore the stamp and seal of her son's DNA, she rewarded me with a gold watch, a brooch, a silver necklace. Medals for meritorious service. I should have thrown them back at her, or at least, refused to go on lying to her blessed son. Karim adrift from his mid teens, throwaway son of a throwaway generation – of course I could have saved him, Aissa. You know that. It would have taken pluck, ingenuity, and money I didn't have. But he'd be alive today, teaching guitar maybe, in some progressive school in the Midwest. He'd be playing subway concerts at the West 81st Street station, peddling his CDs to a disdainful crowd. He'd be . . . this was torture. Aissa offered *rahma*, mercy. I accepted.

'*A bientôt*,' he said, at last, which didn't really mean all that soon, it's just a polite way of signing off.

'*A bientot*,' I parrotted. Then we hung up, in Paris and New York. Amen.

Walt was reading the *New York Times* in bed. 'You were on the phone for two whole hours.'

He often lectured me, for my own good – because he hated to see me brood – about the course of history and how it's always been a chain of horrors, how everyone we know has a story, look at his mother's family, forty-two uncles, aunts, and cousins, deported to the camps. He himself was nearly killed in combat, keen to kill as many as he could first, although violence was against his nature and his principles but it was war; the colonel, as good a man as you could hope to meet, dead of a heart attack before V-J day, what did I think life was?

This time he simply said, 'Get back in bed, you're shivering, I'll bring you something hot to drink,' and returned a minute later with a shot glass full of brandy.

'So early in the morning?' I protested.

'It will help you sleep. Go on. Poor darling, you look terrible.'

But because he's old and too tired for another revolution or a homemade in-house crisis, and maybe jealous and unhappy with my mental infidelities, the backward glancing all consuming passion of the last year, rekindled daily now by the Iraq war, the next day he said something cruel.

'You got off easy.' He had thought it over and concluded it was easier – for both of us – to mourn a missing son than to confront a stranger I had intimately wronged, an unknown soul who could have been a terrorist, a conman, a sad sack, or an irresistible charmer.

'Knowing you,' Walt said, 'you'd give him everything you own, and be left penniless in your old age.'

Was that the crux of it? Money? There spoke the refugee who arrived in the US with ten bucks to his name?

No, there spoke a man who knew his years were numbered. Who would look after me when he was gone? He was not afraid of death, or at least could not express the fear, could not even conceive it probably, except as fear of absence from our shared life, loss of the power to protect me. After so many years together, our imaginations interlocked.

The utter cruelty of what I'd put him through in the past year struck me with full force and I wondered, if I'd known the search would turn up empty, worse than empty, would I have blundered on ahead (Amina's words)?

Sensible, pragmatic Wally invented the story of the fatal bicycle accident as a deterrent, to spare me from learning the worst. The last lap of our shame.

'*Parle pas de malheur,*' he used to say. And he rarely did. In that difficult moment, it was as if he stood beside me, my life coach, telling me, in that sagacious way of his, '*Là, franchement, ma chère Louise, tu exagères. Laisse ton mari tranquil.* Leave your husband alone. He fought in one war, that's enough. Don't drag him through our Algerian failures.'

'Buzz off,' I told imaginary Wally. (Not the first time we communicated across wide distances, on the theory of '*Ce n'est pas la mer à boire.*')

'You don't know my husband. Let me handle this my own way.'

I wanted Walt to retract his words. They were unworthy of him.

'Karim was only twenty-four. Where were you when you were twenty-four?' I challenged him. It was the first time I spoke my son's name aloud for him to hear.

'We were drafted right after Pearl Harbor, I was in basic training in South Carolina.'

'Learning how to handle weapons?'

'They started us on ancient Springfield rifles. Later we got the new M-1.'

'Karim was unarmed. All he had on him was a loaf of bread.'

'*Les salauds*,' Walt said. He could speak French too, when the occasion called for it.

'What will you do now?' he asked me after a pause.

'I am open to suggestions,' I said, relieved to hear he shared my anger and my faithless sorrow. 'I probably won't invade Algeria.'

'As long as it doesn't take you too far away.'

'How about lower Manhattan, that close enough?'

He gave me such a grateful look, I could have wept.

Wounded by my harsh assessments, my father stopped speaking to me around the time I turned sixteen. Before that he was a rich source of useful sayings. (Many came straight out of the Devil's Dictionary.) If he were alive now, I would ask for his advice, just to hear the old saw, 'Don't mourn, organize.'

5

I don't know when Wally saw those early Tracy–Hepburn movies. Maybe right after they were made. In that case he saw them in Oran during the war. His introduction to America, the anti-*Peste*. He wasn't keen on Hepburn, he called her a bony fish. But Spencer Tracy – he said Spansair Trahsi – was his all time favorite. The man had class.

Aissa didn't want to tell me about Wally. I had to beg him, 'If you don't tell me everything, I'll imagine something much, much worse.'

He sighed and offered me a capsule version of what Amina must have told him in the course of their nocturnal ramble. He may have done some editing, in his determination to protect me. But what he said rang true.

Amina was afraid that after the funeral and the memorial her father would go to pieces. When he disappeared into his workroom, in the corner of a friend's garage, she actually wondered if he was building a bomb to hurl at his son's killers. She said she would have helped him, if he'd asked. The highest marks in the province in organic chemistry had to be good for something.

After the riots she postponed her studies although she

251

had been about to enter medical school that year. Too much else was going on at home and in the streets. At home, Mma was on the verge of a breakdown, or perhaps it was an outright breakdown, she was so discreet they couldn't tell. She rose each day and went about her chores, but by midday she began to falter, Amina tried to draw her out, but she just sat hunched over, on the side of the bed, shaking her head from side to side, tears dribbling from her eyes.

Wally's secret project was not a bomb, of course, but an amazing radio: an ancient model with a graceful wooden case in the form of a Moorish arch. The insides too were a miraculously resuscitated anachronism: it ran on vacuum tubes. Amina recognized the subtle act of kindness, the reversion to their early history. Mma simply stared in horror. She knew at once it was her husband's parting gift. She never turned it on.

Sure enough, a few days later, Wally told Amina, '*J'ai la bougeotte*,' the French word for restlessness suggesting a perky optimism. The whole country had *la bougeotte* in 1989. The October children, as they were now called, had paid in blood for a new Constitution, a new democratic opening – sixty new political parties. Hundreds of newspapers and magazines in all our languages demanded reforms. An unheard of freedom of association flowered – human rights, feminism, and cinémathèques in every town and province. The border with Morocco was reopened.

'We had everything a democracy could want, except the rule of law,' Aissa said. And even that seemed within reach. Ready to strike a blow against impunity – a buzzword in the new newspapers – Wally set out on a quest: to locate Karim's murderers and see them brought to justice.

Amina wondered later whether her father believed in the

quest or was just staving off despair. In typical fashion, he ignored the new panoply of pressure groups and set out on his own, a lonesome cowboy, an Inspector Maigret. He returned first to the building where the sniper had been spotted, to see what he could learn from the inhabitants. They had nothing to tell him. He was working on two theories. The gunman was either a nervous sleepy recruit enforcing the early morning curfew, or an agent provocateur, sent to stir up trouble in the sluggish town. Unidentified plainclothes snipers had been spotted in other towns during the riots. Who put them there? Did Amina's father really expect to penetrate the murky feuds between rival factions of the regime that had spilled over into the street?

'The Berlin Wall had fallen,' Aissa reminded me. 'Ceausescu was dead and gone. We thought we were on the same train. We were wrong.'

Wally had an inside source, within the regime: his daughter Nour had married into the upper crust. Her husband was the son of a colonel in the liberation army. An entire province was under the man's control in 1962. His name was in the history books. Which one of Napoleon's marshals was it who boasted, 'I am an ancestor?' This man was an ancestor.

'My father,' Amina said, 'was just my father. To these people, Nour, our queen, was just a pretty girl from the sticks.'

She lived now in a handsome villa in a gated, guarded seaside enclave of the high and mighty, just outside Algiers. They arrived in time to catch the sunset from a high terrace overlooking the bay of Algiers, the most beautiful sight in the world, some say. Amina said the most beautiful sight in the world was Nour, bent over her needlework, fingers

253

flashing. A figure out of Delacroix, in a taffeta vest with ruffles down the front and bouffant trousers, not the frayed old woolen kind their grandfather wore, but some ironic Parisian knockoff. Nour shopped in Paris twice a year.

A bossy little girl when still at home, temperamental, demanding, spoiled, now she was subdued and melancholy beneath that vivid exterior. Her in-laws held her in contempt. That she had given up her studies (medicine, what else?) to raise her daughters earned her no gratitude. This family of self-made nobles required a male heir. Nour could not produce one on command, or could she? She quizzed Amina anxiously. Amina read the scientific journals, what remedies did Science have to offer? In her desperation Nour had paid a fortune to a marabout, for an amulet – a tiny leather pouch sewn shut on all four sides. It smelled of rosewater, orange peel, and dust. She had been instructed to leave it in the pocket of her husband's trousers, hanging in the closet.

Amina was shocked, still more so when her sister asked, 'And why are you here? Have you met someone? Is Baba trying to break it up? You'll have to elope some day, that's the fate of the youngest.'

Amina revealed the purpose of her trip and was sorry at once, because mention of Karim made her sister nervous and evasive. The penniless cousin from nowhere, the street musician, petty smuggler, his death – the scandalously public manner of it – was an embarrassment to her.

Amina made excuses for her sister. She had scarcely known Karim. Her husband's family kept her on a tight rein. She couldn't deny the October violence, but neither could she take it to heart. It stayed out there where the well-tended gardens of the inner circle ended and the dusty crowded highways began.

Prisoner of the glass palace, Wally called his beloved Nour. After a bitter inner struggle he had given up on her and transferred his hopes to his granddaughters.

Nour must have spoken to her husband. He addressed his father-in-law affably that night, 'I understand you're on a little fact finding mission. If it's answers you want, and who doesn't want answers these days, I can get them for you. It may take a while of course. The country is growing up at last but we need to be patient. We're just taking our first baby steps.' And insisted on lending them his car and driver for the following day. The better to spy on their comings and goings, Amina thought. Wally sadly agreed.

On their next trip to Algiers, they ran into the opposite effect, not heavy discretion and secret spying, but scandalous irreverence, unheard of daring that made you wonder where these young reporters for one of the new newspapers, imagined they were living. Denmark maybe or Australia?

Wally asked outright and received this reply:

'A country is at all times a work in progress. We call it into being by our acts. We have been afraid for far too long. We never poured our hearts out, not even to our closest friends, we always kept something in reserve.'

Amina labelled them the pessimist, the optimist, and the bystander. They were showoffs and performers. Perhaps they had already figured out that they were, as her brother Ali would have said, extras in a new experimental film doomed to a short run.

Right straight off they announced with glee that only days before, they'd been summoned to the offices of the dreaded *sécu militaire* and warned by a stern colonel, 'We are the heart of the country.'

'Then this country has no heart,' Wally blurted out.

The troika looked at him, surprised. They were a bit cocky, Amina recalled. Thought they had a monopoly on cleverness.

'Too bad you weren't with us the other day,' the optimist told Wally. 'We were tongue tied, I'm ashamed to say. Old habits of deference die hard.'

'Especially when reinforced with fists and steel-toed boots,' the pessimist amended.

'But they didn't touch us,' the optimist demurred. 'They served us tea and pastries!'

'Of course,' the pessimist agreed. 'But they wanted to remind us that North Africa is not eastern Europe.'

The optimist objected, 'But just in case their days are numbered, they wanted to obligate us by a friendly gesture. We could beat you to a pulp, you know, but we abstain! So that when they stand trial a year or two from now, we can vouch for their decency.'

'Unless we're the ones standing trial,' the pessimist amended.

They were like 'the three stooges,' Amina said, the way they keyed each other up, but then, as if by prearranged signal, they turned serious and somber and asked her father to explain his errand. Which he did, briefly and tersely. Know-it-alls, they had an answer ready.

'Investigations, confessions, and public trials: out of reach for now. But see what you can learn, write it down where it can't be erased and someday there may be an accounting,' the optimist advised.

Wally grew impatient. 'I'm not afraid of taking risks, if that's what you're thinking. At my age I have nothing left to lose.'

The optimist glanced at Amina sympathetically, as if to say, your father overlooked someone. Embarrassed by the unwanted attention, she stared at the floor, covered in stained linoleum.

'That building,' Aissa told me, 'was a French army barracks before the regime turned it over to the press, rent free. What has been given can be taken away again. We stood on borrowed ground that year. We knew that. What we could not foresee was that we were living on borrowed time. Four years later, at the start of the civil war, all three of those young men, were assassinated within a few weeks. The Islamists wanted them gone, but they had other enemies as well. No credible investigation was ever done. Not even the one Amina called "the pessimist" could have foreseen that outcome.'

When Wally asked for their advice, the three men wracked their brains for sources. There had been a shakeup in the regime after the October killings. The dominos were reshuffled. Some higher ups were retired on fat pensions, others vetted to embassies abroad. And a few, for inscrutable reasons, had been moved to remote postings in the desert.

'Those are the men you need to talk to,' Wally was told. 'They have axes to grind.'

'I always meant to see the desert before I die,' Wally said. 'May I count on you for *quelques bonnes adresses*?'

'*Sûrement, monsieur*,' the optimist rhymed Wally's chirpy French with his own.

'And did he get to the Sahara, and what did he find there?' I asked Aissa. On our first visit to Wally's room, Charles and I debated in our childish way, whether his republic was an island or an oasis. What if it was neither? What if the republic of Wally was a battered truck with too many miles on it, like the ancient Citroen abandoned by his friend Fernandez when he returned to Spain in 1978. Wally vowed to keep it running out of dogged loyalty to its

257

owner. He made his children sweat over that vehicle. Amina's brothers did the dirty work, flat on their backs. Her job was the rewiring. The truck repaid their devotion by never breaking down more than ten kilometers from home.

Until that fateful trip to In Salah, where it gave out on the high plains just north of Djelfa, on a day of cold gritty winds. A trucker hauled them into town. They spent the night in the back of a garage, Amina in the cab, Wally in the truckbed, wrapped in borrowed blankets, rocked all night by those same winds.

By next morning the wind had dropped and a steady dry cough had settled into Wally's throat, as if a creature with a mind of its own, a scorpion, were nesting in his windpipe. The truck was in no better shape. It needed a new water pump, one would have to be ordered from Algiers, it could take a week. Amina wanted to catch the next bus southward. Wally dropped another of those breezy French sayings that mocked at his misfortune, Back up and take a flying start. '*Reculer pour mieux sauter.*' A great debunker of superstitions in the past, he claimed the truck's unprecedented balkiness was a sign they were on the wrong track. A sign from whom? Amina demanded. They quarreled in the mechanic's lot, the three of them, Amina, Wally, and that persistent cough of his, totally lacking in human courtesy – it interrupted every proposition with its own insistent message, which she refused to hear.

They took their quarrel into the nearest café, where the TV set above the bar played a rerun of the Harlem Globetrotters trouncing a French team of immigrants' talented sons from Senegal and Martinique, who didn't stand a chance.

'Karim's game was basketball,' Wally remarked after a

258

draft of hot coffee had chased the cough temporarily. 'It goes with the territory.'

And there far from home and everyone they knew, in the not-yet freedom of the not-yet desert Amina's father described Karim's mother. Under cover of the raucous ball-game she heard about an American woman, Jewish, a tangle of black curls, pale skin, like the families who lived mixed in the Arab section of his hometown, when he was a boy. These neighbors relied on him to light their stove on Friday nights. They paid him in pastries and candles. He saw their suffering after the armistice in 1940, when his Jewish classmates were expelled from grade school overnight, their fathers rounded up and deported to internment camps in the deep South.

'She was Jewish?' Amina was shocked, and then ashamed because the hardening of the arteries that afflicted the country beginning in '62 had not spared her.

'Did Karim know?' she asked.

'You know how hard they make adoptions in our country. We avoided the legalities, with a few well-chosen lies. After that, I left it up to Hamid. It was his right.'

'And where is she now?' Amina demanded, and heard an astounding story of a bicycle accident in the New York City streets, in 1975, a young woman sideswiped by a city bus that knocked her to the sidewalk. Her head struck the pavement. She died instantly.

'She died right there in the street,' Amina's father told her. He didn't need to add, like mother, like son. She saw tears in her father's eyes but persisted. It was wrong, perverse, she told Aissa. They had set out on mission to interrogate some semi-retired judge or cop, and instead she was interrogating her own father.

'But you knew her whereabouts, you were in touch?' she cornered him.

259

'We wrote each other steadily, but once she married I decided to break it off for a while. I didn't want to cause a disturbance in her new household. That would have been unfair.'

'And you left Karim in the dark?'

'I didn't like to speak against his mother, so in the end I said nothing,' Wally told his daughter.

'I withheld the truth. I tried to make it up to him in other ways.'

'He wanted to spare me their recriminations. He wanted to spare himself as well. He felt betrayed, and drew a line at the bottom of the page. That's the only explanation. I know him, I knew him. Do you believe me?'

'I only know what I heard,' Aissa said. 'Shall I continue?'

'Please do,' I said. 'I am greatly in your debt.'

'Not at all.'

After the funeral, Amina and Ali unpacked an orange crate full of old slips of paper. Pay stubs from French factory towns named for unfamiliar saints, clippings from *Le Canard Enchaîné* of 1960, a postcard of tall pines under snow with a German stamp and an affectionate salute from Inge. Who was Inge? Of Karim's mother, not a trace. But Ali knew about the woman on the bicycle. In 1989, that hopeful year, his father sent him to the main library in Algiers to check the foreign newspaper archives for some item from the police blotter of the *New York Times*, about a young woman cyclist felled by a New York City bus some years before. The archives were a shambles, careless smokers had started fires in the stacks. Whole years were missing from the files. Ali returned from his fool's errand full of questions he did not ask his father, who volunteered no answers. And there the matter rested.

'So you can see why the letter from New York was such a challenge,' Aissa said. 'Amina didn't know what to do with it.'

'And the desert quest? Did they abandon it?'

'They caught a ride home with a truck driver returning from the oil fields. He was hauling a load of desert sand. He made their cause his own, offered to make a detour to fetch them for the return trip south. But it was not to be. Wally's cough worsened. Doctors, X-rays, diagnoses took over. It was lung cancer. It ruled his life and within months, his death in early 1990. He missed the entire rotten decade of the civil war.'

6

Aissa

A barbaric phone call, may I never make another like it. In Algiers I would have invited her to my mother's place for tea, my mother would have sat beside her on the couch and held her hands while I made my sad report. We do not leave mourners unaccompanied.

What I didn't tell Louise, because there wasn't time or because it seemed out of place, or severely premature ('*Kul ta'kheer fih khir*,' my mother used to say when I was going to be late for school again: lateness has its uses) could fill a book. I didn't tell her that I became fixated on Amina's hair ornament, that yellow number two pencil. If I didn't take possession of it by the end of the evening, I would feel as if life had once more slammed its great double doors shut on our fingers. Claiming that pencil stub by word or deed was out of the question, however. Either it came to me of its own accord, or not at all.

  I didn't tell Louise that Amina nursed her mother through a steep decline, while teaching chemistry in a local high school, till '94, when following her mother's death, she left for France because as she told me, 'the situation was

murky' – a police state euphemism for car bombings, assassinations, the poorest big city neighborhoods under nightly
siege from the police or young Islamist gangs. That she
lived in France on a lapsed tourist visa for several years. As
a woman she was not an automatic object of dread and
loathing, but without papers her employment options were
limited, till she talked her way into her current lab, where
she ran the stockroom, until the professor discovered her
and anointed her his indispensable assistant.

There was no need to tell Louise just yet, what became
of Wally's quest. It didn't end, Amina said. Once the civil
war began, it 'metastasized.' She handed me a sheaf of heavily inked flyers she had just received from over there. A
dozen sheets of postage-stamp size head shots of young
men between the ages of sixteen and thirty, surly, sullen,
smiling (those were the heartbreakers), who disappeared in
the war and are still missing ten years later.

'This boy was sixteen and mentally handicapped. The
militia in Relizane took him away, They locked him in the
trunk of their car. His father begged to take his place, but
they refused.'

For every face a story: Amina seemed to know them all.
She said no, not yet, but someday. The work went slowly.

'Chile, Argentina had their Truth Commissions. We
have gag orders and truncheons.'

No need to tell Louise that at that precise moment the professor phoned, a wakeup call, as milky daylight streaked the
windows. Amina took his call where I could see her and
signaled me with her eyebrows throughout the conversation. I watched her expressive face adopt a small grimace,
a large frown, the ghost of a smile. An eager nod.

'Prof Cellier reminds me we have a committee of

Swedish scientists coming through next Monday. He wants to trim the halls with pine boughs so they'll feel at home.' She was between laughing and crying.

'You see why I love the man? He has no idea! None at all! Do you think that's what my father saw in his American girlfriend? Her ignorance allowed him to take cover . . .' She looked at me with such intense complicity, I blurted out, 'Look, this is going to be hard on everyone. Why don't I contact her to begin with? I can do that much . . .'

'Go right ahead,' she said. But then she relented somewhat, 'I haven't read your book. I don't have time to read. Only scientific papers and a little history. But could you write about Karim? Something short and to the point. His foreshortened life. Can you write about a boy of twenty-four you never met? But you were twenty-four in the same year? Or do I have it wrong?

'He left a mess of tape cassettes. Ali wouldn't let me see them, but he told me Karim switched the labels to confound his customers. The *rai* fans got blazing sermons from some imam out of Yemen, the bigots were polluted by the naked female voice of Cheba Fadela. In the end, Ali knew my brother better than I did. Here, write down his address.'

I didn't tell Louise how when Amina freed the yellow pencil from her hair, a loose garland of dark curls covered her ears. She handed me the unexpected gift.

'What's this for?' That stub of wood, by virtue of its provenance, was charged with masses of subtle information.

'Sorry, I wasn't thinking,' she said. But perhaps she lied. 'Do you think you can fill in the blanks?'

'Blanks are controversial in themselves, aren't they? One man's blank is another man's encyclopedia.'

'There, you see. You are much cleverer with words than

I am. And you have the requisite distance.' And then, because it was another day and time to move on, she invited me to join her on a quick drive into the hills, to cut pine boughs for the Swedish committee. Behind the wheel she turned into a demon, overtaking a Mercedes on a winding mountain road with lethal glee.

'What was that about?' I asked, when we had left the poor man skittering between patches of black ice.

'You didn't see the Paris license plate? They think they own the road. We remind them otherwise. A point of honor.' And that was just the start of a morning that reminded me of trips into the back country with my father, the agricultural engineer whom peasants loved to test and try with all the tricks at their disposal, waiting for him to slip up and confirm their deep-seated distrust of the Ministry that sent him to reorganize their lives.

Amina parked the car at the edge of a steep slope. The trunk contained a neat array of mountain climber's tools: snow chains, pickax, heavy ropes, and a pair of sturdy hiking boots.

'Sorry I have no boots for you,' she said and then led me through a morass of deep mud and melting snow, as if all the glaciers of the Alps had ceded overnight to suddenly mild weather, up a narrow trail and across icy rocks till we reached the stand of pines she sought. She seemed to know this country intimately, like a *maquisard* in hiding.

'Sure you weren't in the hills in 1956?' I asked. Was she putting me to some test, or had the outdoors wiped her mind so clear of useless entanglements, she'd forgotten me outright?

The branches duly sawed, she allowed me to haul my share of them, prickly, sticky, oozing sap. I cursed her professor under my breath for sending us on this fool's errand. The tree limbs loaded into the trunk, she turned to look at me, 'That's good, a little color in your cheeks, but oh, what's happened to your shoes?'

They had disintegrated like cardboard.

'Here, sit down,' she pushed me into the front seat. 'Take off all that wet and let me see.'

Next thing I knew my frozen feet were naked in the Alpine sunlight.

'You could get frostbite, let me, I'll be gentle,' and she proceeded to massage my feet quite capably, although painfully at first. I didn't tell Louise, I haven't even told myself, what happened next.

As my mother used to say, 'Praise lateness.'

Amina dropped me at the train station on her way back to the lab.

'Don't you ever sleep?' I asked, as we said our farewells.

'Life is short, I'll sleep when I am dead,' were the last words I heard from her that day. That was quick, I thought, she disposed of me and Louise, too, in one fell swoop, with grace and sure dispatch.

In the Paris train, I slept at last, and dreamed of a little brown bird of indeterminate species perched atop a tall pine. I have had many conversations with Amina since – both intimate and wide-ranging – but I have yet to hear her say in waking life what that dream figure piped to me, 'Why do you say childless? Karim is our son.'

LAST WORD FROM DOWNTOWN

Tariq

New York, New York
May 2003

Greetings boss,

Glad to hear you may be coming to New York again soon. Be sure to let me know the date and time of your arrival, as you'll need looking after and who better to provide it than yours truly. Meanwhile to give you an idea of current climate, here's a weather report as of this week.

I wasn't planning to be anywhere near ground zero the other day, but in the end curiosity won out, or maybe it's just my ambulance driver past that keeps catching up with me. So, after an early run to the airport I swung by the federal building, a gloomy tower in lower Manhattan. If you saw it in Rome you'd peg it for a Fascist era fortress. This dreary building sits at the edge of a broad treeless sunken plaza, sort of like a drained pool at a defunct zoo. Today it was the rallying point for a single species: Muslim males age sixteen and up, not a huddled mass exactly, in fact there was a distinct lack of huddling, but a ragged assembly of three hundred − by my rough count − sleepy individuals waiting patiently on line outside the tower, although the line curled back on itself into what I hate to call arabesques, but you get the picture. Straightened out, it would have reached all the way to the Brooklyn Bridge, or you may not get the picture, since you don't know the city all that well. But there they were − a bunch of exiles, refugees, tourists, students, bridegrooms (that too!) of all nationalities, races, and social classes commingled. In fact, I don't know where else outside of Mecca during the *hadj* you'd find such a wide spectrum of the faithful gathered to fulfill the law. Not divine law in this case but the law of the land, in fact it was not a law but a decree, or as they call it here an executive order. Problem! In a republic laws are passed by the people's elected representatives in their deliberative bodies, but this was definitely not a law, perhaps it was extra-legal, some even said it was outright illegal. In fact there was some skirmish in the courts, that went nowhere in the end. *Vive la république, pourvu qu'elle dure.* Long live the republic, let's hope it lasts.

None of those present were in any position to question the decree/executive order, or resist the summons to appear, at the same hour, day, month, year, virtually guaranteeing this giant sluggish bottleneck would ensue. In Algiers, where people feel

268

they have nothing to lose, you would have had a stampede on your hands, but these folks, who have a lot to lose, were humble, patient, and orderly. They may have felt they had only themselves to blame. They were given a whole six months to comply with the decree/executive order – since last January in fact. Required to present themselves in person, with their expired visas, their lapsed permits, freshly issued marriage licenses, or whatever piece of paper they could produce to document their right to draw breath in these United Snakes of America, as an old geezer, I once picked up on the return from Kennedy, was pleased to call them.

What we saw today were the procrastinators, answering the final call. Sort of like Judgment Day for Muslims only, Bangladeshis included. That's it, too late, no more leeway, after this, the negligent, slothful, and recalcitrant risk being deported. But so, it turns out, do thousands of others, who hurried up and complied months ago. In fact several hundred are still sitting in some stifling county jail or immigrant detention center as we speak. In my line of work I hear about these places, twenty beds to a room, doorless toilets, rotten baloney sandwiches, handcuffs, shackles, insults, what country is this? *Vive la république, pourvu qu'elle dure.*

In short, you can't blame today's crowd for being slowpokes, worriers, last ditch optimists who were hoping the order would be rescinded and life would go on as in the past, their children would finish high school, study medicine, engineering, or finance, while their fathers went on driving cabs and selling newspapers below ground and halal pilaf and ripe fruit and veg. from

269

street corner stands, like the one where I bought you that juicy mango the day you came to town.

The men at the front of the line had been waiting since two a.m. for the offices in the tower to open! Fortunately, it was a mild night. I wondered why they couldn't give out numbers, the way they do in any well run Jewish deli in this town, so people could go over to Chinatown for breakfast and return refreshed. All this forced milling about on what was getting to be a hot day, no shade, no seats, no fountains, looked like a preemptive punishment of innocents, if you ask me.

And where were the vendors working the lines? A dozen luncheonettes and pizzerias in a two block radius, but not allowed to cart out coffee, cold drinks, cigarettes, lottery tickets – you don't have to be a citizen to win the lottery in the US. In a civilized country there would have been music. Why not, God willing, a Dixieland band playing 'When the Saints Go Marching In', the way they do at certain funerals I have in fact attended.

It's true the crowd idling in this open-air prison – young men in pressed jeans, older men in suits and ties, attended by their nervous wives and capable looking sisters-in-law (their papers were in order, had been for years) were not exactly in the mood for easy listening. They barely spoke among themselves, everyone stuck with their own kin, depressingly few signs of our famous Muslim solidarity! I didn't hear a single joke, just a few discreet, dispirited grumbles. A Pakistani MD dismayed at missing half a day's work (he was being optimistic) in the emergency room of Elmhurst Hospital. A young Moroccan student

270

wondering if he had torpedoed his visa by dropping all his courses except organic chemistry this term. (He also drove a taxi three nights a week. On a student visa? Tricky these days.)

'If they ever took organic chem, they'll have to understand,' an older woman listening in, tried to lighten the young student's mood. He turned toward her by a sort of phototropism, a soft-faced boy of twenty or thereabouts, used to confiding in his forceful mother at home. I turned to look at her too. Over her street clothes she wore an oversize T-shirt stamped in back (not front which would have been awkward on so buxom a woman) with the logo of a Brooklyn civil rights group that had been calling for volunteers on the radio this week. I'd noticed other good citizens in similar T-shirts working the crowd.

'A little vanity wouldn't hurt,' I wanted to tell the poor woman. 'It might actually make you more credible to this group all dressed up for their day in court, as if their life depended on the right necktie.' The T-shirt could have been tied loosely around her neck by the sleeves, for example, and left to flutter behind her like a cape, a banner, a pair of wings. She noticed me noticing her but went on talking to the worried boy.

'Just tell them you won't talk without your lawyer in the room. You have that right. Then call one of these phone numbers,' she handed the boy a flyer from her stack. 'And here's a quarter for the pay phone, just in case. In fact, here's a stack of quarters. You may need them all. And how about you,' she addressed me.

271

'Do you have a lawyer lined up?'

'Louise Berlin,' I exclaimed. It was that woman whose old friend I scraped off the sidewalk uptown a year ago. She was a fan of yours, I arranged an interview. You never told me how it went. I was not surprised to run into her in the plaza this morning. Baghdad on the Hudson has its mysterious trajectories. I would have recognized her sooner, if not for that penitential T-shirt. I have an excellent memory for faces, even faces glimpsed briefly in a rear-view mirror.

She, for her part, did not recognize me. In the end, I had to tell her who I was. When I did, she threw her arms around my neck in a heartfelt American version of a French *bise*.

'Oh Tariq, am I glad to see you. You're just what people need!'

She'd been there since six a.m., handing out flyers to the few takers. Not getting very far, she admitted.

'People are frightened. They don't want to contemplate worst-case scenarios. And maybe they don't trust us. I mean, look at us, we could be FBI plants, how do they know? That group wouldn't even speak to me,' she signaled discreetly toward a trio of skinny young men who looked like a soccer game during half time. Seriously strategizing.

'The idea,' Louise lamented, 'was to collect information from people on their way in, get a headcount – nationalities, professions, age groups, so at the end of the day we'll know how many men and boys have been detained. They're holding teenage boys, can you believe it? You go in and you don't come out. No wonder people are freaked.'

272

I thought she looked sort of off kilter herself. But I could be wrong. The Iraq war has made us all a little crazy, lately. What a botched scenario! She agreed.

'The Baghdad Library is burning,' she said. 'I hate it when they burn the libraries.'

We chatted for a while. She told me Friedrich, the old guy I fished out of the gutter a year ago, was still plying the city sidewalks but has lost his memory.

'All the war talk this year set him off. He thinks it's 1939 again. He keeps running to the park at night. He thinks it's the Berlin train station.'

'Sounds like you have your hands full,' I said and suggested a quick coffee break at a place across the street. No go. I told her my car was parked nearby, if she wanted to go home, rest, and come back later in the day; this was clearly going to be a marathon of patience.

'Dear Tariq,' she said, looking straight at me at last. 'I really want to talk to you. I have so much to tell you. I'm in your debt in ways you can't imagine. But not today, all right?'

'Whatever you say, *chère Madame*.' We shook hands this time, like sensible adults.

'It's really very kind of you,' she insisted. 'But look what's going on,' she gestured toward the crowd that kept on growing. 'I'm here for the duration.'